FATHER'S HOUSE

THE FIRE AWAITS ALL SINNERS,
AND THEIR FLESH WILL MELT AWAY.

THE FATHER'S HOUSE

LARCHE DAVIES

Matador
9 Priory Business Park,
Wistow Road, Kibworth Beauchamp,
Leicestershire. LE8 0RX
Tel: 0116 279 2299
Email: books@troubador.co.uk
Web: www.troubador.co.uk/matador
Twitter: @matadorbooks

ISBN 978 1784623 661

British Library Cataloguing in Publication Data.
A catalogue record for this book is available from the British Library.

Printed and bound in the UK by TJ International, Padstow, Cornwall
Typeset in 12pt Bembo by Troubador Publishing Ltd, Leicester, UK

Matador is an imprint of Troubador Publishing Ltd

For my mother and father
with gratitude

CHAPTER ONE

"I can see you," hissed the Magnifico. "I can hear you. I can watch your every action."

Lucy pulled the pillow over her head as the nightly whispers began.

"The fire awaits all sinners, and their flesh will melt away."

The words swished around the bed and through the pillow. Lucy pressed one ear hard down on the mattress, and put her hand firmly over the other. The voice would go away if she was virtuous, and patience was a virtue, so she waited.

Silence! Lucy emerged from semi-suffocation to breathe in the cold January air that wafted through the open window. Did she dare shut it a little? Surely there'd be no harm in pulling the curtain over to block off the draft. But Aunt Sarah had said she mustn't get out of bed. Would the Magnifico notice if she did?

The more she thought about it the more she felt tempted. She slid out of bed and stepped over to the window. Slipping her hand through the metal bars she paused for a moment as she pulled it towards her, and looked up at the stars in the clear winter night sky. There were thousands of them, millions, big ones and little ones, and clusters of some so small they looked like clouds of dust. Was the Magnifico up there looking down at her at that very moment? Was each one of those stars an eye? He would need millions of eyes to watch all the children in the world, and millions of ears to hear them with.

She pulled the window shut and lingered a little longer, looking over to the common on the other side of the road. The street lamp shaped the bushes around the pond into unfamiliar clumps and eerie figures. Lucy shivered and turned away. She tiptoed over to her little chest of drawers. It gleamed white in the near dark, and her books from the charity shop stood up black along its top like a row of soldiers, held together at each end by large stones from the garden.

As quietly as she could, she pulled open a drawer and took out her non-school uniform jumper and tugged it down over her head. The drawer stuck as she shut it, and she gave it a tap. The row of books shuddered, and a stone clattered down onto the floor. Lucy hastily picked it up and put it back in place. She jumped into bed and strained her ears for the sound of movement from Aunt Sarah's room on the opposite side of the hall.

All was quiet. She relaxed and pulled the blankets up high. Snuggling down into the skimpy bedding she reminded herself that comfort was the shortest path to a life of sin, and that suffering was good for the soul.

Her mind couldn't escape the Magnifico. She imagined him looking down from the sky with his myriad eyes, seeking her out among the millions of children that he watched and heard. Maybe he had a street map. She pictured all the eyes trying to have a look at the different pages all at the same time, pushing and shoving each other out of the way, and her tension gave way to a little laugh.

Perhaps one single pinpoint starry eye would be allocated to her. It would have to roam across the world until it found London with its commons and parks. How would it travel? Would it roll or fly or swoop? When it found the right common, how would it manage to find a girl in a bed in the ground-floor flat at number 3 Mortimor Road? Perhaps it didn't roll or swoop. Perhaps it slithered. Her skin prickled as she pictured it slithering along the narrow path that ran across the common towards the father's house. It would leave a slug's silver trail over the road, under the front door, down the hall to her room, across the bare wooden floor, up the leg of the bed, under the sheet, and onto her face. She stifled a scream and pulled the blanket right over her head.

Aunt Sarah plonked a hard-boiled egg onto Lucy's plate, and a piece of dry toast.

"Eat up," she said, wiping her hands on the apron that spanned her ample stomach. "You haven't got much time." She turned towards the worktop and started preparing two breakfast trays, one for the father on the first floor, and the other for the tenant on the second floor.

Delicious smells of coffee, warming croissants, and bacon with scrambled eggs, mingled together to tickle Lucy's nostrils. She watched as Aunt Sarah put a pot of honey on the father's tray, and wished she could have just a little to scrape on her toast. As she gulped down her milk she told herself firmly that she must be grateful for what was put before her. She thanked the Magnifico for providing her food, and carried her plate to the cracked old butler's sink.

3

Aunt Sarah lifted the trays into the dumb waiter that was set into the kitchen wall, and pressed the button to send it upwards. She turned to look at Lucy.

"Leave that plate or you'll be late. I'll do it later."

"Thank you," said Lucy meekly. She stood still for Aunt Sarah to check that her soft brown hair was pulled tightly enough into her pigtail, and that her tunic still came to at least one inch below her knees.

"Aunt Sarah," she asked tentatively, "has the Magnifico got a body?"

Sarah's tired puffy eyes opened wide in her round red face. "The things you ask! Of course he hasn't got a body. He's a deity – the one and only deity – all-seeing, all-hearing. Now get a move on."

"But if he hasn't got a body that means he hasn't got eyes – or ears. Eyes and ears are part of a body. So how can he be all-seeing, all-hearing?"

Sarah gasped and clapped a plump work-worn hand to her large bosom. She was shocked.

"Don't argue with me. Of course he's all-seeing, all-hearing! Don't you repeat what you've just said at school, or anywhere else, or the other aunts will say I haven't taught you right."

She plopped herself down for a moment into the comfy old armchair in the corner of the kitchen. Even the morning routine was exhausting her these days. And now Lucy with all these unanswerable questions.

"You've really turned into the most aggravating, nosy, inquisitive child I've ever come across, always asking, asking, asking! Why can't you just believe what you're told, same as you used to? I'm not going to tell you lies, am I? It's called 'having faith'. We can't always understand everything."

Lucy wasn't sure if she was supposed to reply. She stood uncertainly and waited, and gently stroked the smooth, warm gold of the reminder bracelet on her right wrist. It calmed her mind and silenced her tongue, and she found it soothing.

"You may well fiddle with that bracelet," snapped Sarah, mopping her face with her apron, "but just you remember it's there to remind you that the Magnifico is always watching and listening, so if he's been listening to you this morning I only hope he can forgive you."

She heaved herself out of the chair and gave Lucy a little push towards the hall. "Hurry up. Go and clean your teeth and get your school things."

Lucy considered it wise to stay silent. Her breath puffed out in clouds of steam as she cleaned her teeth in the icy cold bathroom. Then she went to her room, checked the contents of her school bag, and put on her coat. When she returned to the kitchen Aunt Sarah was still in her apron.

"You'll have to take yourself to school today, and bring yourself back," she said. "From now on I'm going to be too busy to go with you."

Lucy was taken aback and felt a stab of panic. She had never gone anywhere alone. The father must have changed the rules or something, but she didn't dare ask. One more question today and Aunt Sarah's round face might flush up so red it would burst into flames.

Strict instructions were given. Lucy wasn't to talk to anyone when she crossed the common. "Don't trust anyone who tries to be friendly. You can be sure they're up to no good."

The more Sarah thought about it now, the more she could visualise the dangers that awaited an

5

unaccompanied Lucy. "And when you get to South Hill don't go over with that lollipop lady, and don't have anything to do with the primary school children or any other non-followers. Their souls are unclean. Make sure you cross carefully at the lights at the bottom of South Hill."

Lucy shifted her satchel onto her shoulders and nodded. "Yes, Aunt Sarah." As she left the house she turned and gave a little wave, and then walked gingerly down the front path, its black and white herringbone tiles slippery with last night's frost. Sarah's final words followed her. "The Magnifico will know if you disobey me, and you will be punished for the sake of your soul."

Sarah stood at the front door watching as Lucy crossed over Mortimor Road onto the common. Stop worrying, she told herself. Nothing could go wrong. The child had walked that route with her every school day for the last ten years. As for herself, it would give her more time for her housework. Even so, she would miss her escort duties. At this very moment the aunts from the communes would be arriving outside the Magnifico's school with the younger children, and gathering for their early morning chat. That chat was the highlight of Sarah's day. She sighed. There was no room for self-pity. The father had said she must concentrate on a newcomer to the household, and let Lucy learn to do some things on her own. She sighed again. Shutting the front door, she returned to the kitchen. There was no time to waste.

The father had to be obeyed. It was every aunt's ordained duty to follow his instructions, and to raise his children in the righteous path of the Magnifico. Sarah glanced up at the guidance cane that hung on the wall by the kitchen door, and was thankful she had never had to use it on Lucy. Despite all her recent doubts and questionings and lapses of faith, Lucy was a good girl. It was probably just her age. Sarah had heard that girls could become a bit difficult when they reached fourteen – though she herself had certainly never been difficult, and she couldn't think of anyone else in her commune who had been either (apart from one or two naughty boys). It was one of these modern ideas – just a phase that was all, and it would pass. Sarah prided herself on having brought up a polite, well-behaved child who knew right from wrong.

She cleared up the kitchen and took the rubbish out through the back door, then round to the left behind the rear wing, and down the side of the house to the bins. Thomas, the gardener, was just inside the garage doors changing out of his respectable jacket into his gardening anorak. Sarah greeted him but there was no time for a chat, and she never felt comfortable with him anyway – there was something about him, but she couldn't put her finger on it. She hurried back to the kitchen, peeled some potatoes and put them in water.

As she dried her hands she looked up at the clock. She must get a move on. Flicking a switch high on the kitchen wall, she waited for a moment, listening for a voice from the little back room that she had prepared for the newcomer. There it was. Getting a bit scratchy these days. "I can see you. I can hear you. I can watch your every action…" She switched it off and went to check the room. Adjusting a small loudspeaker that emerged from a corner of the ceiling, she turned it slightly more towards the cot. That voice had hissed at her throughout her own childhood and had burrowed into her mind.

7

Even after she was old enough to realise it was recorded, it had kept her on the straight and narrow path laid out by the Magnifico. No child could fail to benefit from it.

She made sure that the bars on the window were firm and rust-free, and straightened the bedding on the cot. The blanket was thin and hard, as were hers and Lucy's. Both she and Lucy knew the importance of stoicism and endurance. They were blessed in that their upbringing would lead to the saving of their souls, and Sarah would do her best to ensure the same for the newcomer.

At eleven o'clock a door upstairs in the rear wing banged shut and Sarah heard heavy footsteps coming down into the lobby behind the kitchen. A key turned in the lobby door and Father Copse appeared, carrying a small child. Towering over Sarah from his immense height, dark eyes smouldering under heavy black brows, he wasted no time on courtesies.

"His name is Paul. He's three. He'll be with you till he's sixteen, and I expect you to bring him up in the teachings of the Magnifico. Should he fail to appreciate his good fortune in any way it will be your duty to be generous with the guidance."

Putting the child on the floor he took the guidance cane down from the wall, flexed it between his hands, and hung it up again. He flicked the switch for the loudspeaker, waited for the Magnifico's voice, and then opened the door to the hall and went to inspect the newly prepared bedroom. Like Sarah, he adjusted the loudspeaker slightly and checked the bars on the window.

"He doesn't need those," he said, pointing to an electric fan heater and a small mat at the side of the cot. "Make sure they're removed."

Sarah nodded silently, gazing down at her rough red hands, unable to look into those burning eyes and wishing he would go. She wanted to comfort the child who was standing alone in the kitchen, rigid with anxiety.

"I must go to work. When I get back tonight I'll send his clothes down in the dumb waiter. I'll keep an eye on his progress over the next few days. If he seems unlikely to conform he'll have to go to the commune, and the aunts there can look after him."

He left through the lobby and locked the door to the kitchen behind him, removing the key. Sarah could hear him unbolting the outer lobby door at the side of the house. She watched through the kitchen window as he strode down the side path that ran between the house and the garage. When he reached the driveway he turned left, and disappeared into the front garden through an arch in the high laurel hedge. She heard the click of the front gate and gave a sigh of relief.

She bent down to pick up the boy and half carried him to the sagging armchair in the corner of the kitchen. He was heavy and she pulled him with difficulty onto her spacious lap. Nuzzling her face into his soft curls, she held him close.

"It'll be alright," she murmured. "Just be a good boy and do as you're told and have faith in the Magnifico's holy word, and everything will be alright. It's your soul that's important, not what happens in this old world."

The child started wailing and Sarah cuddled him to her. What the Magnifico had decreed had to be. It was the written word of the *Holy Vision*.

As Lucy crossed Mortimor Road onto the common she was tempted to nip through the bushes to see if there was ice on the pond, but she suspected Aunt Sarah might be watching. She kept to the path and spoke to no-one. Not that there was anyone to speak to. Her initial panic had gone and was now replaced with a sense of rather nervous excitement. The frost on the common was sparkling in the cold winter sunlight. The sky was an icy blue. All the stars of the night before had disappeared, and she smiled to herself as she thought how silly she had been to think they could possibly have been eyes. The Magnifico didn't seem quite so terrifying in the daylight.

The sense of freedom was very pleasant. Lucy almost skipped along the path towards South Hill, taking in great breaths of the sharp, clean air. Even the scruffy backs of the terraced houses ahead of her looked pretty under the pale blue sky. When she reached the little lane that led between the houses to South Hill, she turned and looked back. Number 3 Mortimor Road glared at her from the other side of the common, and she pulled a face at it. She was glad she was here and not there.

Nearly three doors down South Hill, temptation raised its serpent's head again. Two temptations already this morning, and she'd only left the house a quarter of an hour ago. The Magnifico must be testing her. This time it was the lollipop lady – a delightfully smiling lollipop lady – surrounded by children and mothers and two or three teenagers. They mingled together as though they belonged. There must be something very comfortable about belonging. It surely couldn't do any harm to go over at the zebra crossing instead of at the lights down by the Underground station. The lollipop lady stepped out into the middle of the road and held up her hand. All traffic stopped. What an amazing feeling it must be to have such power, just one little woman against all the buses and taxis and cars of London!

As Lucy approached the crossing, her joy in her newly found freedom was replaced by an overwhelming shyness. These strangers knew each other and chatted together. They would stare at her and wonder why she had pushed herself among them. She knew that they were to be pitied, for they were doomed to suffer the fire of the melting flesh. Even so, she longed to be among them – as long as she didn't have to actually touch them. Luckily the thought of the fire reminded her that she too would suffer that fate if she built up a record of too many sins, and she pulled back.

The lollipop lady called out, "Come on, love, or you'll miss your chance." She didn't reply because she had been told not to speak to anyone and that kind strangers were up to no good, but as she shook her head she couldn't help smiling back.

At that moment she was knocked sideways as a boy shot out of the gate of number 38 South Hill and took a flying leap, landing on the zebra crossing with both feet.

Lucy was mortified. She had been touched, no – actually shoved aside – by a non-follower. What if the taint, the corruption, was catching? She felt dirty.

"George! What do you think you're doing?" A woman with a pushchair emerged from the gateway at number 38. "Don't be so rude!"

"Sorry!" shouted George from the middle of the zebra crossing, tossing his ginger curls and giving Lucy a cheerful wave.

"I do apologise, love," said the woman. "He's so rough sometimes. He's got too much energy for his own good – and for everyone else's good too."

Lucy was surprised. Never in her life had anyone apologised to her. She had always thought it was something children did to grown-ups. She felt embarrassed, so she just smiled and nodded. Perhaps the incident had been a warning to her from the Magnifico for having been tempted. Thank goodness she hadn't succumbed. She made her way down the rest of the hill towards the tube station and waited patiently for the lights to change so she could cross. Children and aunts from the Drax and Copse communes were still coming down the High Street to her right, so she wasn't late. There, on the other side of the road, just a few yards up, stood her school, tall and wide, red and glowering. Apart from a number 10 next to the door frame there was nothing to distinguish it from the other big houses on that side of the road. The Magnifico's school was anonymous.

Children were climbing the steps to the door as Lucy approached. Some of the aunts were turning away having fulfilled their escort duties and enjoyed their morning chats. For the first time Lucy started to wonder why Aunt Sarah was going to be too busy to bring her ever again. It must be something momentous because, as the two temptations had demonstrated, the risk of being influenced by the vice and corruption of non-followers was a very real thing. Lucy hadn't fully appreciated that until now and she felt ashamed, because she had become increasingly irritated lately when Aunt Sarah went on and on about the saving of her soul.

Reluctantly she climbed the school steps and the sun seemed to go in. She followed her fellow pupils down a wide hall, dark with wooden panelling. By the time she reached the cloakroom her stomach was churning and her throat tightening, just as they had done every school day since she first came here ten years ago. She hung her coat on a hook labelled 'Lucy Copse', returned to the hall, and joined a queue waiting to enter the assembly room in an orderly fashion. The boy behind her blew on the back of her neck and made her shiver. She swung her leg back as unobtrusively as she could and kicked out at him with her heel.

"No shuffling!" shouted a teacher.

The children filed into assembly silently, class by class, row after row. The room was large and high-ceilinged, closed in on itself by dreary, grey window blinds. Several dangling light bulbs threw a cold, harsh light on about two hundred children from the age of four to sixteen. The headmaster stood on a platform at the far end of the room flanked by his teaching staff, his long black gown draped over his stout stomach like a musty old curtain. Behind him, across the entire back wall, was a mural painting of the Magnifico's first Holy Envoy, his first representative on Earth hundreds of years ago. He was leaning against a rock with staring eyes and a sword pierced his bleeding chest. The message, 'Martyred for the Sake of your Soul', was painted in large black letters across the top.

Those eyes would be staring, staring, at Lucy, wherever she sat. Today, to her dismay, a sinful question popped up in her mind. How could he have been martyred for the sake of her soul? He couldn't possibly have known about her all those hundreds of years ago when she wasn't even born. She pushed the question away, but his eyes still pierced her as though he could see her most secret thoughts.

As soon as the pupils were seated and the shuffling

and sniffing and coughing had faded away, the headmaster raised his hands high and they all stood up again. Lucy managed to shift her gaze away from the first Holy Envoy, and fixed it on the headmaster's wobbling jowls.

"The Magnifico blesses you, my children," he boomed with his eyes closed, his fat arms outstretched, and his head thrown back.

"We thank the Magnifico, Headmaster," chanted the children.

"The Magnifico watches over you," he thundered.

"We are grateful for his observance, Headmaster," they responded dutifully.

"Sinners must be punished, for the sake of their souls." His voice rose to a bellow then sank to a hiss.

"The sinners are grateful for his blessed guidance," was the murmured reply.

Lucy joined in the chanting but closed her eyes and tried not to look at the guidance cane which hung from a hook at the side of the headmaster's chair. Any child who displeased the Magnifico would be beaten with the cane up on that platform in front of the whole school. Once one of the boys had whispered to Lucy that he'd heard it was illegal, and someone should tell the government about it. But Lucy knew that the Magnifico's word was the true law and that anyone who reported it to the outside world would suffer the fire of the melting flesh.

The thought of that fire burned constantly somewhere in the back of Lucy's mind and she knew the guidance cane was important to the saving of the soul, but she cringed each time it was used on a fellow pupil. It was the same boys every time. David, who sat next to her in class, was one them. The teachers said he was 'insolent'. Lucy liked him, though of course she couldn't be friends with someone who'd had the guidance. His half-sister, Dorothy, had been caned a couple of times too. They must have inherited the same genes for cheekiness. Lucy knew she would drop dead with the shame if the guidance ever happened to her.

Suddenly her heart sank. A small brazier was being wheeled on from the side of the stage. The headmaster, with a flourish, poured a scented liquid into it and it burst into flames. John, the skinniest boy in her class – in the whole school – was being called up yet again. She closed her eyes and quickly ran her fingers back and forth along her reminder, trying to soothe the beating of her heart. Would he remember what she had told him? "Just stroke your reminder and the Magnifico will help you. It always works for me."

The headmaster stood John in front of him and looked into his eyes. "What do we have here, Boy?" He waved his hand towards the brazier.

John's face twitched as he whispered, "The fire of the burning flesh, Sir, or melting flesh, Sir."

"And why is it here, Boy?"

"To remind us what awaits the sinner, Sir."

"And what is this for, Boy?" said the headmaster, unhooking the guidance cane from the side of his chair.

"To guide sinners along the path towards righteousness, Sir."

Lucy could barely hear the response. She was willing John to listen to her mind. *Stroke the reminder, stroke the reminder.*

"Roll up your trouser legs, Boy." Red marks from the previous caning still showed on John's calves. This was the fourth time in two months

Lucy's lips moved silently as she begged the Magnifico to forgive John's sin. She remembered the first time he had pulled a face when the teacher spoke to him in class. His mouth had twisted and his right eye twitched. The other children had looked on horrified at his impertinence, and then someone had giggled. Despite the first beating he had done it again, and again, and the twitch got worse each time. Once Lucy had asked him why he didn't stop, and he said he couldn't.

"Don't be silly. Of course you can!" she had said.

Now she opened her eyes and held her breath. John's face was twisting and twitching. His fingers ran frantically back and forth along the full circle of his reminder. Then, as he silently accepted the grievance, Lucy knew he had spoken the truth. He genuinely couldn't stop. A wave of shame swept through her as she remembered what she had said. She looked sideways at David and saw his fists were clenched till they were white to the bone. The entire assembly was silent.

When it was all over and the brazier had been wheeled back into the wings, and the closing hymn to the Magnifico had been sung, the subdued children shuffled down the hallway to their various dreary classrooms. Lucy settled herself at her desk and pulled out her books for the first lesson. She looked neither right nor left. Each child stared straight ahead, at the teacher or at the board. All hands rested on the desktops. No-one whispered to his or her neighbour, or giggled, or sniggered, or fidgeted. Absolute silence reigned until the teacher spoke, and then the school day started on its usual routine of prayers, maths, English, prayers again, Spanish or French, geography, then prayers and the lunch break. After lunch there would be reading from

16

the Magnifico's *Holy Vision*, followed by computers or carpentry for the boys, sewing or cooking for the girls, and more prayers.

The morning dragged. Lucy couldn't concentrate. The board, and even the teacher, were eclipsed by John's poor twitching face and the reminder round his skeletal wrist. At last it was geography, which meant it was nearly lunchtime. Lucy perked up a little. She liked geography because sometimes the class would be allowed to watch documentaries on a television set perched high up on a shelf in the corner of the classroom. Father Copse didn't allow television at number 3 Mortimor Road as it corrupted the soul, but geography programmes were carefully chosen and educational and showed the various countries where the current Holy Envoy had his offices. Lucy loved those documentaries, and would sit and imagine herself wandering through some exotic bazaar dressed in crimson silk and feeling the warmth of the sun on her back. Her secret hope was that one day the Magnifico would give her permission (through Father Copse of course) to travel to different places. It would be sad to have to stay at home till she was an old lady and look after everyone, like Aunt Sarah.

In today's class, despite the television, Lucy couldn't focus. She was just wondering if she could pluck up courage to approach the headmaster and explain to him that John couldn't help twitching, when she nearly jumped out of her skin. Aunt Judith Geography was shouting.

"David! Come to the front. Bring me your books."

What on earth had he had done? He was sitting right next to Lucy, but she hadn't noticed a thing. David stood up nonchalantly. She would have been mortified, but he didn't seem to care. He scratched his leg, tossed back his ash-blond hair, and picked up his books, sliding a scrap of paper sideways onto the floor as he did so. Giving Lucy's pigtail a little tug, he passed behind her chair to reach the aisle. Aunt Judith Geography checked through his books but couldn't find fault with them. She looked down at his wrist.

"Where's your reminder?" she snapped. He pulled up his shirt sleeve. "You know it should be exposed at all times. Sit down right here where I can see you, and pay attention."

As Lucy glanced across his empty seat his friend, Matthew, caught her eye and winked. She turned away and fixed her gaze attentively on the teacher. After a few minutes she dropped her pen and leaned down to retrieve it – and the fallen piece of paper. There was nothing on it except over and over again, *pigs, pigs, pigs*. Lucy put it into her blazer pocket and, when lunch time came, she hurried to the cloakroom and squeezed it under the tap into a tiny ball of indecipherable mush. She then went to search for John, but couldn't find him anywhere.

After lunch she looked for him again during the compulsory hour out of doors. The entire school population was milling around in the field at the back of the building, but John was nowhere to be seen. The sense of guilt was gnawing at Lucy. If only she hadn't been so unsympathetic. Her tongue had been as sharp as Aunt Sarah's. Poor John! She felt she would burst if she couldn't comfort him and tell him how sorry she was. For some reason his reminder hadn't worked, and this gave her a terrible sinking feeling because she knew it must have been the Magnifico's will. If it hadn't worked for John the time might come when it wouldn't work for her. She was still looking for him when Matthew came towards her across the yard, his good-natured face eager for information.

"Hi there!" he said cheerfully. "What was David writing on that bit of paper?"

Everyone liked Matthew. He was always happy and full of jokes that were so silly one couldn't help laughing. But today Lucy wasn't in the mood. He annoyed her. How he could be so perky after what had happened to John? He was actually laughing now! She remembered his wink in the classroom with indignation. Why should she satisfy his curiosity?

"It was nothing," she said with a shrug. "Just something about Glory to the Magnifico. I put it in the bin." She turned away.

Despite the wintry sunshine the field was bleak and cold, and the black thorny branches of the leafless hedges closed in on the children like a prison wall. Aunt Mavis Mathematics was organising a game of rounders. Boring! Lucy felt too miserable to join in. She crept out of sight round the side of the school building to a quiet spot between the bicycle shed and the garden wall. The sun was still shining but the ground was cold and hard. She was just in the process of folding up her coat to make a cushion when David's half-sister, the cheeky Dorothy, escaped the game of rounders and plonked herself down next to her.

"I saw you come to school on your own today," she said, arranging herself carefully so that she managed to sit on a bit of Lucy's coat. "I'm being nosy. I want to know why your aunt wasn't with you."

Lucy felt flattered. Dorothy was fifteen and lived in Father Drax's commune, so Lucy didn't know her very well. It was nice to be noticed by someone from the class above. All the same, she was embarrassed. It wasn't against the rules but she didn't mix with people who had received the guidance cane if she could help it – apart from poor John of course, and that was because she felt so sorry for him. She didn't feel sorry for Dorothy or for David because they never seemed to care, and really they ought to care if they valued their souls.

"Aunt Sarah was too busy to bring me," she said shyly. "I'll be coming on my own from now on."

"Nice!" said Dorothy. She plucked at a blade of withered brown grass and twisted it round a twig. With the twig between her lips, she took a puff on an imaginary cigarette and then craned her head to peep round the corner of the shed towards the playing field. "What did you think of today's assembly?"

Lucy's face fell. "Horrible!"

Aunt Mavis Mathematics was clapping her hands and calling people in, and the two girls jumped to their feet. Dorothy ran out towards the field, but Lucy waited until she had gone and then sidled out, and walked as unobtrusively as she could towards the rear door of the school building. She hoped the Magnifico hadn't noticed her chatting with a past recipient of the guidance cane.

CHAPTER TWO

School ended at five o'clock, and Dorothy was standing outside the bicycle shed waiting for David. He emerged pushing his bike, and they made their way in miserable silence over the junction and up the High Street towards Drax House.

"I feel so guilty," he blurted out after a few minutes.

"Me too," muttered Dorothy.

"I just sat there and didn't do anything to help him."

Dorothy sighed. "Don't wallow in your own guilt," she said. "We all just sat there. You're not the only one." She caught a powerful whiff of exhaust fumes and spluttered. "Ugh! Just look at that traffic!"

David struggled to push the bike through the throng of workers as they poured down the pavement towards the Underground. He veered left onto a small patch of grass and plonked himself down on a bench with the bike at his side.

"Let's sit here for a few minutes," he said, "till the crowd has gone. Lucky things!"

They watched as the non-followers went by, on their way to proper homes with proper families, and Magnifico-free lives.

"It's obvious he can't help it," said David eventually. "He just twitches more and more each time they do it. Why can't they see that?"

"Perhaps they do see it, but if they accept that he's ill they'll have to hand him over to the good doctors," said Dorothy quietly.

They both digested this thought.

"We've just got to get out of here!" exclaimed David. "I can't stand it any longer. Why do we just keep going on about running away instead of actually doing it?"

"Where can we go? The infiltrators are everywhere. We'd only get caught and brought back, and then things would be worse." Dorothy shivered. "They might even send us to the disposal cells."

"There must something we can do. We've just got to plan it properly."

"Well, I still think our original idea was best," said Dorothy slowly. "Me to disappear first, find a job, and get a message back to you when it's safe to come."

She knew David wanted them both to go at the same time, but they had to be practical. They were more likely to be caught if they were together, and at least she looked nearly old enough to get a job – or so she hoped. The problem would be how to get the message back to him when she had found somewhere safe to live.

"I was trying to talk to Lucy Copse today," she said, "because if I go first we'll need an outside friend to get a message through. We can't trust anyone in the commune now. They've just started training some kid to be an infiltrator, which means whoever it is will practise by spying on the rest of us."

David groaned. "How do you know?"

Dorothy glanced over her shoulder, not that anyone could have overheard above the traffic noise. "The aunts were talking about it last night," she whispered, "when I was hiding in the linen cupboard. For all we know there might be others being trained too, so we've got to be really careful. Lucy can't spy on us from Father Copse's house and we might be able to trust her. We'll have to try and get to know her better."

They sat in silence for some time, both minds running through a mental list of possible trainee infiltrators. The traffic was still at a standstill, but the crowd on the pavement had dwindled slightly and was now bulging out of the entrance to the tube station. "Come on," said Dorothy standing up. They walked slowly up the hill, comfortable to be with each other, and in no hurry to reach the commune.

"I'm not sure about Lucy," said David after a while. "I don't know what to make of her. It's three months since they put me to sit next to her, and it's like sitting next to an empty space. I do try talking to her, and she's always terribly polite and she does laugh at my jokes, but she never shows what she's thinking."

He stopped as a shocking thought came to him. "That would make her a good spy. Perhaps she's already an infiltrator for the Magnifico!"

Dorothy laughed. "Lucy's OK," she said. "She's just got a really bleak life. Worse than ours, I think. It knocks the stuffing out of you. It's because she's so quiet that they put you there – to calm you down."

"Well, Matthew's on the other side," David pointed out. "He's certainly not quiet. He laughs louder than anyone!"

"He's good fun, so they probably hoped he'd draw you away from me. It was when they were threatening to send me to another commune. Remember?"

David nodded. He smiled to himself at the thought of anyone entrusting secret plans to Matthew. It'd be all over the place in no time. He'd be fooling around and it would just pop out before he realised. Disaster!

"Yeah, you're right. We need someone from outside. Lucy never lets out secrets because she hardly ever speaks to anyone. In fact, she's like a secret herself."

"I wonder what does go on in Father Copse's house. It's probably even more miserable than living in a commune." Dorothy straightened her back. "Right! Decision made. I'm going to try and get closer to Lucy and find out what she's like. Someone who hardly ever speaks is discreet, if nothing else."

The primary school children had gone home long ago. It was almost dark, and bitterly cold, but Lucy was not in a hurry. She had managed to put John's face to one side temporarily, and was intending to savour the novelty of going home on her own.

A school bus drove up. She stood on the steps above all the bustle, and watched as pupils from faraway communes clambered on board. Suddenly the pavement cleared and she could see the older boys from the Drax and Copse communes fetching their bikes from the shed at the side of the building. The girls were already crossing over the junction and traipsing up the High Street chattering among themselves.

She watched as Dorothy and David walked together up the High Street towards Drax House and melted into the crowd. They were so lucky to have each other, she thought. It must be much more fun living in a commune. She waited until they had disappeared completely, and then pulled herself together. It was time to get a move on, or Aunt Sarah would be cross and say she wasn't to be trusted on her own. She crossed at the lights. The

24

traffic seemed to be stuck and people poured up and down the steps of the Underground station. Lucy would have enjoyed feeling inconspicuous as she was briefly swallowed up by the crowd, if only she hadn't had to try and avoid actually touching the non-followers. That was impossible. No doubt she'd get used to it in due course. She dawdled up South Hill, looking into front gardens and brightly-lit rooms. Children were sitting at tables eating their tea, or doing their homework with mothers hovering over them. Fireplaces glowed, and television screens flickered like fingers inviting her in. It all looked so cosy that Lucy had to remind herself firmly that these were corrupt households. Television corrupted the soul.

At number 38 South Hill a boy was climbing a curtain. He looked out and saw Lucy, and stuck out his tongue. She recognised that awful boy, George, and hastily moved on, embarrassed at being caught staring – especially at a non-follower. Aunt Sarah would have said, "Non-followers' lives are their lives and our lives are ours, so mind your own business." Only yesterday she had said, "When we rule the world they'll all come under the Magnifico's blessed guidance and their souls will be cleansed, but until then we are the elite, so don't get involved."

Lucy had smiled to herself as she pictured all the non-followers in the world trooping onto the headmaster's stage, and knocking him over in their haste to be cleansed by the guidance cane.

"Why are you smiling?" Aunt Sarah had said.

"I don't know."

"Then don't be cheeky."

Remembering this incident, Lucy turned round and stuck her tongue out at the non-elite George. Just as she did so the curtain pole collapsed and George, the curtain and the pole all disappeared simultaneously. Lucy burst out laughing and then hastily turned away as his mother appeared in the window looking crossly down at the floor. What a stroke of luck to have witnessed that! She passed the next two houses with a big smile on her face and turned into the little lane that led between the terraced houses onto the common. It looked very dark from where she stood. Creepy. She took a deep breath and ran. The sky seemed to grow lighter as the streetlamps of South Hill receded behind her. When she reached 3 Mortimor Road she was out of breath, but she felt good. The porch light was on. She jumped with both feet over the covered hole in the front path where men used to pour coal in the olden days when people had heating in the ground floor flat. Father Copse didn't allow heating, but it didn't matter today because the running had warmed Lucy up nicely.

She had forgotten about poor John in the dash across the common, and she felt almost happy. It had been fun coming home on her own. Then, remembering that the Magnifico expected females of all ages to walk with dignity, she stepped sedately into the front porch and tried to subdue her panting. The door had been left slightly ajar for her. She pushed it open and made straight for the kitchen. Aunt Sarah was just beginning to get anxious.

"You took a long time coming home," she said accusingly.

"I had to wait ages at the lights," said Lucy.

She hoped the Magnifico was too busy with more important things to notice the lie. It would have been nice to be able to tell Aunt Sarah about George and the curtain, but it would have led to a lecture on dawdling.

Sarah had put the oven on to heat up the kitchen. The father need never know, and she was sure the Magnifico wouldn't want that poor little boy going down with pneumonia just as soon as he'd arrived. Lucy pulled off her coat. As she did so her happiness turned to astonishment and concern. There was a child in the corner of the room. She stared in amazement. He stared back for a moment and then opened his mouth wide and yelled. He stopped for a moment to glare at Lucy, and then howled louder, gripping the bars of the playpen as he tried to climb out.

"This is Paul," said Aunt Sarah, her voice raised above the noise. "He lives with us now."

"Where did he come from?" asked Lucy.

"He has been sent to us by the Magnifico."

Lucy approached the playpen. The screams became more frantic. She paused.

"He's afraid," she said.

"We must all be afraid," said Aunt Sarah. "Afraid of the evils of this world so we may be free of sin for the next. He's got to get used to it."

She turned away and set out Lucy's tea. There was a small piece of cold meat, some bread without butter, and a glass of milk. Also, there was a banana.

Bananas were a treat for special occasions so Lucy guessed that Paul's arrival was a cause for celebration, though he obviously didn't think so. Her old high chair had been brought in from the garage, and it now stood at one end of the table with Paul's supper laid out for him. Sarah picked up the screaming child, struggling with his weight, and hauled him over the side into the chair. He threw his plate on the floor and shut his mouth firmly, and a beautiful silence fell briefly on the kitchen.

27

Lucy needed to think. There were three important matters to digest. One, of course, was the boy's arrival, and another was Dorothy's surprising and novel display of interest in her. The most important of all was poor John, who was once more weighing heavily on her conscience. She was disgusted with herself. How could she have preached at him when he needed comfort?

"May I go in the garden?" she asked Aunt Sarah.

"But it's dark."

"Just for a minute, so I can pray quietly to the Magnifico."

Paul opened his mouth to yell and Sarah zoomed a spoon towards it.

"Don't be long," she shouted over the noise. "I don't want you going down with a cold. I've more work than I can cope with as it is."

Lucy let herself out through the back door. Light fell on the lawn from the kitchen, but beyond that the garden was an ocean of darkness, and the eight-foot high surrounding wall was barely visible.

There were rustlings in the bushes and scuttling sounds that made Lucy's skin crawl. Glancing back through the glass in the door she could see Aunt Sarah struggling to make the boy eat, and she dared to hope that his arrival might mean more freedom than just going to school on her own. Perhaps she'd be allowed to help Aunt Sarah by going to the shops for her sometimes. Of course she would never speak to the non-followers, she assured herself, because she knew that would be wrong, and she would certainly ignore that rude boy George if she ever met him again.

Her eyes became accustomed to the dark and she ventured further out across the grass and round the back of the rear wing. She leaned against the trunk of the huge lime tree that spread across the lawn behind the garage and over the wall into the next-door garden. Closing her eyes and running her fingers back and forth over her reminder, she asked the Magnifico to forgive John. The gentle rubbing didn't soothe her as it normally did, and she couldn't help asking herself why He hadn't done something to stop the beating. Poor John, with his mousy hair and pale skin and glasses! He'd never harmed a soul in his life. What on earth was the Magnifico thinking of to allow him to be treated like that?

Only last week she'd pulled him away from some horrible bully-boys from the class above, and though she'd been scared at the time she was glad now that she had done it, or she'd be feeling even more guilty. "Mind your own business," they'd shouted, "you don't even live in a commune!" Since then they had jeered every time they saw her. "Watch out! Here comes the fire of the burning flesh!" or "The FOBF is coming!"

Aunt Sarah had told her to ignore them. "There's worse things waiting for you in life than a bit of name-calling," she had said, and she was right because what had happened to John today was far worse. "Though mind you," Aunt Sarah had added, "I'm proud of you for helping that little boy."

Lucy felt a flash of anger as she remembered that the Magnifico hadn't helped John escape the bullies on that occasion either, but she hastily pushed it away. As Aunt Sarah would have said, He had a purpose which ordinary followers like themselves shouldn't even try to guess at. At school tomorrow she would look for John again. She would ask his forgiveness, and try and help him think of a way to master the twitch.

The decision went a little way towards soothing her conscience, and she forced her mind to switch to something else. She looked up at the side of house. The first floor was in darkness. Father Copse would not be home from work till about seven o'clock. Lucy wondered briefly what he did in the evenings, but tried not to think about him too much.

She shifted her gaze to the second floor. There the blinds were open, and the light was on. All she could see was a lamp dangling from the ceiling. Against the light she could see bars on the windows. Her own room had bars, but she was on the ground floor and it was for her own safety Aunt Sarah had said, to keep out intruders. Lucy couldn't see why bars were needed on the second floor. It was too high up for intruders. Obviously the first-floor windows weren't barred. No-one would ever dare creep in on someone as frightening as the father, with his powerful shoulders, his burning eyes, and the thunderous voice that froze a person's heart.

Lucy wanted time to think about the little boy and Dorothy, but the sky had clouded over and it started to rain, and she shivered. She ran back to the house just as Aunt Sarah appeared at the door.

"That was a very long prayer," said Aunt Sarah.

Lucy said nothing. She washed her hands at the sink, and sat down at the kitchen table to eat her tea. The best thing, the banana, was left till last, and she ate it slowly. She thanked the Magnifico for her meal, washed up her mug and plate, and then settled down at the table to do her homework. Paul had stopped crying, and was lying on his back in the playpen staring silently at the ceiling. When Lucy had finished her homework and had put her books back in her bag tidily ready for tomorrow, she lay on the floor by the playpen and put her arm through the bars. She stroked Paul's listless hand.

"Don't be afraid, little boy," she whispered. "I'm going to be your friend." He didn't move.

CHAPTER THREE

Dorothy lay in pitch darkness under the bottom shelf in the linen cupboard thinking about what had happened to John that morning. This was a good place for thinking, but an even better place for listening

Years ago, when she was very small, she had been locked in the cupboard in the dark as a punishment. She had felt her way along the bottom shelf on the right and crawled under it and curled up into a ball. Voices had floated into the blackness around her like ghosts, and she was rigid with fear until she recognised Senior Aunt Sonia's imperative tones, and realised that they came from below her. When her heart had stopped thumping she explored with her hands and discovered a small section in the furthest corner where the floorboards had been cut too short and didn't quite reach the wall.

An eternal optimist, she was always telling David that bad things sometimes happen for the best, and this was her favourite example. Whenever they were feeling really down they would remind themselves that if she hadn't been locked in the cupboard she would never have picked up all sorts of interesting and important information over the years, information that they hoped would help to lead them to freedom.

Now she had wiped in the corner with a tissue as usual to make sure there were no spiders waiting to spin webs in her hair, and had pressed her right ear to the floor. Whoever was in the kitchen below her must have been on their own because all she could hear was occasional clattering and sighing, and the humming of a dreary hymn tune. She knew she wouldn't have to wait long because it was always busy just before supper. This was the best time for her to come.

Her mind switched from John to Lucy while she waited. She and David really needed to find out more about her. If they were lucky it might be that her strict upbringing had secretly made her react against the Magnifico. On the other hand she could well be a zealous believer only too ready to report on sinners – for the sake of their souls. They would have to tread very carefully.

She was startled out of her thoughts as a voice below said, "How's it going? Have you stirred the gravy?"

The humming stopped. "Mm. It's a bit lumpy."

"Let me have a go. What's the matter? Is it John?"

"The good doctors came for him," the hummer said sadly. "They took him down through the passageway."

The hair prickled on the back of Dorothy's neck. There was a long silence.

"Poor little fellow," said the other voice eventually. "I suppose it was the best thing for him in the long run. It was the Magnifico's will."

More voices floated upwards, but nothing was said about John. Dorothy lay too shocked to move until Aunt Sonia's brisk bark snapped, "Take that laundry up to the cupboard, please. It should have gone up hours ago."

She scrambled hastily out of her hiding place and groped her way past the shelving. With her ear to the door she listened for a second and then slipped out and shut it behind her. She was sauntering nonchalantly down the stairs as one of the aunts came up with a pile of sheets.

Later that evening in the first-floor flat Father Copse, dark and sombre, sat at his desk staring at the window. Now and then the rain-washed twigs of the leafless lime tree caught the light from the room and glistened, piercing his reflection like twinkling pinprick stars. But he saw nothing, nothing but a black pool of money, ambition, and the hurt that swamped his soul.

The expense of maintaining his family was troubling him. An open file lay in front of him. It contained records of the fifteen children born to his wives on instructions of the Magnifico. Apart from two deceased, and the girl and boy downstairs, all were living in his Copse House commune. Also, there were the aunts and the discards – extra children dumped on him because their fathers had died or been sent abroad. And of course he had to maintain his own private household. His income just wasn't enough. He wanted more from life than just to be able to make ends meet. Admittedly he earned a fortune as a lawyer in the outside world, and the Holy Envoy paid him well for infiltrating the legal profession, but it seemed that no matter how hard he worked, whatever he earned, he needed more.

As he gazed blankly ahead his brilliant brain was working but, unusually for him, it was failing to come up with a solution.

He would have to make economies but he couldn't see where. Sarah didn't receive a wage, and nor did the aunts who worked in his commune. Like Sarah, they toiled for the glory of the Magnifico, and would receive their reward in the next world. It was enough for them that the father fed, clothed and housed them. They were truly blessed. As for the children, fortunately his religion preached austerity so their food was plain and their possessions few, as his had been as a child. Nevertheless, they were a necessary expense because he had a duty to the Magnifico to make sure that they grew up healthy and strong, and fit to further the Holy Cause.

There was one major extravagance. It was crippling him but he couldn't even contemplate giving it up. It was the woman upstairs. He bought her books and magazines, and beautiful clothes and jewellery. She had music and television, and whatever foods pleased her. For all his generosity she had never shown him any gratitude or tenderness.

All he wanted was to see her smile, and to stroke her hair.

Outside the rain beat on the window and the bitter wind blew through the branches of the lime tree. Despite the warmth of the room, he shivered as he imagined how cold life would be without the knowledge that she was there just above him, and could never escape. He stood up and closed the curtains against the bleak winter darkness, then crossed the room to the opposite window and looked out over the garden. The shrubs were dark and wet and depressing. There was nothing to cheer him. He sighed. Everything was too big – the garden, the house, his family. Why did he have to be responsible for a house with status, and for so many wives and aunts and children in whom he was not really interested? Happiness would have been one wife in a little flat in the Temple near the High Court so he could walk to work, and a couple of kids that he could send to good schools and take on skiing holidays.

He pulled himself together. It was not for him to question the Magnifico's will. He drew the second set of curtains to shut out the night and was immediately comforted by the warmth and luxury of his surroundings. Crossing back to the desk he put the file to one side and took another out of a walnut cabinet to his left. He turned to a section labelled 'Disposals'. It recorded the deaths of some wives who had been abducted for their brains and beauty, and had been brought to him unwillingly. They had refused to be converted to the Holy Cause and had to be disposed of. The woman upstairs should have suffered the same fate, but he had managed to persuade the Holy Leaders that there was a possibility of more children, and that he still had hopes of her conversion.

What was it about her? Was it just her hair? He felt warm when he touched it. It was soft and cloudy and dark, and it reminded him of his mother.

Also under Disposals were the names of three commune aunts who had succumbed to ill health and ceased to be useful. And there were two children who had suffered physical or mental frailties. The Holy Leaders had arranged everything for him with the good doctors. He didn't like to think about that, but it had to be done. There was no room for weakness in the service of the Magnifico, and the lethal injection was very humane. Of his thirteen living children, and the extra hangers-on, he could not think of one who was not hale and hearty, and he couldn't justifiably dispose of any of them. Today he'd heard that the good doctors had taken one of Drax's boys. It always reflected badly on a father if his kids weren't up to scratch.

To his left, at the far end of the room, a purring sound announced the arrival of the dumb waiter. He moved towards it, catching his foot on the Persian carpet as he went. For a split second he wondered if he should sell a couple of his valuable carpets, or some of his antiques or paintings, but immediately put the thought out of his head. He liked to be surrounded by lovely things.

He opened the door to the dumb waiter and lifted the top tray onto the sideboard. Then, closing the door, he pressed a button and sent the other tray up to the second floor. The food looked and smelled good. However many aunts he might dispose of he would never get rid of Sarah. He'd inherited her from a much older father, and she was a wonderful cook. He lifted a bottle of wine out of the rack next to the sideboard and poured himself a glass. Then he put on some Vivaldi and set the tray down on a small table next to the big leather chair by the fire. He was glad he had had that fire fitted. The flames were so realistic. He settled down to his meal. It was pleasant to be comfortable.

He gazed up at the Van Gogh over the fireplace. So crude. Perhaps that could go. He would never have bid for it except that he knew Father Drax wanted it for his own private collection. It could go back into auction, now that he had had his little triumph. He smiled as he thought that Drax might bid again and have to pay more for it than he had. Even with the auctioneer's commission he might make a profit out of Drax. That would indeed be amusing.

The wine was a lovely colour. He swirled it around in the glass and allowed his mind to roam beyond the little world of his own household to the wider and more fulfilling world of ambition. The deputy to the current Holy Envoy would be retiring soon, and the post would be open to candidates. If he were to be elected his income would double and his troubles would be over. He could think of only one possible rival of equal calibre to himself, and that was Drax. It was always a pleasure to get one up on him.

All of a sudden his eyes filled with bitter tears. He had been just three years old when they took him from his mother. Her face was a blur, but he could see and smell her hair now, and feel its gentle warmth. Of course he'd had to leave her, he understood that. Most children left the breeding rooms at two, and the Magnifico had been generous in letting him stay until he was three. But when he turned at the door to blow his mother a final kiss, she wasn't looking at him. She already had another little boy on her lap – a toddler – and she was smiling down into his blue, blue eyes, and stroking his golden curls.

OK. So Drax's mother had died. Bad luck. But there was no need to steal his.

CHAPTER FOUR

The next morning, as Lucy was crossing at the lights, Matthew and David came out of the bicycle shed.

"What were you writing on that bit of paper yesterday?" asked Matthew.

David hardly heard the question. His head felt heavy.

"What bit of paper?"

They reached the school at the same time as Lucy.

"Hi there!" called Matthew cheerily, just behind her as she started up the steps. "If you're still looking for John, he's gone."

She turned and looked at him. "What do you mean?

"John's gone. The good doctors took him away."

Relief flashed over Lucy's normally inscrutible face.

"Wow! That's great news! They'll get him well again." She smiled. "Do you know how long it's likely to be?"

Matthew was taken aback and his smile disappeared.

"No. Sorry."

"Well, thanks for letting me know."

As she moved off she glanced at David and stopped in her tracks. Her relief switched to concern.

"Are you alright?"

He nodded.

"Well you don't look it. You should ask the surgery aunt if you can lie down."

He nodded again, and she ran on up the steps. Matthew looked at David.

"Did you see her face when I said about the good doctors? She hasn't got a clue, poor fool," he said, genuinely surprised. "That's what comes of living in Father Copse's private house instead of in his commune. Just so ignorant!"

David too had seen the look on Lucy's face. It was obvious no-one had ever told her about the good doctors. But what was worrying was that he and Dorothy had thought they were the only ones who knew that John had gone. One of the aunts must have been blabbing. He nearly blurted out that he knew already, but stopped himself in time. If he let on he might find himself giving an explanation about the linen cupboard.

"How do you know the good doctors have taken him?" he mumbled.

"I don't," replied Matthew. "I just assumed she knew what it meant, and thought it would be fun to wind her up."

"That's really mean."

"Yeah. I realise that now." Matthew looked contrite, then brightened up. "Still, she won't know that's what I was doing. If John is at his desk today, I'll tell her it was just a rumour, and if he isn't I'll be proved right."

Well, you are right, thought David to himself. The horror of it sickened him.

CHAPTER FIVE

"He's dead."

Lucy grabbed the back of her chair. "What d'you mean?"

"Well, I can't put it any more clearly than that," said Matthew a little crossly. "You asked if I knew when John was coming back, and I told you he's dead. What that means is he's died. Gone. The Magnifico's taken him."

He looked at Lucy's ashen face, and grabbed David's arm. "Come on. Let's go, before she faints or something."

David shook him off. "Listen, Lucy," he said quietly, "I'll explain it all to you." But she turned sharply, and started weaving her way through the rows of desks towards the door.

"Leave her alone," said Matthew. "She'll get over it. Let's go and get some food. It's Father Copse's duty to educate her, not ours."

As they watched, a boy jumped up from his chair and shoved it backwards into Lucy's right hip.

"Hey!" he exclaimed. "It's FOBF, knocking into innocent people."

Two of his friends loomed up alongside him.

"Holy Magnifico! She looks like something the cat sicked up!" laughed one of them. "What's the matter, FOBF?"

Lucy hardly heard them. John's face was swimming

before her eyes. She moved on. One of the boys grabbed her arm and swung her round to face them.

"We're talking to you, FOBF. Don't you turn your back on us."

Trying to clear her head, she looked at the three grinning faces.

"We'll be fathers someday, and you'll just be a kitchen aunt, so show us some respect."

Slowly, Lucy took in what they were saying.

"Oh, I thought fathers were chosen because they were clever and handsome, not stupid and ugly," she said contemptuously. "The Holy Leaders must have changed the rules!"

She didn't wait for a response. As she turned one of the boys pulled her back by the neck of her jumper. David leaped forward between the desks and pushed him away. "Leave her alone!" he growled.

Matthew grabbed him from behind. "Come away, you idiot!" he muttered in his ear. "Let's go and get our lunch."

"Ooh! Sir Galahad!" jeered one of the boys, and all three laughed and whooped as Lucy walked towards the door with as much dignity as she could muster.

David couldn't see Lucy in the canteen. He left Matthew at the counter and took his plate over to where Dorothy was sitting on her own at a window table.

"I think we'll have to give up on our idea of making friends with her," he said, after he had described Lucy's reaction to the news about John, and the incident in the classroom. "She hasn't got a clue what goes on, or what the good doctors do. An outside friend who doesn't know things won't be much use to us." He looked past Dorothy and noticed that Matthew had settled himself down with two buddies, and was talking nineteen to the dozen. Probably telling them about how stupid Lucy was, thought David.

"Yeah, I know what you mean," Dorothy checked over her shoulder. "But I think we should make one big and final effort, very subtly, to educate her. There isn't anyone else. Otherwise we'll just have to leave together at the same time."

"Well, I've been making a really big and final effort for the past two months. It's like talking to a rubber wall. Whatever I say to her some polite response bounces back at me and that's it."

"We've got to keep positive."

"I know." David watched the runny stew dribble off his spoon into the bowl and gave it a stir. "Yuk!" he said, pulling a face. "I hope it tastes better than it looks."

They ate in silence for a while.

"She'll get suspicious if I'm too friendly," said David when he had finished, "and I don't want Matthew to think I fancy her! He'd blab it out to the whole school, and she'd never speak to me again."

"We'll have to think of a strategy."

David looked out of the window. The sky was a miserable grey. "Look how dark it is, and it's still only lunchtime!" he remarked forlornly. "Everything's so depressing."

"Mmm," Dorothy was thinking. Her face brightened. "The clocks go forward on Sunday, and it'll be light in the evenings. You boys'll be allowed to take your bikes on the common after school."

"Good! I'm fed up with having nothing to do except homework."

"Count yourself lucky," remarked Dorothy. "I wish girls were allowed to ride bikes."

"Ah, girls would be tempted to ride away! The Magnifico wouldn't want to risk that."

Dorothy laughed. "You're so right! We'd be off like a shot." She lowered her voice. "You'll be going up South Hill to get to the common, and that's the way Lucy goes home."

The significance sank in. David nodded. "Ah! Right. I see."

"You might get a chance to talk to her."

"Maybe," he said slowly, "as long as I can do it without looking suspicious."

"And I might be able to too." Dorothy's voice had dropped almost to a whisper. "Some of the girls will go up to sit on the grass and pretend to do their homework while they watch whoever they've got a crush on – poor fools." She tossed her head scornfully. "A waste of time seeing they'll be forced to marry a father! Anyway, if I come up with them I might have a chance to talk to Lucy on her way home."

They finished their lunch in silence and stood up to leave.

"Change of mind!" Dorothy announced suddenly. She dropped her voice. "I'm not going to wait till the clocks go forward. I know where she'll be now. She'll be behind the bike shed digesting the news about John. Being subtle takes too long. I'm going to be direct. I know it's risky, but I'll suss her out a bit before I say anything stupid."

Lucy was huddled up with her chin on her knees. There was a huge pain in the pit of her stomach. Big tears rolled down her cheeks as she tried to reason with herself. It was not as if she had been friends with John. And the

Magnifico must have a purpose. Even so, she felt her heart would burst. How could He be so cruel?

She looked up nervously as Dorothy slipped round the corner of the shed. "Oh, it's only you," she whispered with relief.

"Only me," said Dorothy quietly, sliding down next to her and putting her arms round her.

Lucy wriggled away. She used to cry on Aunt Sarah's shoulder sometimes years ago before she started school, but now Aunt Sarah would have told her sharply to pull herself together this minute! Sitting up abruptly she wiped her face with her sleeve. "Sorry," she mumbled.

"Don't be daft." Dorothy handed her a tissue. "David told me what Matthew said. We're upset too, but it's not such a shock for us because we already knew about the Magnifico's ways."

"It's his purpose, isn't it?" sniffled Lucy. "Why use poor harmless John to carry out his purpose?"

She stopped, aghast at what she had said, and looked around, almost expecting to see the fire licking towards her and melting her flesh.

Dorothy hesitated. This could all go terribly wrong. "There isn't a purpose," she said.

"Yes there is." Lucy sniffed and wiped the crumpled tissue all over her face. "Aunt Sarah told me. She knows. It's called having faith."

Dorothy was wondering if she dare say more when the bell rang, and they could hear the playground aunt clapping her hands for them to go in. "Having faith isn't the same as knowing," she said as she jumped to her feet. "And listen," she added hastily, "David and I want you to be our friend. We'll talk about it some other time." She walked quickly away.

Lucy waited behind and then sidled out on her own, and made her way back to class. It was impossible to concentrate. Her mind switched back and forth from John to Dorothy. The astonishing offer of friendship had brought fleeting joy followed by puzzlement and suspicion. She'd never had a friend and would love to think she could be seen as potential friend material, but why? After all, they'd known her for the past ten years. Anyway, she couldn't even contemplate it. They'd both had the guidance cane and there was the risk of being tempted to their ways. It would be wrong to put herself in the way of temptation. Perhaps there could be a sort of friendship if she were to make it her task to persuade Dorothy that there was such a thing as the purpose. But was there? She wouldn't dare ask Aunt Sarah, so she'd have to ask Thomas.

Thomas wasn't there when Lucy got home. She was disappointed, but not surprised. He only came to do the father's garden when he could fit it in, and he couldn't always stay long because he had two proper jobs – one as a corporation gardener, and one as a nurse at the Mortimor Hospital at the end of the road. Even so, she sat down on a pile of sacks inside the garage door and waited, just in case he did come. Sometimes he called in after his shift at the hospital finished.

Lucy thought she loved Thomas. She wasn't sure what love was, but she certainly knew that she liked him very much. He wasn't good-looking or clever enough to be a father, but he worked hard and was useful to the Holy Envoy, so he must be a good man. Not only did he look after the local parks and do three days a week as a nurse, but on top of that he was paid by the Holy

Envoy as an infiltrator into the local authority and into the health service. If anyone knew what was going on it was Thomas.

He was skinny and pimply with thin, sandy hair, but he had such a kind face. Leaning up against the garage wall he would roll himself a cigarette and chat, asking Lucy about herself and Aunt Sarah and the father, and how things went on at the house. He was the one person in the world who seemed interested in her, and what was more he always answered her questions if he could without making her feel guilty for asking. And he told her things. Once he had shown her the secret hand signal the infiltrators used if they needed to make themselves known to other infiltrators. He'd crossed his right thumb over his palm and dropped his hand to his side in a twisting movement. It had to be done very subtly and quickly so people wouldn't notice. According to Thomas some of the councillors used it when they came to meetings at the town hall.

Lucy had practised it over and over again, and he'd told her she might make a good infiltrator one day. They were always looking for people to train.

Sometimes he gave her a sweet, and she would hide behind a shrub to eat it, for the sweet things in life were forbidden. Lucy knew that when she was sixteen, less than two years from now, she would have to marry some unknown father she had never met before. She would rather marry someone like Thomas.

After waiting a good ten minutes she scrambled to her feet. He'd have turned up by now if he was going to come. When she entered the kitchen Aunt Sarah was sitting with Paul on her lap playing 'round and round the garden' on the palm of his hand, and they were both laughing. Lucy couldn't remember when she last saw Aunt Sarah laugh. Paul reached up and fingered the gold circle that hung from a chain round Sarah's neck.

"Pretty," he said. "It's got flowers in the middle."

"Three daffodils. My mother put it round my neck when I was taken from her, just your age. The Holy Leaders were kind and let me keep it."

Lucy hung up her coat and went to her room to change out of her school clothes. When she returned to the kitchen Paul was standing in the open doorway looking out into the back garden and chanting, "Holy Leaders, Holy Leaders," over and over again to himself. Aunt Sarah was briskly setting out the tea table.

Lucy fetched some mugs.

"John's died," she said.

Aunt Sarah's face softened. "Yes, I heard," she said sadly. "Aunt Martha told me. Poor little fellow!" She looked at Lucy's stricken face and touched her hand. "It's the purpose. We must try not to grieve. He's probably sitting at the Magnifico's right hand at this moment, and is happier than he ever was in this sad world."

Paul clambered up into his high chair with Lucy shoving him from behind, and Sarah put a fish paste sandwich on his plate. "Now come along and eat up both of you. We're running late as it is, and I've got the upstairs suppers to cook yet."

"Where's my mother?" asked Paul with his mouth full.

"You were taken from her just after you were born."

Sarah sighed. Already she could see the questions in Lucy's eyes. "Some fathers think it's cruel to let children remember their mothers, so they let the mothers name them and nurse them for a month, and then they're put with the foster aunts till they're two or three, same as you were, except you were lucky. You didn't have to go to a commune. It was the same for Lucy too."

She took down a saucepan from the shelf above the sink and started laying out supper ingredients onto a wooden board. "Mind you, it's not cruel for everyone. I'm glad I can remember my mother. I'll know her when I see her."

Lucy couldn't stop herself. "Where is she?"

"She's in Paradise," said Aunt Sarah, "waiting for me." Her face lit up with a flash of pure joy. "And when I get there she'll hold me close."

CHAPTER SIX

It was April, and today was adult achievement day at the school. An atmosphere of suppressed excitement filled the hall. Lucy's class sat near the front and she had to crane her head up to look at the stage. In the centre, seated on a splendidly carved chair, was a Holy Leader, one of the Magnifico's worldwide body of priests. He stroked the wispy beard that straggled over his black robes, and his small hooded eyes darted back and forth over the rows of children, penetrating their souls and prising out their sins. To his right stood the headmaster, head thrown back, eyes closed behind little round glasses, and the palms of his hands held up to the ceiling. His pink chins quivered and shook and the little tuft of white hair on his head stood upright pointing towards Paradise. No-one would have guessed he was wondering what was for dinner.

When complete hush had fallen over the congregation the headmaster lowered his arms and spread out his plump hands. The twelve boys and girls who had reached their sixteenth birthdays by the beginning of March were lined up in the aisle that ran down the centre of the seating area. The girls were dressed in white and the boys in suits.

Calling them up one by one the headmaster cut off their reminders with holy pliers and dropped them with an elaborate gesture into a sacred woven basket. He sent each child to the right, left, or middle of the stage. As they stood staring in embarrassment at their toes or the ceiling, or anywhere except at the audience of smirking school fellows, he began a long speech to the effect that they were now men and women and would be required to do their duty in the service of the Magnifico. His voice droned on and on.

The first Holy Envoy stared accusingly at Lucy from the mural at the back of the stage. A cobweb hung down from the ceiling just above his head. It must have been difficult for him to rule the world if he was stuck with a sword and leaning on a rock. The current Holy Envoy would probably find it difficult too, even though he wasn't stuck with a sword. How could anyone rule the whole world when everyone in it had a different way of looking at things? Lucy tore her eyes away and tried to focus on something else. A boy to her left was annoying the girl in front by gently tapping the back of her chair.

Suddenly the headmaster's voice changed.

"And now," he announced in triumphant tones, "we move on to the most significant moment in the lives of these young ladies."

Next to him the Holy Leader rose to his feet and came forward to a lectern at the side of the stage. Lucy pictured him washing his beard and drooping side curls in a wash basin. She didn't like to think of him having a shower. It wouldn't be respectful. Supposing he went bald? Would he have to wear false curls? She hastily pushed the thought away. Disrespect to the Magnifico's servants was a sin.

The *Holy Vision* lay open on the lectern. The Holy Leader's voice was deep and solemn as he read.

"And when a female has reached her seventeenth year, she shall be wed to the Magnifico body and soul to serve Him faithfully either as a mother or as an aunt to His children, or as His agent infiltrating the world of non-followers in furtherance of the Holy Cause."

He then turned to the girls and asked them to stand in a line before him. They stood meekly with their heads bowed, some gawky, some buxom, and some nothing in particular. He passed along the line placing his hand on the head of each of them in turn saying, "Do you promise to serve the Magnifico faithfully as his wife in whatever capacity he may allocate to you for the rest of your life?"

Each girl murmured a promise.

After a very long prayer and a hymn the young brides trooped awkwardly off the stage and down the centre aisle to the recorded sound of an organ. The boys followed, looking sheepish and self-conscious. One winked at the congregation and someone sniggered. Then came the headmaster and staff in solemn procession. As the ponderous music thundered out, the Holy Leader remained on the stage waving incense from side to side. Then he raised his hands, palms facing the audience, and said, "Bless you, my children. Now return to your classes."

That evening, after supper, Lucy sat in her hidey-hole in the back garden under the bush with the green and yellow spotted leaves. It was nearly dark and there was a nasty little wind, but she had a great deal to think about.

The thought of marrying a father, once a distant curiosity, was now an utterly depressing reality. The fathers that Lucy had met at prayer meetings had all been chosen for their brains and their looks so that the Magnifico's children would be clever and handsome. She had no reason to doubt that they were clever but as for their looks, well, they never smiled and, to her, their faces seemed terrifyingly severe or even cruel. She had noticed the bitter submission in Aunt Sarah's face as she stood with her eyes downcast, listening to Father's Copse's ferocious instructions. Once she had even heard Aunt Sarah mutter a prayer to the Magnifico to forgive her evil thoughts against the father that had been allocated to her.

Now Lucy decided firmly that if she could serve the Magnifico in any other way she would not marry a father. She would study the *Holy Vision* word for word. There must be exceptions – especially if she could make herself really ugly and useless at cooking so that none of them wanted her. There were no mirrors in the father's house or at school, but she had seen herself in shop windows and her face had looked so pinched and plain that she was sure she could make herself hideous. She twisted her mouth round now as the first step of a practice regime.

Soft fine rain brushed against her skin, and she shifted further back into the shelter of the bush. She mentally assessed the beauty of today's brides. A few were pretty, but some of the plain ones had nicer faces. She wondered whether her own mother was both pretty and had a nice face. A twig caught in her hair and pulled at her pigtail. Her mother would not have had boring brown hair. It would have been a luxurious chestnut, or black, or blonde, or auburn. Lucy could picture the hair, but not the face. She would certainly not have had a face like Lucy's because the shop windows wouldn't have lied. Aunt Sarah had told her many times that she was plain, and always scraped her hair back as severely as she could so as to emphasise it. Vanity was a sin she said.

The clouds were heavy and it was getting darker. Aunt Sarah switched on the light in the kitchen and it poured out in oblong shapes through the glass panes in the back door. Lucy knew she should go in before she had to be called, or she would get the sharp edge of Aunt Sarah's tongue. As she moved forward there was a creak at the back gate and she froze. The latch lifted with a little scratching noise and the gate squeaked slightly as it slowly opened. A hooded head appeared and looked around. Lucy held her breath as a figure emerged and slid along the side wall till it reached the back of the house. It darted across to the kitchen door and crouched down, peering in through the panes.

The sound of blood thumping in her ears was so loud that Lucy wondered why whoever it was didn't hear it.

Very quietly the figure made its way across the back of the rear wing and vanished round the corner to the further side of the house. Lucy didn't dare move. For the first time in her life she wished that Aunt Sarah would come out, or even the father. Her wish was granted because at that moment Aunt Sarah opened the back door and called her in. Lucy was torn between the terror of being caught by the figure as she ran across the lawn, and the terror of incurring Aunt Sarah's wrath if she disobeyed the summons.

From inside the kitchen Paul started to yell.

"Come in quickly. It's cold," shouted Aunt Sarah.

Her stout frame filled the doorway and she seemed to be taking gulps of the cool night air. Then she turned back into the kitchen and slammed the door. Lucy waited. The figure must have waited too, because an eternity passed before it slipped back round the corner and behind the wing. It paused to take another furtive look into the kitchen, and then dashed over to the wall to the left of the garden and out through the gate. Lucy waited a few more seconds then shot across the lawn with what felt like a thousand demons behind her.

Aunt Sarah was busy with Paul, and Lucy slipped in almost unnoticed.

"Just praying," she muttered, and went to her room to fetch her homework.

She opened a drawer and pulled out her extra jumper. Aunt Sarah was right. It was cold. Everything was cold – her room, the school, Aunt Sarah's stern face. Every morning the sight of the lollipop lady made her feel warm, just for a moment. Sitting behind the shed with Dorothy made her warm too, but that didn't happen very often.

In the kitchen a small electric heater softened the chill. Lucy plonked her satchel on the kitchen table, and drew up a chair.

"You were much too long out there," said Aunt Sarah. "I've got enough on my plate without having to nurse you through influenza. Tomorrow you must come in sooner."

"Yes, Aunt Sarah," said Lucy.

"And just look at you! You're as white as a sheet. Don't expect me to be sorry for you if you come down with a cold."

"No, Aunt Sarah."

Lucy pulled her books out of her satchel and sat down at the table.

"Take this out to the bin before you start, will you." Aunt Sarah handed her a plastic bag full of potato peelings. Her throat felt tight. She tried to swallow but couldn't.

"Come on. Get a move on," said Sarah. "I haven't got all night." She gave her a little push, and turned to the stove.

Lucy hesitated. "Can I do it when I've finished my homework?"

"Do it now and it's done. It won't take a second."

"Shouldn't we save it for Thomas's compost?"

"I'm not telling you again."

Lucy grabbed the bag and peered out of the back door. Beyond the shafts of kitchen light the garden lay in darkness. The familiar bushes had vanished, and the world was a black nothingness from which goblins and hooded figures might leap and grab a girl by the hair and pull her down into a burning brazier full of sinners.

"Hurry up! You're making the place cold with that open door," called Sarah.

"Can I take the torch?"

"Yes, but be quick and don't waste the battery."

Lucy took the torch from the shelf by the door and shone it onto the darkest areas before stepping out into the garden. Its light was feeble. Her eyes and ears strained as she followed the path round the back of the wing and down the left side of the house towards the garage. The bin was in its usual place under the kitchen window. She threw in the plastic bag hastily and closed the lid. A rustling sound behind her made her jump and turn. In the light of the torch something darted between the shafts of a ladder that leaned against the garage, and disappeared into the gap between the garage and the garden wall. She ran back to the kitchen with legs like lead weights.

"Good heavens!" said Sarah. "Are you ill?"

"No," she mumbled. "It's cold, that's all." She sat down to finish her homework. "And I saw a rat. It went down the far side of the garage."

"Nonsense," said Sarah. "Get on with your work." She made a mental note to put some rat poison down tomorrow.

Father Drax was sitting in his private residence just off the High Street, two doors up from the Drax commune. His feet were propped up on the fender in front of a dying log fire, and in his right hand he held a tumbler of whisky. He was listening to Mozart and thinking about his childhood tormentor, Father Copse.

The post of Deputy Holy Envoy would be coming up some time this year, and today Drax had learned that Copse was going to apply. He mentally sized up all other possible candidates. The only one with the brains, qualifications, and the experience to match his own, was Copse. But Copse had something extra. He could turn on the charm – which was why he made such a brilliant infiltrator. In the courts juries melted at the sound of his voice, and in social gatherings he was the fascinating magnet that drew establishment figures towards him. In the interview process for the deputy's post no-one else would stand a chance.

Somehow Copse had to be put out of the running. If he could be discredited in some way the path would be clear. The Holy Envoy would never touch someone with a scandal to his name.

There was a tap on the door. He called out, "Enter!"

and in came a thin wiry man with spots and lank sandy hair. Father Drax waved him to a chair by the fire and rose elegantly to his feet to fetch him a drink from an exotically carved sideboard covered in bottles and decanters and crystal glasses.

"Well, Thomas, did you manage to see anything?" he said, placing a whisky on a small inlaid table next to his guest.

"No, Sir. Father Copse hadn't come home and there was no light in his window. The light was on in the upstairs flat, and I was just about to get into the tree to have good look when I realised the girl was somewhere out there because I heard Sarah call her. I waited long enough for her to go back in, but I thought it best to come away and try later when she'd be in bed and Father Copse would be home."

Father Drax paced up and down on his long legs, his feet sinking softly into the plush fitted carpet.

"Right," he said at last, smoothing back his thick golden blond hair. "We'll wait. There's no immediate rush, but we need to find out all we can about Copse. What is he up to in his apartment, and how many wives has he got in the top flat? Chat to Sarah, and the girl, and find out any little bits of gossip they might have about him."

"They never gossip, Sir. Sarah rarely speaks to me, and the girl seems to know nothing about Father Copse except that he frightens her."

"We must try and discredit him somehow. There must be something we can use to blacken his name. Can we use the girl? What's her behaviour like?"

"Impeccable. I'll keep my eyes and ears open, Sir," said Thomas, getting to his feet. He pulled a woolly hat over his head and stood by the door.

"I'm not going to pay you for tonight because you misjudged the timing and found out nothing. When you can bring me enough information to knock Copse off his pedestal, I'll be generous enough."

Thomas was disappointed, but not surprised.

"I'll let you know when I find anything," he said, and left. He turned into the High Street and stood in a shop doorway to roll himself a cigarette. If only that child had not been around he could have got up into the tree and waited till Father Copse came home. Kids always spoiled everything. They were worse than garden pests.

CHAPTER SEVEN

"Blessed be the Magnifico, blessed be His holy name."
The headmaster's fruity voice sang out over the assembly.

"Blessed be the Magnifico," responded the children.

Lucy's mind was on last night's incident. The skin on the back of her neck prickled as she thought of the hooded figure. The rat was nothing in comparison. Her throat tightened up and the words would not come out.

Next to her David bellowed out the chant with gusto. The headmaster threw his arms up heavenward.

"Guide us with your holy word."

Something cut across Lucy's thoughts. Suddenly she was alert. Had she heard what she thought she heard? She held her breath and waited for the next response.

"Magnifico, the holy word," cried the headmaster.

"Magnifico's a silly nerd," sang David, his cracked newly husky voice drowning in the universal chant.

Lucy was rigid with shock.

"We thank you for your holy writ."

"No we don't you stupid git!"

Lucy was horrified. She started to giggle. The more she tried to stop the worse it got. In panic she grabbed at her reminder and rubbed it frantically, but she still couldn't stop. She shook uncontrollably as the giggles exploded in snorts and sniggers and tears began to stream down her cheeks. David stood poker-faced beside her and the headmaster lowered his arms and stared. The silence that fell on the entire congregation was broken only by Lucy's uninvited splutters. Her purple face switched from mirth to sobriety and back to mirth as she tried to suppress the horrible hiccups and choking sounds. When at last it was over, she lowered her eyes and hoped she was invisible. But of course she wasn't, and she waited for the storm.

Sarah took the guidance cane down from the hook on the wall and held it firmly.

"When she gets home, use it," the father had shouted down the phone. "She's brought dishonour on our household. We're disgraced."

Sarah agreed. She was appalled. The stick swished through the air as she tried to get the feel of it. What on earth had come over the child – the model child who prayed so dutifully? Never since she had arrived in Sarah's kitchen all those years ago had she disobeyed, or answered back, or shown disrespect to Sarah, to the father, or to the Magnifico (other than with her constant questions). And now the humiliation of a whipping with the guidance cane in front of the whole school!

All the aunts in the communes would have heard about it by now, and would be tut-tutting and wondering where Sarah had gone wrong. They would whisper behind her back when she went to the Wednesday night prayer meeting, and say she was unfit to raise the Magnifico's children. They would say she should return to the commune and let some other more dedicated aunt enjoy the privilege of serving Father Copse in his own home.

Paul ambled towards her and tried to take the stick

from her hand. She put it on the bare wooden table and pulled him up onto her lap. He nestled against her, just as Lucy used to do before she started school, and she hugged him close. If they took him and Lucy away from her she would have nothing. Tears flowed down her cheeks.

Rain started to patter on the window, and the kitchen grew dark. Sarah was as stern with herself as she would have been with Lucy. She must stop feeling sorry for herself and pull herself together. There was more reason to feel sorry for poor Lucy than herself because her soul was now in danger. She put Paul down and stood up wearily. Despite the privilege it sometimes seemed too much. There was still such a lot to do before she could lie down and sleep – the children to feed, the father's and the tenant's meals to prepare, Paul's bath and bedtime and, horrible thought, Lucy must be punished.

It was nearly six and Lucy should be back by now. Sarah was starting to worry that she might be too frightened to come home. As she began to peel the potatoes the front door clicked, and Lucy came slowly into the kitchen. Sarah looked at the white face and huge hurt eyes, and the hair in rats' tails dripping with rain, and she longed to hold and comfort her.

"You're wet," she said sternly. "Go and change before you catch your death."

Lucy crept to her room and rummaged in her drawers for dry clothes. She sat on the chair to pull off her socks but quickly stood up again because the backs of her legs hurt. Twisting round to see what she could of the strips of red, she felt sick. Slowly and carefully she pulled off her socks and her school tunic, and climbed gingerly into her trousers. They would rub, but at least

62

they would hide the shameful marks. She wanted to lie down and sleep forever, but Sarah called her from the kitchen. Her food was ready on the table and she knew she would not be able to eat it.

Paul was in his high chair, stuffing bread and jam into his mouth. He was pleased to see Lucy.

"You're late," he said.

"Am I?"

Sarah knew why she winced as she sat down. She remembered her own school days when one of the boys would step down from the stage with wheals up as far as the hems of his short trousers. She knew she could no more whip that child than fly to the moon.

"Eat your food," she said. "You've got your homework to do yet."

"Yes, Aunt Sarah," whispered Lucy.

CHAPTER EIGHT

David lay in the dark under the bottom shelf in the laundry cupboard. The remorse was eating him up. Why had he done it? What a fool! A cruel fool. It was a dare. Matthew had done it first and it had seemed funny to watch the girl in front of him tense up – but he'd never even thought about Lucy. Now he realised of course that she would have reacted somehow or other, her being so weird and everything, but it would never have occurred to him that she'd have laughed! Even Matthew had been shocked.

He knew he shouldn't have come here – he and Dorothy had agreed it was too risky for them both to use the linen cupboard – but he just couldn't face anyone yet. Him and his stupid-trying-to-be-funny jokes! Funny to him and Matthew maybe, but not to anyone else. And look at the damage they'd caused.

Gradually the heat of his shame subsided, and he started trying to think of how he could make amends. But there was nothing. She'd never speak to him again, and their plan to be friends with her had been totally destroyed. Serve them right. They could have seen that she needed a friend for the past ten years if they'd bothered to look. If they were honest, they'd really only wanted to use her.

The kitchen aunts were clattering away below. It

must be nearly supper time and he'd have to get moving, but first he had work to do. They were bound to be gossiping about the latest scandal. He rolled over with difficulty in the confined space and put his ear to the listening corner.

When the father arrived home at seven o'clock Lucy was struggling to concentrate. The words in her text book stared up at her meaninglessly. As she heard the heavy footsteps enter the side door something gripped her chest and she could hardly breathe. She shrank into her chair as Father Copse turned the key to the door that led from the lobby to the kitchen. He strode in, but didn't look at her.

"Did you use the guidance?" he asked Aunt Sarah.

"Yes," she said.

"How many strokes?"

"Seven." She mentally asked the Magnifico to forgive the lie.

The father turned to Lucy. "You mocked the Magnifico and disgraced this house."

He grabbed the back of her collar and pulled her to her feet and shook her. Her head felt as if it would fall off. He dragged her into the hall and opened the door to the coal cellar. The wooden steps disappeared down into a black hole.

"Get in there and stay there till I say you can come out." Picking her up with both hands, he threw her down the steps and shut the door. The key turned in the lock.

Lucy lay where she fell. Her back and shoulder hurt and her legs were stinging. She lay very still. Everything was so black she didn't dare move in any direction. She closed her eyes and opened them but the blackness didn't go away. Her ears strained for the sound of rats, or beetles, or monsters, and her skin prickled. Her hair was still wet from the rain and felt like a cap of ice. For a while she lost consciousness.

When she came to her eyes seemed more used to the darkness. Looking up she could see a faint ring of light in the roof at the far end of the cellar. Stiffly she rolled over onto her hands and knees and groped her way towards it. Something scuttled away from her. She knocked against boxes and bits of wood. Her hands and knees crunched into fragments of coal, and the smell of mould and damp coal dust filled her nostrils. As she approached the ring of light the shapes beneath it became faintly visible, and she could see that the floor rose upwards into a steep slope. She lay against the slope, her arms outstretched, searching for a grip on the rough concrete.

A push with her left knee and then the toes of her right foot took her part way up towards the light, only to slip back grazing her legs in the process. She sat on the floor and felt around for something to climb on. Her frozen fingers sank into a damp mass of cardboard. The smell of mould was overpowering. Her fingers scraped against the splintery side of a wooden crate. Before she had time to pull it towards her she heard the key turn in the lock and the cellar door opened throwing a beam of light down the rickety steps.

"Come on out wherever you are," called the father.

She crept towards him. Her hands, face, legs, and her clothes, were black.

"Get yourself cleaned up and then go to your room and pray for forgiveness," said the father. "To mock the

Magnifico is a deadly sin. Those who cannot be forgiven must perish."

Lucy pulled herself up by the rail of the wooden steps. With her head so bowed that she was almost bent double, she skirted round the father and stumbled down the corridor towards Aunt Sarah.

"The same again tomorrow night, and the next," he said to Sarah as he departed through the kitchen and into the lobby, locking the door behind him.

Sarah longed to hold Lucy, coal dust and all. But that was forbidden. She fetched clean towels and started to run the bath. The water was cold, as always.

"Make sure you rinse your hair thoroughly." She closed the bathroom door and went back to the kitchen to prepare the dinner trays for the upstairs flats.

Lucy couldn't sleep. She lay on the bed and shivered. Her mind raced round and round reliving the nightmare day. The trip into the cellar was nothing when she thought of the assembly and the public humiliation of the guidance cane. She didn't blame David. It was her own fault for losing self-control. Why on earth hadn't she used the reminder straight away? But even now, when she thought of David's words and visualised the deadpan innocence on his face, a hysterical splutter escaped her.

In the middle of the night when the house was very still and the distant traffic over on South Hill had ceased to rumble, she climbed out of bed and silently opened the door to the hall. Moonlight sparkled through the coloured glass in the front door and made patterns on the herringbone floor tiles.

Sarah's room was at the front of the house, on the opposite side of the hall from Lucy's, and she paused outside the door to listen carefully. There was no sound. She tiptoed to the kitchen, took the torch off the shelf, and returned to the hall. The cellar door was shut and the key was still in the lock on the outside. She turned the handle. The door gave a little creak as it opened and she stood for a second, her heart in her mouth.

She switched on the torch. The click sounded like an explosion, and again she paused and listened. Then, standing on the top step, she shone the beam down to the far end of the cellar. On the right the floor sloped upwards till it touched the ceiling just beyond the circular plate that was letting in the light. A wooden crate and a pile of disintegrating cardboard lay near the base of the slope. There were other crates and boxes, a chair with only two legs, a heap of old clothes, and what looked like a piece of rolled-up rug.

Lucy tried to take in the position of every item. Then she closed the door silently, crept back to the kitchen, and put the torch in its proper place on the shelf. She stood at the side window for a while looking over to her right at the huge lime tree. On one side its branches stretched over the high brick wall into the next-door garden, and on the other side they spread across the lawn and disappeared behind the wing. Lucy glanced over to the left. The ladder was still propped up against the garage. She remembered the rat and tiptoed back to bed.

CHAPTER NINE

The next morning it was cold. Lucy put on school trousers instead of her tunic. They rubbed against her sore legs. She was stiff all over and had bruises on her arm and shoulder where she had fallen down the cellar steps. The walk to school was more difficult than usual.

The lollipop lady smiled. Lucy managed a sort of smile back, and went miserably on down to the lights. She was a pariah to be despised, not worthy of kindness – she who had mocked the Magnifico. Looking neither left nor right she climbed the school steps, her head bowed.

"Welcome to the guidance club," called a cheerful voice behind her.

Dorothy caught up with her and smiled.

"What do your legs feel like?"

"Sore," said Lucy.

"You'll get over it. I did. Stop shrinking in to yourself like that. Stand upright and show you don't care. Be proud. That's what I do." She demonstrated by tossing back her dark curls, straightening her shoulders, and giving a cheeky wink. "What set you off?"

"David."

Dorothy stopped in her tracks and stared. "What?"

"It wasn't his fault. My reminder didn't work. I didn't use it in time."

In the playground other children looked at Lucy furtively, too embarrassed for her to say anything. She sat on her own behind the bike shed during the break. The pain inside her was worse than the pain on her legs, and she wished Dorothy would come so that she could ask her how long it would take to stop hurting.

Dorothy didn't come. Lucy could see her in the distance looking bored and fidgety as she joined in the eternal game of rounders. When Aunt Mavis clapped her hands Lucy crept out from behind the shed, and joined the queue to go in. The other children shuffled away from her, as though they might catch some of her pariah disease. She'd been like them once. Now she knew what it felt like. David surreptitiously passed her a note in class saying, 'Sorry'. She nodded, but the threat of the cellar hung over her, and by this time she couldn't smile at all even though she tried.

George was in his front room looking out into the road. He waved at Lucy but she didn't wave back. A few moments later he came running up behind her, shoelaces undone and one arm through a sleeve of his anorak.

"Wait!" he shouted. "I want to talk to you."

Lucy pretended not to hear him. If she were seen talking to a non-follower in the street the three nights in the cellar might be increased to four.

"Why are you so snooty?" he panted, pulling on the other sleeve.

Lucy stopped and stared at him. How could a pariah be snooty?

"Why should I be snooty?"

"Because you won't cross with us with the lollipop lady. Because you go to private school."

"What's private school?"

"It's where you go. Anyone can go to our school, but not to yours. So it's private."

"Oh, I didn't know that." She started walking on. George followed her.

"I mustn't talk to you," she said, not looking at him.

"See! That's what I mean. You're snooty." George nodded his ginger curls in vigorous emphasis.

Lucy stopped again.

"I'm not snooty," she said crossly, "It's just that I'm not allowed to talk to strangers in the street." She carried on walking, and George tagged along beside her.

"Why are you bothering me?"

"It's because you belong to that sect," he said. "I wanted to see what a person from a sect talks like."

"What's a sect?"

"My dad says it's a bunch of nutters who don't let girls have jobs and shut them up to have babies and pray for the rest of their lives. And he knows everything."

"Go away," said Lucy. "I don't like you."

"I'm just curious, that's all. Curiosity is a sign of intelligence." He didn't sound at all offended, but to Lucy's relief he turned back.

She hurried as fast as her sore legs would let her, up the hill then left through the little lane, and over the common towards the father's house – supposedly her home. It was not her home. A home was a haven. This was simply the place where she lived. Turning to look at the cheerfully painted backs of the houses on South Hill, Lucy stood and counted three down from the lane. That was where George lived. He had a mother and father and little sister in a pushchair. His house was a home.

There was no light on in the hall as she approached

the father's house. Aunt Sarah and Paul would be in the kitchen. The father wouldn't be home yet. Perhaps a miracle would happen and he'd never come home, and they'd have the house to themselves. There'd still be the tenant on the top floor, but that wouldn't bother them. She wondered briefly what he (or she) did all day, but she didn't really care.

She walked reluctantly up the front path, pausing only to look at the coal hole cover with an interest she'd never felt before. Her indignation at George's remarks was banished by the dread of the evening to come.

Aunt Sarah had made a cake for tea, and Paul was already picking crumbs off his plate and asking for more. Cake was normally something special for birthdays and holy days, but today Lucy couldn't eat it.

"Eat up," said Aunt Sarah. "I made it especially for you."

"Thank you, Aunt Sarah," Lucy whispered, but the crumbs caught in her throat.

Her homework stared up at her from the page but refused to jump into her head, and her ears strained for the sound of the father's arrival. At seven o'clock he passed the kitchen window and entered the lobby, and Lucy heard the stairs creak as he went up to his flat. A few minutes later the footsteps creaked downwards and she cowered over her school books. The key turned in the lock, and his huge frame appeared in the kitchen doorway.

"Get up."

Aunt Sarah turned away towards the kitchen sink, and started to run the tap over the children's teatime crockery. Lucy stood up and meekly made her way towards the cellar door. She did not wait to be thrown down, and clutched on to the wooden rail as the door closed behind her. Sitting on the steps she listened as the father's footsteps returned to the kitchen. He said something to Aunt Sarah, and then the door to the lobby slammed shut.

Lucy closed her eyes and when she opened them the darkness gradually softened and she could see the ring of light at the far end of the cellar. Clinging to the rail and feeling each step carefully with her foot before treading firmly, she reached the bottom of the stairs. The smell of mould and damp and coal dust was as oppressive as ever. She fixed her eyes on the ring of light and stumbled forward, her hand outstretched to the wall on the right. Her fingers scraped through cobwebs and her legs knocked against unseen objects.

As her eyes grew used to the darkness the ring of light gave shape to the concrete slope below it. Sinking to her hands and knees she felt around for the wooden crate, and dragged it to the base of the slope. She pushed herself up with one knee as her hands scrabbled to get a grip on the concrete. Pausing to gather all her strength, she pushed with her toes and then the other knee, and up. As she stretched out one arm to touch the ring of light, she slid back onto the wooden crate.

She sat down on it to think. What she needed was something to give her a grip. She looked around at the faintly visible shapes around her. Her hands were numb with wet and cold as she groped past rotting cardboard and musty clothes and touched the rubber underlay of a piece of old rug. She laid the underlay flat up the slope and wedged the crate against the bottom end to hold it in place. She put a smaller wooden box on top, and climbed up. At that moment the father's booming voice and Aunt Sarah's faint response floated through from the kitchen.

Lucy jumped down from the box and hastily scrabbled her way back into the darkness. When the door opened she was sitting on the bottom step. She emerged as filthy as the night before, her eyes screwed up against the blinding light. The bath water was running, and she made her way to her room to fetch her night clothes.

When the father had departed Aunt Sarah fetched a kettle of boiling water and poured it into the bath. Lucy was surprised and silently grateful. Aunt Sarah took away the dirty clothes. There was no washing machine and no dryer, but the extra work would be nothing if she could only ease the child's misery without displeasing the Magnifico.

Later, Lucy lay in bed and thought of George's mother who'd made him apologise. His father thought Lucy was a nutter, but he was called Dad. No way was Father Copse a dad. She couldn't even call him her father. He was *the* father, not hers, just the Magnifico's agent and nothing more.

She waited until long after Aunt Sarah had gone to bed, then crept out to the kitchen and found the torch. Its light moved over the table and chairs and cupboards and worktops, but there was nothing that could help her climb the concrete slope in the cellar. She tried the back door and the door to the lobby but they were both locked and the keys were hidden in Aunt Sarah's secret hiding place. Lucy switched off the torch and put it back on the shelf by the door. She sat down at the table and laid her head on her arms.

For a moment she slept. She was woken by a dragging sound outside near the bins, and sat bolt upright. The window looked out onto the side path. She stepped over and peeped cautiously through. To the left she could see the side and back of the garage. A hooded figure was shifting the ladder slightly and steadying it at the bottom. It climbed the ladder and stepped over a small turret. Crossing over to the further side of the flat roof of the garage, it dropped down on all fours, disappeared briefly, and then reappeared crawling very gingerly along the high garden wall towards the lime tree to the right. It clambered onto a bough that stretched over the wall towards the next-door garden, and then vanished into the darkness of the branches that faced the windows at the side of the wing.

Lucy watched and waited for what seemed like an eternity. She knew she should go and tell Aunt Sarah, but couldn't move. Suddenly the figure reappeared along the bough. Lucy could see it clearly in the moonlight. Instead of returning along the wall it swung down from the branch's lowest point, landed with a faint thump on the lawn, and disappeared behind the wing. Lucy ran to the back door and looked through the glass panes. She caught a quick glimpse of it before it vanished through the back gate into the alley that ran along behind the houses.

Her mind was suddenly alive and clear as a bell. She remembered the candles that Aunt Sarah kept in the dresser drawer. Taking one candle and a box of matches, she put them in an old plastic bag retrieved from the kitchen rubbish bin. She picked up the torch and made her way quietly to the cellar door. Silently she turned the handle and switched on the torch. She went down the wooden stairs and put the plastic bag with its contents under the bottom step. Shutting the door carefully behind her she crept back to the kitchen, put the torch in its place, and tiptoed down the hall to her room. She switched on the light and checked her clothes for coal dust. There seemed to be no visible signs of the cellar. Giving the clothes a good sniff she decided they didn't smell of the cellar either. She was almost looking forward to tomorrow. Despite the strange behaviour of the hooded figure she slept well.

CHAPTER TEN

Lucy tapped at the shell of her boiled egg. "Aunt Sarah," she said. "What's a nutter?"

Sarah's stern brow wrinkled for a moment, and she looked perplexed.

"I don't know. It's not a word I've heard. Is it someone who gathers nuts?"

"I think it's supposed to be an insult," said Lucy. "Yesterday in the street a boy called someone a nutter, and it sounded rude."

"Well, I wouldn't know about that then. Was the boy from your school?"

"No."

"I hope you didn't talk to him."

"No. I was just walking past and I heard it."

"Good. Now eat up and get a move on."

In the lunch break Lucy found Dorothy sitting behind a pile of rubble at the rear of the bicycle shed. Her heart lifted as soon as she saw her. Dorothy, with her rosy cheeks and laughing eyes, always made her feel better, even if she didn't have faith in the Magnifico's purpose. But something was wrong. Those cheeks were pale and the eyes were dull.

Dorothy looked up as Lucy approached. "Ah, there you are," she said.

"Why are you sitting here?" asked Lucy. "Are you feeling sad?"

"It's only so they can't see me," Dorothy explained. "I've got something to tell you – to warn you about."

Lucy felt a stab of fear. Dorothy shifted up a bit to make room for her and gave her a little push. "Come on. Get further back out of sight. If we're seen they'll think we're plotting. That's why I didn't come yesterday."

"What would we be plotting?" asked Lucy, squeezing herself further along. She sat down gingerly, carefully adjusting her legs to avoid the sore bits.

"I don't know, but they'll think we are. Running away perhaps."

"What!"

"Just joking."

Dorothy peeped over the pile of rubble and then leaned towards Lucy.

"You can't imagine how awful David feels and he's really, really sorry."

"It's done now," said Lucy quietly. "There's worse things in life. Look at poor John!"

Dorothy nodded. "Thanks."

They sat in sober silence for a while. "No-one could help John," said Dorothy eventually, "but we thought if we warned you about something it might help make amends, not that anything could really make up for what David did."

The stab of fear jabbed at Lucy again. She held her breath.

"We've discovered something, and I know you believe in the purpose and all that, but I can't not tell you, and if you report us it's what we deserve because of what David did yesterday."

The fire of the melting flesh flickered before Lucy's very eyes.

Dorothy leaned closer and dropped her voice to a whisper. "You know how when we're sixteen we have to marry the Magnifico?"

Lucy nodded.

"You probably don't know that girls with a bad conduct record, like me, aren't considered fit to be his wives, either as mothers or as aunts."

"No. I didn't know that," said Lucy, immediately wondering if she could make use of this piece of information herself to avoid having to get married.

"Well, what David and I have just found out is that if a girl isn't fit to be a wife she's disposed of. She just disappears. They can't take the risk of letting her free in the outside world because she might damage the Holy Cause."

Lucy ignored the pain in her legs as she tried to struggle to her feet. "What's the matter with you? You're mad. You're just trying to frighten me."

Dorothy grabbed her arm and pulled her down. "I'm not," she hissed. "I'm trying to help you. You've only had the guidance once so you might be alright, but I have to warn you in case. You've got to save yourself. It's easy for them to get rid of girls because we don't have birth certificates, only the boys. People who don't have birth certificates don't exist in the outside world."

Lucy felt sick. "That can't be true. The headmaster said some girls would be trained for careers."

"It is true, because I've heard the aunts discussing it. Some of them don't think it's right, but they have to obey the Magnifico. Girls who are trained for careers are given fake birth certificates, and whatever documents they need to get a job. But that'll never happen to you or me, because we're a risk – we've had the guidance."

"I don't believe you."

An expression of utter bleakness passed over Dorothy's face. Her voice caught in her throat. "I'll tell you something else, and then you might believe me." She stopped.

There was a long pause. Lucy waited.

"Well, once when I was little, one of the aunts said if I didn't behave myself I'd go the same way as my mother, and I didn't know what she meant."

"Well?"

Dorothy swallowed hard then sat up straight. She spoke quietly but firmly. "Did you know that the mothers in the breeding rooms are always selected for their beauty and brains – same as the fathers – except that some of them are abducted, kidnapped?"

Lucy shook her head.

"Well my mother was one of them. She was abducted off the street but she refused to be converted to the Holy Cause, so after I was taken away from her they disposed of her. I can just remember her a little."

Lucy's stomach was churning.

"How?" she managed to whisper.

"By lethal injection."

Dorothy stood up. Lucy watched as she unsuccessfully tried to retrieve her usual cheeky expression. She bent down to whisper. "I'll be sixteen in September, and it's April now, so I've got five months. I don't know what happens in the outside world if I can't get a job, but I'd rather starve to death out there than wait to be disposed of here."

As she edged her way along past the pile of rubble she turned back to Lucy.

"It's David's fault you had the guidance. Although we won't blame you if you report him, we beg you not to – or to repeat what I've told you today."

She sidled out into the playground. Lucy waited a moment and emerged just as the bell was ringing.

Lucy crossed at the lights and started walking uphill. Her mind was buzzing with the horror of what had happened to Dorothy's mother (if it was true and if Dorothy wasn't completely crazy). There was a long queue at the bus stop, and she looked at it longingly, wondering if she dare join it just to stand there among people who belonged to the outside world. A bus was a wonderful thing, she thought. It could carry her away for ever. But if she wasn't registered, if she didn't exist, she would never even be allowed to earn the money for the fare. She'd have to walk.

David pushed his bike and followed at a distance as Lucy trudged despondently up the road. Matthew called after him from outside the school, but he just waved and pointed up and to the left, towards the common.

"Lucy!" called David, when she was halfway down the lane between the houses. "Wait for me."

"You'll get into trouble," she said when he caught up with her.

"I'm really, really sorry," he said.

"I'm not going to report you if that's what you're worried about."

"It's not. I'm just truly sorry. I'll go and tell them it was my fault if that's what you want."

Lucy stopped and looked at him. "I don't want that," she said at last. "It wouldn't take what happened away." She twisted her reminder. "And it's made me learn something."

81

She turned away from him, but he followed. They slowly crossed the common together. Her mind was on tonight's visit to the cellar. It held no terrors for her now. It almost gave her a sense of adventure.

"Which is your house?"

"It'll never be my house even if I live there for ever!" She exclaimed bitterly, pointing at number 3 Mortimor Road. "It's the father's house, and look how furiously angry it is! It's watching me now all the way from over there, and when I get back Aunt Sarah will say she told me to hurry home and disobedient children will be burned in the fire of the melting flesh."

Self-pity turned to anger. "I shall be trapped for ever in that house, and it's not right. Why should I be stopped from having a registered birth and being an existing person and getting a job and earning my own money?"

David was surprised. He had often wondered what lay behind the inscrutable calm of that exquisitely delicate face. She had a sense of humour he knew, because sometimes when he was particularly silly at school, a suppressed laugh would bubble from her lips, but he had never really got to know her. It was as though she was trapped inside an invisible wall.

He leaned on his bike and studied the house, thinking.

"Does Father Copse live with you?" he asked.

"No. He lives in a flat on the first floor."

"Do you ever go into his flat?"

"No. We're not allowed upstairs. They keep the door to the lobby locked, and that's where the stairs are. Why d'you want to know?"

David was thinking.

"Just because you don't exist in the outside world

doesn't mean you don't exist in the Magnifico's world," he said slowly. "All the fathers have to keep records of the births of their children, and report on their welfare to the Holy Leaders. Somewhere up there in Father Copse's flat he'll have a record of your birth. In a box or a file or something. If you could find it and escape you could take it to somewhere official, as long as it wasn't infiltrated of course, and ask them to give you a proper birth certificate. A court perhaps. Then you'd exist."

Lucy caught her breath and stared at him.

"How do you know?" she said, hardly daring to believe him.

"Dorothy hears things no-one else knows about."

As they came nearer to the house Lucy moved off the path, towards the bushes by the pond. "I'm allowed to play here with Paul," she said.

"Who's Paul?"

"I don't know. He lives with us. The Magnifico sent him in January. He was with a foster aunt before that."

Once they'd reached the bushes, out of sight of the house, Lucy relaxed a little and took time to think. "I don't know how I'd ever manage to get into his flat," she said. "Even if I could get up there I wouldn't know where to start looking, because it must be enormous. It stretches over the back wing, and over the whole of our flat to the front. Maybe Thomas the gardener would have some ideas."

"Whatever you do, don't tell a soul!" exclaimed David fiercely.

Lucy was taken aback. "But he's my friend," she said.

"It doesn't matter. You must promise me you'll never, ever, tell anyone what I told you – or what Dorothy told you." He caught Lucy by the arm and looked earnestly into her green eyes. "All it takes is one slip of the tongue, and not only will you be in danger of disposal, but so will Dorothy and so will I."

She felt shaken. "Let go of my arm. OK. I promise."

"You're lucky," said David, "because you've got a chance. If you were in the Drax commune you'd never be able to get at your records because Father Drax doesn't keep them there. They're in his private house."

"I must go in or I'll be in trouble." The curtain of inscrutable courtesy came down. "And thank you for what you've told me. I'll try and think of something."

David watched her go. She was fourteen, the same age as he was, but had the body and the crushed vulnerability of a little girl. It was easy to believe the rumour that Father Copse kept her half-starved. She turned, and her face lit up briefly as she smiled. He smiled back, waved, and jumped onto his bike. For a moment he'd caught a glimpse of the real Lucy. He sensed that despite her fragility, she was tough.

As Lucy crossed over the road to the house, she gritted her teeth and was determined. When she got at those records nothing would hold her back. Who did they think they were to decide what she should do with her life? If the Magnifico was reading her mind at this moment, she hoped he read so much he went blind! It would serve him right.

CHAPTER ELEVEN

Lucy entered the cellar meekly. As soon as the father's footsteps had died away she took the candle out of the bag, taking care not to rustle it. The matches slipped out of her hand but she felt around in the dark and found them on the bottom step. She lit the candle and, stepping over and round the various obstacles, made her way to the far end of the cellar.

She blew out the candle and placed it with the matches against the base of the wall at the side of the slope so that it would be easy to find again. Then she stepped onto the crate and onto the box. Laying her body flat and digging her left knee into the disgusting bit of underlay, and pushing with the toes of her right foot, she worked her way up from the top of the box until she reached the ring of light. She felt with her fingers and pushed at a heavy circular bit of metal. It moved upwards and sideways. All it needed was a good shove.

Light poured in from above. With a final push with her toes Lucy grabbed the rim of the coal hole and pulled herself up. Her head poked above the path and she immediately recognised the street lamp which, together with the moonlight, had so obligingly provided the ring of light. She pulled herself out on to the path and stood up. The air was no colder outside than it was in the cellar, and was considerably fresher. She breathed deeply and looked around. The common lay silent just over the road. Its trees made sharp shadows in the bright March moonlight.

Lucy crossed the road and slipped into the bushes surrounding the pond. The water was a black mirror speckled with stars, and reflected a big round moon. She stood listening to the rustles and sighs of the earth and the shrubs, and was not afraid. Lying flat on her back on the ground, she closed her eyes. Out here in the open the stars no longer frightened her. The cold was nothing, and she felt at peace.

As she breathed in the sharp pure air and the sweet scent of the grass, she found it easy to believe, just for a moment, that the Magnifico did not exist and there was no purpose. Perhaps Dorothy was right after all. She pushed the heresy away. Aunt Sarah would not have lied to her all these years.

Something woke her. There was a noise at the house. She jumped up and peeped through the bushes. The automatic gates to the left of the house had opened and a long elegant car with blackened windows was purring up the drive towards the garage. The gate shut behind it and Lucy darted across the road to peer through the diamond-shaped holes that ran horizontally across its upper section. The car stopped before it reached the garage and an outside light was switched on over the lobby door. As the driver stepped out the father appeared. A giant of a man climbed out of the passenger seat and came round the car to speak to him. Was Lucy imagining things or did they each give a quick flick of the infiltrators' hand signal?

The man then opened the right-hand rear door and started pulling at something heavy. Lucy saw a shoe dangling off one foot, a rucked up trouser leg, and then two legs. Out came the body of a woman. The man threw her over his shoulder, her head and arms dangling. Her thick auburn hair fell loosely down his back. Aunt Sarah appeared at the lobby door and the father spoke to her briefly. The big man disappeared into the lobby with his burden, and the father and Aunt Sarah followed. A minute later a light shone out from a small side window up in the second-floor flat.

What Dorothy had said about her mother flashed cross Lucy's mind, and a shiver ran down her spine as she thought she might be witnessing an abduction. She pushed the idea aside. Aunt Sarah was there, and she would never be involved in something like that. It must have been a new tenant arriving. Perhaps she'd been taken ill. Even so, the possibility of Dorothy's disposal and her own suddenly seemed more real.

The driver of the car was leaning against the bonnet and rolling a cigarette. He wore a chauffeur's livery with a peaked cap which hid his face as he bent forward to light the straggling bits of tobacco. The way he used his hands reminded her of Thomas, and she smiled as she tried to imagine him in a chauffeur's outfit. He'd be chuffed to have the chance to drive a car like that. Shaking out the match the man looked at his watch, and Lucy suddenly remembered that she was supposed to be in the cellar. She had to make a quick decision – whether to go back, or run away.

Her head buzzed rapidly with pros and cons and she realised that a hasty escape without preparation could be disastrous. She needed to find her birth record first. Also, Thomas had once told her that the police were infiltrated with the Magnifico's agents. If they picked her up they would bring her straight back, and her punishment would be far worse than three nights in the cellar, especially if what Dorothy had said about disposals was true.

Once in her own bed she'd have time to think about what she had just seen. There may have been some reasonable explanation. It would be wrong to jump to conclusions. At least she would have a roof over her head while she made her plans. Now that she knew how to get through the coal hole she would always have an escape route via the cellar if she needed it.

Running low along the pavement past the privet hedge that hid the front garden, she reached the path and slipped down into the coal hole. The cover was heavy but not too difficult to pull over, and it settled into place as though it had never been lifted. Back in the pitch darkness she slid down the underlay on the concrete slope, groped to her left for the candle and matches and, in the flickering light, made her way back to the wooden stairs. She snuffed the candle and put it and the matches back in the plastic bag, and hid them under the bottom step. If she ever needed them again the plastic bag would keep them from getting damp.

She was only just in time. Footsteps approached and the key turned. Lucy stood up blinking and stepped out into the hall. As she emerged Aunt Sarah was on her way to the bathroom with the towels. She looked at Lucy's inscrutable face, and was proud of the child's dignity. When she took the dirty clothes away and shook them out, she wondered why there was grass on the back of the jumper.

Lucy was on tenterhooks and burning with curiosity. She wondered if Aunt Sarah would say anything about the new arrival. When she was clean and sitting in the kitchen in her pyjamas, Aunt Sarah handed her a mug of hot chocolate.

"Tomorrow, make sure you and Paul play quietly if you go in the garden after school," she said. "We've got a new tenant on the top floor, and she's not at all well."

Later, as she lay in bed, Lucy heard the opening creak of the big double gates on the further side of the house. The car crunched down the gravel drive and out into the road, and the gates slowly shut. Who was the woman with the lovely auburn hair? Lucy wondered. More importantly however, she started making, discarding, and remaking plans, for getting hold of those records.

CHAPTER TWELVE

Father Copse checked the girl on the bed in the second-floor flat. Her breathing was even and her colour was good. Her wonderful red hair was a mess and there was mud on her clothes. She had been chosen for her looks alright! Drax would be green with envy if he ever found out. He had a penchant for redheads. Part of her sleeve had been torn away, and her arm was bruising rapidly. She had obviously put up a struggle, so she had spirit. Copse liked strong women. It was such a triumph to master them.

His wife, one of many, stood in the doorway watching him with sorrowful green eyes.

"At least she'll be company for you," he said

She sighed. "Poor thing," she said sadly, and turned away.

Back in his study he sat at his desk with the 'Wives' file in front of him. He recorded the date, and the name 'as yet unknown'. He wrote a brief description of the girl's colouring and approximate height. Tomorrow he would find out her name. Certainly she was a beauty, and whoever had tracked her down would have ensured she had brains. But he didn't really want another wife. He wanted fewer, not more. He had had enough of wives. And he didn't want more children either. Now he'd have two women upstairs living in the lap of luxury and costing him a fortune. If she proved amenable to conversion to the Holy Cause, he'd send her over to the commune. It'd be cheaper.

All his hopes now lay with the post of deputy to the Holy Envoy. If he were to be appointed he would be able to hand over his domestic responsibilities to another father. He would just keep the woman upstairs, and, of course, the two children in the flat below. He had plans for them. The boy was the most handsome of all his sons, and he intended grooming him to become a father. As for the girl, well, she didn't look up to much at the moment but, judging from her colouring and bone structure, she was going to be strikingly beautiful one day in an exotic sort of way. If he proved right about that he'd be able to use her for negotiating purposes with other fathers. He cursed when he remembered Lucy had brought dishonour on the household. It was just the sort of thing that could hamper his chance of promotion to the Deputy Envoy post, and would greatly please his fellow candidates, especially Father Drax.

He sighed and rose to put the file away. The prospect of another wife and yet more children was an indication of the Magnifico's trust in him as a true and valued follower, and he must bear his burden with gratitude. But he was so tired! A hot circle of pressure was squeezing his head. It came more frequently these days – his ring of fire, his crown of pain. The Magnifico was trying to tell him something, He picked up the intercom and phoned down to the kitchen for some coffee and a piece of chocolate cake.

Sarah had just finished hand-washing Lucy's clothes for the third night running. They were now dripping on the wooden airer over the bath, and she was about to go to bed. She pushed away the thought that the father had two hands and could have made his own coffee, and that he had two legs and could have come down to get his own cake.

Lucy's incarceration had upset her deeply, though of course it was not for her to question the Magnifico's instructions. Bitterness raised its ugly head for a moment, but she managed to slap it down. She pushed some loose wisps of hair into the bun at the back of her head, washed her hands, and prepared the tray for its upward journey. Her reward was yet to come in the next world, and she looked forward to that.

The woman upstairs peeped in on her new companion. She'd sleep for a while yet, the father had said when he left. Sleep? A charming euphemism for drugged up to the eyeballs.

Wives had come and gone before, and Maria intended do all she could to persuade this latest one to pretend to take up the Holy Cause. If she could act convincingly enough she might be transferred to the commune where there was more chance of escape, perhaps even with her own child.

With a sinking heart she realised this new arrival meant that the Holy Leaders would come, and the brainwashing would begin all over again. The videos and the recordings would tell the stories of the discovery of the first Holy Envoy as a baby in an empty fruit crate. He, an abandoned child of destitution, was destined to lead his followers to a life of strict morality and, through his martyrdom, to Paradise. In the name of the Magnifico, he and his successors would rule the world and cleanse it of sin. The only music would be hymns of praise. There would be one race, one language, one religion and one ruler.

She sat down by the bed and held the girl's hand. It was the hand of a very young woman, perhaps nineteen or twenty, on the threshold of adulthood and full of hopes and plans – just as Maria had been when they brought her in fifteen years ago. Now all hopes and plans would come to nothing unless there was some means of escape. Her only joy would be to nurse her child for a week or two, if she had one. Maria studied the porcelain skin and delicate features, and smoothed the glorious hair. Somewhere, someone would be desperately searching for a daughter or sister or lover. She thought sadly of her own beloved parents, far away in the west of Wales. Their hearts must have broken long ago.

She rose from the chair and went to the window. It looked out over the back garden, but was too high and too small to give much of a view. Looking down into the branches of the big lime tree, she longed to see its leaves burst forth again, a fresh green reminder of the seasons of the outside world. The window sash pushed up easily, and she breathed in the night air. She studied the steel bars minutely and gave them a tug or two as she had done many times before. They were criss-crossed and set into the surrounding concrete. There was no way she could remove them.

There was a rustling sound and she looked towards the bed. The girl's hands were fluttering slightly and her lips moved. Maria approached and took her hand, and her eyes opened dimly.

"Where am I?"

"I'll explain later," she said gently. "What's your name?"

"Claudia." The girl's eyes closed. "What's yours?"

"He took my name away long ago. I used to be called Maria."

She stroked the smooth hand as her mind travelled its never-ending journey searching for ways to get out of here. Once she had tried to climb into the dumb waiter but the space was too shallow, and that woman, Martha, who came to clean once a week, was always accompanied by a minder, so there was no chance of overcoming her. Martha would never have helped her even if the minder hadn't been there. She was rigid with religion and devoted to the service of the Magnifico.

Claudia opened her eyes again.

"I'll fetch you some water." Maria's soft lilting voice was soothing. "When you've woken up properly I'll explain where you are."

•

CHAPTER THIRTEEN

By the time spring came Paul had grown into a quiet and solemn child. He followed Lucy round like a little dog, and when the school holidays began at the end of April she was put in charge of him.

"I've got enough to do without running around after a little busybody all day," said Sarah. "You can look after him. It'll be good practice for you for when you're an aunt."

If it was raining they would sit at the kitchen table drawing, or would squash together in Aunt Sarah's sagging chair and Lucy would read to him from her old book of fairy stories. Sometimes she would teach him his ABC and how to count on his fingers. When it was fine they went over the road to the common and played by the pond, or they would kick a ball in the garden or dig their flowerbeds.

Lucy had her own plot where she grew the seeds that Thomas brought her from his job with the corporation gardens. Paul was given a plot too, and together they marked it out with little white pebbles gathered from the drive in front of the garage. Thomas offered to make them a swing. With Aunt Sarah's permission, he screwed rings into a fine strong branch of the big lime tree, pulled ropes through and secured them tightly. He made a seat like a box that Paul could sit in safely and yet was big enough for Lucy, with holes for their legs to stick out. Paul loved the swing. Lucy would push him back and forth, higher and higher, and he was happy.

Lucy didn't have time to be happy. Her mind was constantly working on how to get away. The prospect of marriage in less than two years' time preyed on her mind. Also, since her three nights in the cellar, and the new tenant's arrival, Dorothy's talk of abductions and disposals seemed more credible. If she didn't manage to get into the father's flat, she'd just have to leave without her birth record and hope for the best, but the more she thought about it the more difficult running away seemed to be. It was not just a matter of walking out of the door, because of Paul. She would never leave him behind, but how would she feed him, and keep him warm and clean if she couldn't get work? And how would she find out who was the proper person to go to for documents? Was it a policeman, or a court, or someone in the government? She wouldn't be able to ask any of them because they were all infiltrated. And she was just so ignorant! She knew absolutely nothing about the outside world.

These thoughts ran continuously through Lucy's mind as she and Paul played. The garden was huge, and full of places for hide-and-seek. She would shout to give Paul a clue from wherever she was, behind a shrub, or under the sacks in the garage, but her mind was elsewhere. If they went on the common no-one could see them behind the bushes that surrounded the pond and Lucy loved the privacy of their own secret world, but even there the same old questions were hammering away inside her head. Paul was fascinated by the tiny frogs and funny little insects that darted about on the water's surface, but it was hard to snap out of her own thoughts and share his enthusiasm. She tried her best, because his pleasure gave her pleasure and she adored the sweetness of his smile, his big hazel-green eyes and his soft curly hair.

One day, when the sun was shining and the night-time figure and rat were winter memories, and the leaves were beginning to unfold on the lime tree, Lucy climbed the ladder at the side of the garage and stepped over the turret onto the flat roof. She crossed over towards the garden wall and looked down into the gap between it and the garage. There was no sign of the rat. Perhaps she had imagined it.

A narrow wooden platform spanned the gap at one end creating a little bridge from the garage to the wall. Cautiously, Lucy tested the bridge with her foot. It tipped slightly towards her. She jumped back and tried again, planting her foot well into the middle. It seemed steady. Looking over the back of the garage she checked that Paul was playing happily with the earth and singing to himself. Then, with one firm step onto the middle of the bridge she took another step that reached the top of the wall. It was about eighteen inches wide. She lowered herself onto her hands and knees and, not daring to look down, crawled towards the overhanging branch of the lime tree.

Once in the tree she felt safe. The branches spread out comfortably in all directions from a good wide trunk that provided plenty of room for sitting. Lucy wondered if she would be allowed to ask Thomas to build her a tree house – though there was no point because she would be leaving. She would have to remember to say goodbye to Thomas before she went.

Looking at the ground below, she reckoned she

would be able to swing down safely if Aunt Sarah were to call her. She climbed a bit higher and, seating herself comfortably between two boughs, she had a good look over the wall at the house next door. There was a large garden like the father's but with nothing of interest, just a big lawn marked out in faded white lines for tennis, and flowerbeds all round. The grass needed mowing, and the beds were full of weeds. According to Aunt Sarah the owner was a diplomat, and was always away in other countries. He should have arranged for someone like Thomas to come in and look after the garden. The father's garden was nice and tidy in comparison, and much more interesting with all its shrubs and trees and secret places.

She turned round in the hollow of the branches and looked up at the house. From an angle she could almost see into the father's flat on the first floor. If only Thomas's ladder were longer she'd be able to smash the window and climb in. It was a pity the drainpipe wasn't closer to the window because she could have climbed that easily. Pulling herself higher she moved up and over until she found a niche which gave her a better view. Her skinny little figure fitted nicely into the fork of a branch. The first-floor window was big and from here she could see down and into what she guessed was the father's living room. There was a desk under the window and beyond that two armchairs and a sofa. In fact, she could see right through the room and out through a window on the other side. It was lucky he was at work because he would have been extremely angry if he'd caught her staring in.

On the second floor the windows were small and the bars made it difficult to see anything more than the white sides of the casement, and the fringed edge of a partially drawn blind.

It was interesting to see the world from a different angle. Lucy sat there watching Paul as he pottered around humming to himself. She called to him and waved, and he laughed to see her in such a strange place.

A black cloud went over the sun and a breeze blew up. The bright spring leaves fluttered and Lucy felt a heavy drop of rain. As she was about to turn herself around ready to climb down she had one more look up at the second-floor window, and a face appeared. She didn't move. The tenant was looking down into the garden. Lucy could see that it was not a man, but a beautiful woman with dark brown hair.

She had been told many times never to bother the tenant, and she knew that if there was a complaint about her she would be punished, and the sin would be added to her record. Dorothy's warning about the dreaded disposal was never far from her mind. She pressed herself back against the tree trunk and hoped that her own brown hair was acting as a camouflage.

The woman looked up at the sky. The sun had gone behind a cloud. Perhaps it would rain, perhaps not. It would make no difference to her. Seasons would come and go, the leaves on the lime would change colour and fall and grow again. Nevertheless, as she looked at the tree, its sprouting spring foliage gave her pleasure. Suddenly she realised that gazing up at her through the lacework of twigs was a pair of big anxious eyes.

Lucy stayed still. She knew she had been seen. Two arms appeared next to the face and struggled with the window. The bottom section shot up with a bang and the face pressed itself up against the bars. Lucy twisted herself round to face the tree trunk and slithered down until she reached the lowest branch. For a moment she swung from her hands and then dropped. As she reached the ground she heard Aunt Sarah calling for her. Hot in the face, she sauntered as casually as she could over to the back door. Aunt Sarah emerged with a brush and pan in one hand, looking cross.

"Where have you been? You're supposed to be looking after Paul."

"I was just looking for another trowel to dig my garden," said Lucy. "Paul's been using mine."

"Well, don't leave him like that again. Goodness knows what he'll get up to. I'm much too busy to be watching you all the time. Quick, come in both of you. It's raining."

Paul was humming his little tune, and singing the one and only song that he knew. "I can see you, I can hear you, I can watch your every action," he sang. He abandoned his garden and followed Lucy into the kitchen.

"Aunt Sarah, I saw Lucy up in the sky."

"Did you indeed!" said Sarah. "Come and play indoors now while it's raining, both of you, and don't get under my feet."

CHAPTER FOURTEEN

There's something up with that child, thought Sarah.

Lucy was tense and fidgety for the rest of the school holidays, and hardly ate her food. Each day she waited for the tenant to put in a complaint about her, and for the father's massive hand to grab the back of her neck. She couldn't help wondering how unsuitable girls were disposed of. Would it be the lethal injection, the same as Dorothy's mother? Lucy longed for the beginning of term so she could ask Dorothy more questions – even though she might not want to believe the answers.

When the summer term began in the first week of May Dorothy was no longer there. Lucy looked for her in the corridor and in the cloakroom but there was no sign of her. At lunch time she searched in vain in the bushes surrounding the playing field and behind the bicycle shed. Nobody referred to her absence, and eventually Lucy asked one of the girls from the Drax commune where she was.

"We don't know. She went to bed one night and wasn't there in the morning. We're not allowed to talk about it." The girl ran off.

That evening Lucy waited in the corridor for David to come out of the boys' cloakroom. She studied the noticeboard with one eye on the cloakroom door. There was a note saying that the Wednesday prayer meeting had been cancelled because the Holy Leaders were away on the Envoy's business. Why on earth couldn't people pray without the Holy Leaders? Next to it was list of the last end of term exam results. There was her name, and she'd done well. In fact she had by far the highest marks in her class. At least the father couldn't be angry with her for that.

Dorothy's name was not listed.

A group of boys emerged from the cloakroom shifting their satchels onto their backs and pulling on their caps. Lucy moved as casually as she could away from the board, and stood aside as they went past. David was among the stragglers. His blazer was spotlessly clean and his silvery-blond hair was neatly combed down ready to face critical inspection by the aunts at Drax House. He and Matthew were whispering about something a teacher had said. Matthew put an arm round David's shoulder.

Catching Lucy's eye David wriggled away and put his satchel down on the floor and rummaged through it. "You go on," he said to Matthew. "I haven't got my homework book. I'll have to go back."

Matthew joined the group of boys in front and disappeared down the steps. Lucy walked past David and he fastened up his satchel. Out on the steps she slowed down until he was alongside her.

"Do you know where Dorothy is?" she asked, looking straight ahead and scarcely moving her lips.

"Gone," muttered David through clenched teeth. "But I don't know where."

He moved one step down ahead of her just as the headmaster emerged from the front door. At the bottom of the steps he turned left as always, towards the entrance to the bike shed, and Lucy stepped over to the traffic lights. The headmaster waddled past David and climbed into a car parked at the side of the building. David lingered until he had driven off, then fetched his bike. Instead of following the other boys as they aimed for the High Street he pushed his bike towards the lights, and stood behind Lucy.

The green man appeared and, as Lucy moved off, Matthew looked back.

"Hey! David! Why are you going that way?" he shouted.

"Bike practice!" David called back.

He was too late to catch the green man and Lucy had already crossed. She glanced over at him, and walked on slowly up the hill.

He bent down and fiddled with one of his tyres. Out of the side of his eye he watched as Matthew cycled up the High Street towards the Drax House commune. When the green man came again he crossed and waited until a red double-decker bus blocked Matthew from view, then he hurriedly pushed the bike up South Hill. When he caught up with Lucy she was talking to a scruffy-looking little boy of about ten who sat on the gate at number 38.

As David came up George turned towards him. "Here's another snoot from the snooty sect. A nutter from the nuthouse."

"Nutter yourself," said Lucy, and moved on wishing she had a better vocabulary for dealing with insults. David ignored George. He hastened up the hill alongside her.

"He's right," he said. "They're a bunch of nutters. They're crazy and they're evil."

"I don't know what to believe," said Lucy. "I just wish I knew where Dorothy was."

"So do I. But she'll be alright, as long as she doesn't get caught. All I know is that if some of the mothers manage to get away they have to make sure they're not caught."

"What happens if they are?" asked Lucy, hardly wanting to hear the answer.

"Disposal."

Lucy's heart plummeted. She didn't want to believe it, but she was terribly afraid it might be true. Fear for Dorothy clutched at her insides.

"How will we ever know what happened, if we never hear from her again?" she asked tremulously.

David's voice cracked. "We won't."

They turned into the lane towards the common.

"Listen," said David. "You can trust me for ever because you didn't tell on me about the hymn singing, but don't trust anyone else. I must go back now."

He jumped onto his bike. Lucy stared after him. The silver-blond hair that he had smoothed down so neatly was now blowing all over the place in the wind, and his shirt had come out at the back. The aunts at Drax House would not be pleased. They took pride in their reputation for clean and tidy children. As Lucy walked over the common all she could see was Dorothy's cheeky smile, and she felt bereft. If Dorothy could have seen the misery on her face at this moment she would have said, "Stop looking so dismal! Hold your head up and be proud. You'll think of something." When she was halfway along the path Lucy turned round and could see George sitting on his back wall, staring after her. He waved.

Sarah scooped blue rat poison into one end of a bit of plastic piping. She squeezed her large hips into the gap between the garage and the garden wall, and carefully put the piping down on the ground. This was the fourth time she had done so since Lucy told her about the rat, and she hoped it would be the last. The poison had disappeared from the first dose, and a few days later she had found a dead rat near the bin. Last time only half the dose had gone so it looked as though there might be no more rats. If none went this time she would know that they were all dead and she could relax.

She straightened herself up, looked upwards and wondered briefly why there was a wooden cover over part of the gap above her head, and then backed out. It was hard to turn round in the narrow space. She jammed a piece of hardboard across the entrance and then secured a piece of wire fencing over it, to keep Paul out. She dragged one of the bins up against it just for good measure.

Back in the kitchen she washed her hands thoroughly and started to prepare Lucy's tea. Paul would wake up soon and there wouldn't be much peace for quite a while. Acting on an uncharacteristic impulse, she cut two small slices from the father's favourite coffee and walnut cake and laid them on the children's plates. He would never know, and she hoped the Magnifico had too many serious matters on his mind to bother about it.

Lucy noticed the cake as soon as she came in. The anxious look in her eyes vanished briefly and she smiled. Sarah was glad. She longed to ask Lucy what was troubling her but knew she could not. The Magnifico had decreed that children must receive no comfort from those about them. They had to find the strength within themselves to deal with their own difficulties.

After finishing her homework Lucy sat at the table with Paul and admired his drawings. They were much too good for a little boy of three. "You'll be a great artist one day," she said, and he was pleased. Sarah was wringing out washing at the sink. She put it into a plastic tub and took it to the back door.

"Watch him while I hang this out."

"Yes, Aunt Sarah," replied Lucy.

Paul knelt on his chair with both elbows on the table, intently focusing on his artistic efforts. He wrote PAUL and drew a picture. "Look. It's me. Fluffy hair."

Lucy smiled. Her mind was far away. How would Dorothy manage in the outside world when she'd only ever lived in a commune?

Aunt Sarah returned with the empty washing basket. She was in a good mood tonight. Lucy risked asking some questions.

"What's a sect, Aunt Sarah?"

"It's a sort of religion," said Sarah. "You do ask strange questions."

"Do we have a sect?"

"No. We have a religion, the only true religion, the Holy Cause. We are the elite."

"Why have we been chosen to be the elite?"

"So we can be saved when all non-followers perish. Now get along with you. You've got school tomorrow."

Lucy lay tense in her bed. Wouldn't Dorothy perish in the outside world? She would surely be safer back in the commune. Wasn't Lucy safer too, in the father's house? What else had she ever known? There was a distant memory, perhaps only a dream. She was high up in the doorway that led from the lobby to the kitchen, held in the arms of a giant, and looking down at a fat woman who stood by the window. Then she was on a lap and could feel a gentle face nuzzling down into her hair, and a loving voice was saying, "It's going to be alright. Just be a good girl and everything will be alright."

She had been a good girl, but nothing felt all right. It felt all wrong.

CHAPTER FIFTEEN

In the second-floor flat Maria was listening to the Holy Leaders. They sat in the armchairs like three crows, spilling out the familiar mantra as they stroked their beards and twisted their side curls round their fingers. Claudia lay on the couch, too listless to care what they said. If they wanted her to believe them she would. It didn't matter to her one way or the other. All she wanted was to get out of here. Maria moved quietly around the room pretending to dust, tidying books, stacking magazines, no longer a target of the conversion techniques. The oily voices painting their pretty picture of Paradise would have made her laugh out loud years ago when she was young and free. Now they sickened her.

"The Magnifico has a special place in Paradise for the mothers of his children," one Holy Leader was saying.

Maria thought of the pinched little face and the huge eyes that had stared at her out of the unfurled leaves of the lime tree. Every day, many times a day, she looked out of the window to see if it came again, but it never did.

"The warmth of his eternal love will wrap itself around their souls and bring them comfort." The voice droned on and on.

"Their sacrifices in this world will be rewarded in the

next. They will dwell in palaces, and feed on delicious foods. They will wear beautiful clothes and precious jewels, and bathe in crystal pools."

Claudia suddenly sat up.

"Oh, for God's sake just bloody well shut up!" she screamed. "You're making me sick. What do I want with jewels? And I hate swimming, in crystal pools or anywhere else." She swung herself off the sofa and stood up.

The Holy Leaders were stunned into silence. Maria put her hand over her mouth and rushed into the bedroom slamming the door behind her. Throwing herself on the bed she tried to smother her splutters in the pillow, but gave up and rolled onto her side clutching her stomach. She gasped and wailed and laughed out loud till her sides ached.

A few minutes later Claudia came into the room, tall, slender, straight, and electric with energy.

"They've gone. What a bunch of revolting old windbags!" she said, dropping down on the bed beside Maria and joining in her laughter.

Eventually Maria sat up, tears streaming down her face. With ever diminishing gasps she fished under her pillow for a handkerchief.

"How do we get out of here?" said Claudia.

Maria wiped her face and blew her nose. She put her finger to her lips.

"Shush." She pointed at the ceiling, the walls and the floor.

"We don't even try," she said loudly. She stood up and beckoned. Claudia followed her to the sitting room.

"Music!" announced Maria cheerfully. "That's what we need. It'll help you think about what the Holy

109

Leaders have told you. You may see things differently when you've had time to absorb it all."

She chose some Wagner from her collection and slipped it into the player.

"Just lie down and rest," she called loudly over the music. "Just relax and this'll help empty your mind of all your troubles." Then she added, "I'm just going to have a shower."

She beckoned Claudia into the shower room that led off the hall, shut the door loudly, and turned on the tap.

"I've been trying to tell you, but you didn't seem to hear me," she whispered, against the sound of the spraying water.

"Tell me what?"

"You've got to pretend to believe them and you've got to be convincing, or you'll end up like me and never get out. Don't make the mistake I made by refusing to be converted. I'm here forever until that horrible Father Copse gets sick of me and has me disposed of."

"What do you mean?"

"If you can convince them that you're happy to give up the comforts of this world in return for the future delights of Paradise, and that you're a sincere convert to the Holy Cause, you've got a good chance of being sent to live in the commune to be a mother or an aunt to Copse's children. If you can be an aunt you may get an opportunity to escape. It's more difficult if you're a mother because they keep the ones they're unsure of locked up on the upper floors."

"What happens if I don't convert?"

"You'll be disposed of. By lethal injection."

Claudia looked at her in horror.

"How come you're still here?"

110

"He's besotted with me. I don't know why. I'm never nice to him. I've had children by him, but all he does these days is stroke my hair, and I grit my teeth. He says it's like his mother's hair and he calls me by her name – Belinda. The rest of the time he just calls me 'woman'."

Claudia gasped. "He's crazy!"

"Whatever you do, pretend to try and please him."

Maria turned the shower off, then quickly turned it on again.

"The whole place is bugged, but I've never been able to find out where. Those idiot priests are probably in the flat below listening out for us at this very moment. He's at work all day, but he'll listen in the evening because you're new, so be careful what you say. Always put the music on, or the shower, or rustle a tissue near your mouth if you want to say anything that you don't want him to hear."

She switched off the shower again, waited a moment and then opened the door.

"That was a lovely shower, I feel so much better now," she said loudly, turning down the music.

"Good," said Claudia equally loudly. "That music has done wonders for me too. Inspiring! I'm so glad I've had time to think. I'll have to ask the Holy Leaders to come and explain it all to me again. Perhaps they'll forgive me for my rudeness."

Downstairs the Holy Leaders listened with interest.

"It's all a sham," said one of them.

"Perhaps so," said the other, "but it's our holy duty to keep trying."

Later that evening the father changed out of his formal work suit and slipped into loose velvet trousers and an

111

embroidered jacket. Crossing over to the sideboard he took his tray out of the dumb waiter then pressed the button to send it back to the kitchen. He settled himself down at the dining table and opened his napkin. He poured his wine and lifted the covers from the plates, taking pleasure in the sight and smell of a beautifully prepared meal.

A few minutes later the whirring noise of the dumb waiter on its way up to the second floor reminded him to turn on the sound from upstairs. He had lost the habit of listening while the woman had been on her own, but now there were two of them up there it might be wise to hear what they had to say. Reaching over to the wall near the door, he pressed a switch and then took up his knife and fork. Music floated gently down and he could hear the soft murmur of women's voices chatting about the colour of Claudia's hair.

So Claudia had recovered from her state of decline. Now he would get to know her. The Holy Leaders would no doubt report on today's visit. If they were beginning to persuade her to the Holy Cause, his own striking good looks and charming manner should speed up the process. Maybe he could even make Belinda jealous by showering a younger woman with his attentions. Reaching out to the little side table, he pulled a hand mirror out of the drawer and practised his smile. It was still there, but it took more of an effort these days. He tried to crinkle his eyes a little more, but wasn't really satisfied. Never mind. The pain in his head would pass off when he'd had something to eat.

Upstairs Maria carried the tray over from the dumb waiter and set it down on the table. She winked at Claudia.

"Sarah is a wonderful cook," she said. "You'll enjoy the food while you're here."

"I'm so glad you persuaded me to think over what the priests said." Claudia spoke clearly, but stopped for a moment to stifle a little laugh. "I was so unreceptive at first, but I think it was because I was still in shock from finding myself here. Now that my mind has cleared, I can see the logic of what they say. We really do need a new order to this world. All the corruption that goes on is quite shocking."

Maria smiled, and nodded her head. Down below the father thought Aha! So the Holy Leaders had trouble with this girl, but now all was well. She was beginning to see the light, thanks to Belinda. What an amazing lady! Too honourable to pretend to believe when she could not, yet she was prepared to support others who might be able to do so. If only she herself could be persuaded. She would be a prized convert after so many years of doubting, and would ensure him a position at the Holy Envoy's right hand.

The voices floated back and forth. "Father Copse is very kind to me," Belinda was saying. "So generous."

Claudia's response was clear. "He's certainly very handsome. I'm looking forward to getting to know him better." The music became louder and smothered the splutter of laughter.

Putting aside his financial problems and his promotion aspirations for a while, the father felt satisfied with his lot, and with himself. He switched off the sound. There was nothing there to disturb him, though it might be wise to remove their music player just in case it drowned anything he needed to hear. If all went well Claudia might produce a child fairly quickly and then she could be passed on to the commune as a convert. The Holy Envoy might even increase his expenses.

113

CHAPTER SIXTEEN

One day in the middle of July a rumour swept through the school that Dorothy had been caught.

"What happened?" Lucy asked David in the playground as she handed back the ball he had kicked in her direction.

He answered hastily in a hoarse whisper. "They say she went to the police, but one of them was an infiltrator." He ran off with the ball and Lucy joined a game of rounders.

When they came out of school that evening he muttered as he passed, "The aunts are saying she might have to be disposed of."

Lucy's skin crawled. She stopped on the steps. "If anyone asks," she said quietly, "say we're talking about the homework." David nodded and took a maths book out of his satchel and opened it up between them. Most people had gone home already.

"Can we find out where she is?" asked Lucy quietly. "Perhaps we can save her."

"I listen to the kitchen aunts every night," David whispered, "except when there's a risk I might be seen. I shall just keep listening. At the moment even they don't know where she is. She's probably in the upper rooms of some other commune."

"I could get out through the coal hole in the middle of the night and go and look for her."

"No. You'd never find her. We'll certainly know if she gets taken to the disposal cells because they're just behind Drax House, and the kitchen aunts will have to take her food and they'll be gossiping about it non-stop. Until she's taken there we'll know that she's alive."

Lucy was gripped with fear for Dorothy. She couldn't eat her supper, and her homework was a meaningless scribble. "What's the matter with you?" asked Aunt Sarah in exasperation. "You're shuffling around like a zombie, and you've not uttered a word all evening."

"Sorry, Aunt Sarah," mumbled Lucy, and made an effort to pull herself together. She changed the subject. "Why does the father live upstairs?"

"He wants peace and quiet, like all men."

"We don't make a noise."

"No, but men have very important things on their minds, so they find women and children a nuisance unless they're out of sight."

"Why can't I go with you when you go into his flat?"

"Because it's private. Now don't ask any more silly questions."

Lucy risked one more question. "Will I be allowed to earn money when I'm grown up?"

"No. Your place will be in a commune. You'll be taught all the skills and, if you listen to what you're told, you might be a really good cook like me."

So what Dorothy had said was right. A lot of the things that Dorothy had said seemed to be true. Lucy wouldn't be allowed to leave. She would never have the money to take a bus to the outside world. As for being a good cook, so what? The meals that went up on the dumb waiter certainly looked and smelled as though they had been prepared by a really good cook, but the food that went on her plate didn't, nor did the food on Aunt Sarah's plate. In fact Lucy often wondered how Aunt Sarah had grown so fat.

Tonight was Wednesday, prayer evening. After supper Sarah and the two children tidied themselves up and walked across the common. They emerged into South Hill via the little lane, just up from George's house. As always, Lucy hoped George wouldn't see them passing or, if he did, that he wouldn't shout anything about snoots or nutters. There was no sign of him thank goodness, and they marched purposefully down to the lights, over the junction and up the High Street.

Copse House was on the right, a few hundred yards up the hill beyond the shops. Drax House stood almost exactly opposite, and behind Drax House were the woods where Aunt Sarah had sometimes taken Lucy to play when she was little. Tonight the prayer meeting was to be in Copse House, and all the aunts and children from both communes would gather together.

Aunt Sarah loved visiting Copse House. It was her one and only social event. The men would be holding their prayer meeting in the school building tonight because they had important business matters to discuss. They would finish much later than the women and children, so there was plenty of time for Sarah to gossip with the aunts and for Lucy to play with the children.

The Copse boys were circling round and round the tarmac parking space on their bikes, showing off as they rode with no hands or on one wheel. The girls were not allowed bikes. Tonight they were skipping and playing hopscotch, and Lucy joined in. Now that they were not in the school building some of the girls made her

116

feel welcome, and if she hadn't been worrying about Dorothy she could have felt happy.

"It's more fun living in the commune," she said to Sarah on the way home.

Sarah was offended.

"You should be grateful for what you've got," she snapped.

"Yes, I am," said Lucy humbly, "but they've got each other to play with."

"They're probably jealous of your life, all the attention on you and Paul."

"Yes, I expect so."

"You don't know how lucky you are," said Aunt Sarah after a moment's silence. "I was brought up in a commune. You can't imagine how hard it was." She shook herself briefly. "I suppose it was all for the best."

Lucy was irrationally surprised to hear that she had had a childhood.

Paul was grumbling about having to walk so far.

"It'll make you strong," said Sarah. "You don't want to grow up a weakling, do you?"

"Aunt Sarah?" ventured Lucy. "Do you think I would be allowed to have a bike?"

"Never!" exclaimed Sarah. "Of course not! Decent ladies don't ride bikes."

On Wednesday nights the father would call in on his way back from the prayer meeting to hear Sarah's weekly report on the children's behaviour. Lucy had decided that in preparation for her birth-record-finding plans, she was going to note carefully the details of these visits.

The father never entered the ground-floor flat by the front door. He would stride up the side path past the garage, past the kitchen window and into the lobby. Lucy would listen as he first unlocked the outer door to the lobby, and then the door to the kitchen. He would stand in the doorway, tall and fiercely handsome with his shining black hair and eyes like smouldering coals, putting questions to Aunt Sarah and giving her instructions. She would respond respectfully with a minimum of words, because men didn't like talkative women.

Sometimes he would call Lucy and Paul to stand in front of him so that he could have a good look at them. He rarely spoke to them, or asked them to speak. Then he would leave, locking the door behind him. Lucy would listen to his footsteps going through the lobby and up the stairs to his flat on the first floor. She would hear him unlocking his own front door and closing it after him.

Tonight, as soon as she saw the father pass the window, Lucy got up from her chair and, as casually as she could, positioned herself so that when he entered the kitchen she could see past him into the lobby. As the door opened she could see the stairs that led up to the upper flats, and the outer door of the lobby with its three bolts. She had passed that door on the outside many times when she took rubbish to the bins round the back of the house or played in the garden, but she had never thought much about what lay inside it. Now it intrigued her, and she studied it with interest. It was solid oak with small coloured glass panels at the top, and there was no letter box even though it was the front door for the first and second-floor flats. Not only did it have three bolts, but there were two keyholes.

It was obvious that Lucy would never be able to get

into the lobby from the outside door. If she only had the key to the kitchen door and, of course, the key to the upstairs flat, it would be simple. She imagined herself nipping up those stairs in a tick, finding her birth record lying on the desk open at the right page, and running off to catch a bus with Paul under her arm.

"Why doesn't the postman ever go up the side path?" Lucy asked Aunt Sarah when the father had gone. "Doesn't the father ever get letters? Even we get letters – from the school or telling us when to put the rubbish bins out."

"He gets all his letters addressed to his work, I expect," said Sarah. "Men don't like to be bothered with business in their own home."

"What's so special about men?" asked Lucy.

"It's the Holy Order of things."

"Oh, I see."

CHAPTER SEVENTEEN

The evenings were light and Lucy lingered longer on her way home. The tea would already be laid out when she arrived, but Aunt Sarah was often too busy to eat with her and Paul. She seemed to be finding her work more and more difficult. Occasionally Lucy would hear her grumbling to herself about having to wash and cook for so many people upstairs and downstairs, followed by a muttered prayer for forgiveness.

Sometimes, when Lucy dawdled up South Hill, George would be swinging on the front gate at number 38, watching the traffic or calling out insults to any of his friends who happened to pass.

"Hello, snoot!" he shouted one evening as Lucy approached. "You need a nutcracker to crack all those nutters."

A large ginger cat was sitting on the gatepost next to him. Lucy stopped and looked over her shoulder. There was no-one watching her.

"Is that your cat?" she asked.

"Yes, and his name is Marmalade, Marma for short."

He turned to stroke the cat and made a purring noise right into its face. It turned its head away.

"Actually, he's not just mine. He belongs to me and my sister, but I'm older so he knows me better."

Lucy put her hand up to stroke Marma.

"He's beautiful," she said. "I'd love to have a cat."

Marma purred.

"What's your sister called?"

"Elizabeth."

"I've seen her. In the pushchair."

"Yeah, well I'm lucky because I live in a normal family, not in a sect with a bunch of nutters."

"I don't live in a sect," retorted Lucy sharply. "I live in a private residence. And as you're so clever, Mr Clever Clogs," she added, nipping round behind the gate, "perhaps you can tell me something."

Her unexpected foray into his territory silenced George for a moment.

"I want some information," said Lucy hurriedly, huddling down into a hydrangea bush. "And I want sensible information, not some stupid remark."

George gaped. This was trespass.

"I want you to find out how to get at a key if it's left in the lock on the other side of the door."

He looked at her so blankly she wondered if he had understood.

"Like burglars," she added.

"How would I know that?" he said, racking his brain for what he had seen on television.

"Your dad," said Lucy earnestly. "You can ask him."

"My dad's not a burglar!"

"Of course he's not, but you said he knows everything. You must ask him, but don't say why. Just say you're writing a story for school or something. When he tells you, write it down as though you're taking notes, otherwise you might get it wrong. I'd like the information on paper please, so you can pass it to me as I walk past looking the other way."

121

Lucy was surprised at her own authoritative tone. She sounded just like Aunt Ann who taught them English.

"What'll you give me for it?" asked George.

"I can't give you anything, because I don't own anything. But one day you'll get your reward."

Remembering Aunt Sarah's oft-repeated promise she chanted, "If you act righteously now, your reward will be great." She stopped herself from saying it would be great in the next world, but added, "It will be great sometime in the future."

George pondered over her strange request. Perhaps she wanted to be a burglar, he thought, in which case she might steal something wonderful for him as a reward. That would be exciting but, after some consideration, he hoped it wouldn't happen because his mother would be sure to find out.

"OK," he said, "but I don't want any stolen goods or I might be put in prison."

Lucy laughed. "Of course not! When can you get it?"

"I'll try and get it by tomorrow."

"Thanks."

Lucy peeped through the bars of the gate and looked up and down the road. Then she slipped out onto the pavement and ran up South Hill.

The next day was Wednesday. George was not at the gate. Lucy didn't wait in case she was seen by some old busybody turning up early for the prayer meeting.

That night, after she and Paul and Aunt Sarah had arrived home from Copse House, Lucy was putting away her books when she saw the father's tall figure pass the window. A moment later he was in the kitchen, and the door to the lobby was wide open. Aunt Sarah was saying something about "not enough time in the day," her eyes downcast and her hands clasped together.

"Then make time!" he thundered.

"Yes, Father," replied Sarah with a meekness that contradicted the high purple colour in her face and the downward glare of her eyes.

Lucy watched unnoticed, afraid to move. The father was horrible to shout at Aunt Sarah. Lucy looked past him through the open door into the lobby, and up the stairs that led to his apartment.

When he had gone Aunt Sarah looked upset. Lucy wondered if she dared to ask what it was she had to make time for.

Sarah was muttering to herself.

"What's the matter, Aunt Sarah?" asked Lucy nervously.

Sarah let go of her usual stern expression for a moment, and even looked resentful.

"I can't do everything," she said, almost to herself. "Look after him, two children, two tenants, do all the cooking, washing, shopping, and now he wants me to clean his flat because Martha's got a bad back."

"I'll help you," said Lucy promptly.

"You've got school," said Sarah, "but you're a good girl. Thank you. You can help in the holidays by looking after Paul for me, and doing some shopping." She sighed. "I must look upon it as a duty performed in the service of the Magnifico."

She sat down at the table and put her head in her hands.

"I'll make you a cup of tea," said Lucy, putting on the kettle. "And I'll give Paul his bath."

When Paul was in bed Lucy stepped out into the

123

garden. It was a lovely evening. She sat on the swing and gently pushed herself back and forth with her feet. The side gate clicked and she thought for a second of the hooded figure, but it was only Thomas.

"Hello," he said. "Shouldn't you be in bed, or doing your homework or something?"

"No, I've done it, and I don't go to bed till nine o'clock nowadays because it's so light."

She jumped down and joined him on his way to the garage. A rolled-up cigarette dangled from his lips dripping loose wisps of tobacco. It reminded her of the chauffeur on the night the new tenant had arrived. She realised to her surprise that she had never mentioned that night to him.

"Why have you come so late?" she asked.

"I've just finished my shift at the hospital. Today it was sad work because somebody died. A bit of gardening will help take my mind off it."

Lucy stroked his hand. "Poor Thomas," she said. She wished she could comfort him.

She followed him into the garage. Picking up his torch from the window sill near the door, he went over to the shelves at the rear. He switched on the torch and shone it into his toolbox, poking around for a screwdriver and a hammer, and other bits and pieces. Lucy stood beside him, watching with interest.

"What's that for?" she asked, when he picked up a small tool with a round wooden handle and long piece of pointed metal.

"It's an awl, for making holes where I want to put screws."

Stumbling over some old tins of paint he made his way back towards the entrance. It was surprising, thought Lucy, that he kept the garden so tidy and yet the garage was always in a mess. He put the torch back on the window sill, and threw the tools down onto a pile of sacks near the door. His working anorak hung from a hook in the corner by the window. He pulled it on and hung up his respectable jacket in its place.

"See what I've got," he said, taking a small gadget out of the jacket pocket. "It's a mobile phone. You carry it around and can phone from anywhere you like."

The two of them sat down on the sacks and Thomas showed Lucy the various tricks this wonderful invention could perform. He took a quick photo of her to show her the camera, but it was too dark in the garage to make a clear picture.

"I'll do it again outside," he said. "Look, this is where I put in all my phone numbers, then all I have to do is press a button and their phone rings. It saves me having to look up the numbers. And if I just want to send a message, I can do something called a text. See?" He tapped in some words onto the tiny screen.

"Can I ring Aunt Sarah?"

"You'd better not. She might think you're wasting her time. Come on outside, quick, and I'll take another photo."

Lucy stood with her back to the setting sun.

"Smile!"

She smiled. He showed her the photo. It was the first she had ever seen of herself, and she laughed. "Is that what I look like?"

"I'll make you a copy to keep," said Thomas. He took the phone back into the garage and put it in his jacket pocket.

"If you lose it, you'll lose all those numbers," said Lucy.

"Don't worry. I'll take good care of it, but I've got

125

them all noted down, just in case." He picked his tools up off the pile of sacks. "Right! I've come to work, not to chat. I must get a move on."

Outside the wheelbarrow was in its usual place, leaning against the outside wall of the garage. Thomas turned it over onto its wheel and placed the tools and a fork and spade inside.

"I want to mend some gaps in the back gate and do a bit of digging," he said.

"Have you noticed how my pansies have grown?" asked Lucy.

"Of course," he said kindly. "They've come on really well. And your carrots. Here, have a sweetie. What's Father Copse up to these days? Did you know he's applied for the Deputy Envoy's job?"

With a quick glance at the kitchen window Lucy stuffed a toffee into her mouth.

"No. Does that mean he'll go away?"

"If he gets the job he might."

Lucy's heart lifted for a moment. Thomas smiled at the expression on her face.

"It'll be OK. He's got a really good chance. There's no-one to beat him when it comes to preaching. It curdles the blood in your veins."

Lucy shuddered.

"And he's a brilliant infiltrator," Thomas continued. "It's the charisma – the charm." He laughed. "Don't look so astonished. Everyone has more to them than what you see. All the top judges and civil servants, he mixes with them and what they don't realise is, he knows their secrets and passes them on. He knows more about them than they know themselves!"

He ruffled her hair.

"Let me know if you hear anything. You know I'm always interested in how you're getting on."

"Of course I will. And thanks for the sweetie."

"It's a pleasure."

He stubbed out his cigarette and trundled off with his barrow leaving Lucy to wonder what a civil servant was, and to ponder over the truly amazing information that the father could be charming. The way he spoke to Aunt Sarah certainly wasn't charming. And the way that poor red-headed tenant had been bundled into the house hadn't been charming. But it must be really interesting to be an infiltrator. Perhaps she could be one. She wished she had some information to pass on to Thomas – just to practise. After a while she followed him. He was busy with the awl and a screwdriver doing something to a loose board in the back gate.

"Thomas," said Lucy, appearing behind him.

"Yes?"

"Did you know we've got another tenant? We've got two now."

A startled look passed quickly over Thomas's face and immediately changed to puzzlement.

"Two tenants?"

"Yes. In the top-floor flat." She turned and pointed up at the barred windows.

"No, I didn't know," said Thomas. "I suppose there's no reason why I should. Perhaps the father needs the income. What do they look like?"

"I've never seen them properly, though I know one of them has long red hair. And I'll tell you a secret. I once climbed into the lime tree from the wall over there, and I saw a lady's face looking out at me."

A flash of annoyance passed over Thomas's face and quickly vanished.

"You shouldn't have done that," he said firmly. "Supposing you got caught?"

"I know," she said, "I've not done it again. But it was like how you imagine a lunatic asylum in a book with the lunatic gripping the bars trying to get out."

"Listen to me," said Thomas, crouching down in front of her and gripping her arms. "Don't tell anyone about this, promise me. And don't tell anyone how you got so high up into the tree – or that you got into the tree at all. Promise me!"

"OK, I promise," said Lucy, somewhat shaken. Thomas knew perfectly well that there was one tenant because they had often talked about it. So why should it upset him to hear that there were two – or was he just cross that she'd climbed the tree?

She went back to the swing and pondered on the significance of these tenants for whom Aunt Sarah had to cook, and who never came downstairs to do their own shopping, and for whom the postman never called, and who looked out from behind bars like lunatics. She had considered telling Thomas about the hooded figure who had shown her the way into the tree, and how it was that she knew one of the tenants had red hair – and how she had briefly wondered if the new tenant had been abducted – but she decided not to. She had obviously irritated him enough for the time being.

After school the next day George was swinging on the gate. Lucy didn't look at him. He dropped his hand down. She reached hers up and took a scrap of paper from between his thumb and finger.

"Thanks," she muttered. "You'll get your reward in

due course," and walked straight past without looking back.

When she arrived home she tucked the bit of paper between the pages of her homework book. She didn't dare read it straight away in case Aunt Sarah came suddenly to look over her shoulder. There was no supper that night because they were supposed to be fasting to celebrate the discovery of the first Holy Envoy as a baby in his wooden box sixteen hundred years ago. The evening seemed very long. Lucy wandered round the garden for a while. There was no sign of Thomas. He was probably still at the hospital. She went back to the kitchen and sat down to do her homework, but it was difficult to concentrate. Her mind was on George's note. Why on earth hadn't she stopped by the pond on the way home from school and hidden in the bushes to read it? Perhaps Aunt Sarah wouldn't notice if she slipped out again. She shuffled her books around and felt for the bit of paper, but withdrew her hand quickly.

Aunt Sarah was always irritable on a fasting night – though you'd have thought she'd be happy not to have to cook. "What's the matter with you tonight?" she snapped. "You're as restless as a box of wriggling eels. Just get on with your work, and then you can help Paul with his reading."

When she had finished her homework Lucy sat down with Paul at the table, and they practised his letters.

"A is for apple," she said, drawing an A and a picture of an apple.

"I know that," said Paul. He opened his mouth wide. "Apple. I'm hungry."

"B is for boy." She drew a picture of a round little boy with curly hair.

"I can spell boy," said Paul. "I can spell Paul."

"C is for cat."

"I know all that already." Paul grabbed the pencil and drew a picture of a boy with an apple standing next to a cat.

"You draw much better than I do," said Lucy admiringly. "I'll read you a story instead." She fetched her book of fairy tales from her bedroom and they sat together on Aunt Sarah's chair.

"Once upon a time…" began Lucy.

"I can read that," said Paul. "Once upon a time there was a beautiful princess." Lucy couldn't help smiling to herself. It was hard to tell how much Paul could genuinely read and how much he knew by heart.

The evening dragged by. When Aunt Sarah took Paul to bed Lucy gave up and said she was going too.

"You're very early," said Sarah.

"I just feel a bit more tired than usual."

"Well you won't sleep while it's so light, but it's up to you."

Sarah had her hands in the sink, and a delicious smell emerged from the oven.

Lucy's mouth watered. "Are you cooking for tomorrow, Aunt Sarah?" she asked.

"No, it's for tonight, Miss Nosy Parker. The father's just had a message direct from the Magnifico saying he and the tenant are exempt from fasting for some reason." Aunt Sarah's nose wrinkled. Did she actually mutter, "I don't think!" under her breath?

No of course not. Lucy must've heard wrong. "Can I help you with anything before I go?" she asked.

"No. You go. I can manage better on my own, but thank you."

Aunt Sarah turned and a smile flickered over her stern face. Lucy noticed that her legs were swollen, and thought how tired she looked.

Lucy washed, cleaned her teeth, and laid out her school clothes ready for the morning. The curtains let in some light, but she opened them a bit further so as to read clearly. Rosy pink rays from the sunset fell across her room. She climbed into bed and sat with her homework book open in case Sarah came in. Peering down at George's rather imperfect writing she managed to decipher his instructions:

To retreev key from other side of lock – First, push large sheet of niwspaper or carbord under door keeping just enouff back to get hold of it on your side of door. Second, poke wire or thin rod such as niting needle into keyhole and jigle it about till key falls out other side and lands (you hope) on niwspaper or carbord. Third, pull niwspaper or carbord towards you and key will apere on your side of door.

Of course! That was brilliant, thought Lucy. What a clever man George's father was. He was so, so lucky to have a father like that, full of useful information. She tried to picture the process of getting at the key to the lobby exactly as the instructions stated. If only she could be sure that it didn't fall too far away, it should be quite straightforward.

Her mind was too alive for her to sleep. She got up and went back to the kitchen. Aunt Sarah was still rinsing out clothes by hand in the deep butler's sink.

"You were right, Aunt Sarah. It's too light to sleep."

"Put the kettle on then, and make us a cup of tea. I've

nearly finished these." She gave them a final wring, and pulled them out onto the draining board. "I'll just hang them out. We'll each have a biscuit, fast or no fast, but you'll have to clean your teeth again."

Lucy put the kettle on and took the biscuit tin out of the cupboard. Her tummy had been rumbling hopefully ever since the smell of the father's supper had tickled her nostrils. The thought of a biscuit was quite delightful, and she hoped Aunt Sarah would be quick because she was starving. She stood at the back door and watched as Aunt Sarah puffed with her load of washing and vanished round behind the wing to the clothes line. Moving back across the kitchen to the side window she could see Thomas with his wheelbarrow making his way across the lawn towards the garage. He stopped under the lime tree and looked up into its boughs. Then he went into the garage and reappeared with three saws of different sizes. Perhaps he was going to cut the branches. It didn't matter to Lucy. She would never climb that tree again.

Aunt Sarah hung up the last of the laundry and picked up the empty basket, but instead of coming straight back so that Lucy could have her biscuit she went over to talk to Thomas. She looked cross, and they seemed to be arguing. Eventually Thomas rolled his eyes and shook his head, and took the saws away.

"He wanted to cut that big branch," said Aunt Sarah indignantly, when she came into the kitchen. "Anyway, he'd never be able to do it with those silly little saws. It's much too thick." She opened the lid of the biscuit tin. "Right!" she said, "Two each."

CHAPTER EIGHTEEN

After school the next day Aunt Sarah was complaining about the stairs. Her face was shining with sweat and her hair fell in lank wisps away from its bun. She had had a bad day.

"I've not only got to clean his flat while Aunt Martha's away with her bad back, but I've got to do all those stairs, all the way up to the top floor."

"Did you take Paul up with you?" asked Lucy.

"No. Of course not! He's no more allowed on those stairs than you are. I had to leave him in his room. No harm can come to him there. Anyway, the father says he's got to get used to being without company, same as you had to. It gives you time for quiet contemplation and brings you closer to the Magnifico."

Lucy thought she would prefer not to be close to the Magnifico. In fact, ever since Dorothy had been captured she had wanted to escape him altogether.

"Well, I'll be looking after Paul in the holidays," she said.

"That's true. Though I hope Aunt Martha is back by then."

Lucy knew she was being selfish, but she couldn't help hoping that Aunt Martha would stay away for a little longer. The thought of being asked to do the shopping was very appealing. Her mind was already working out what she could do with her freedom on the days that Aunt Sarah was upstairs. If she could find out how to use the Underground or the buses she might be able to plan her escape. As for money, well, she had no idea where that would come from. Perhaps Thomas would lend her some. In the meantime she wanted to find out if there was any news about Dorothy. The only person she could talk to about it was David.

"Can I have a friend over in the holidays?" she asked.

"It depends who it is. I'll have to ask the father first. Who is it?"

"It's David from Drax House. He's very well-behaved. He used to have the guidance cane, but he doesn't any more."

Sarah wrinkled her forehead.

"I doubt that you'll be allowed. You shouldn't be seen to mix with people who've had the guidance, even if you have had it yourself. It might make matters worse. Anyway, for some reason I think the father disapproves of Drax House these days, even more than he used to. But I'll ask him."

After that Aunt Sarah felt she had talked too much and too leniently for one day, and drew her lips into their usual stern line. She shut Paul in his room, to which he objected, and told him to be silent because we all have to do things we don't want to do at times.

The following morning Lucy ran all the way to school hoping she'd see David before everyone went in. She checked that there was no-one near enough to hear them, and caught him as he was going up the front steps.

"I've asked if you can come to my house in the holidays," she panted. "If the father gives permission we can be friends. Then you can let me know if you hear anything about Dorothy, and you can help with suggestions for my escape."

David stopped and looked at her doubtfully.

"I'd have to get permission too, and I have a feeling from things I've heard that Father Drax and Father Copse don't like each other. In fact, I think they hate each other, which of course is a sin, but I suppose they're above all that. I'll wait till you've heard what Father Copse says."

Needless to say, the father refused permission. Aunt Sarah was not told why. The result of Lucy's request was that Father Copse asked the school to discourage any friendship between Lucy and children from Drax House, particularly David.

Lucy wondered how she could have been so naïve as to think of such a thing, let alone get so excited about it. If only she had been more subtle! Now everyone would be on the lookout to make sure she didn't talk to David. What made it all the harder was that there was no news of Dorothy, except that she was being kept somewhere, awaiting a decision as to her future.

The summer holidays came, and on the days that Aunt Sarah had to clean upstairs the door from the kitchen to the lobby would be firmly locked behind her before she went up to the first-floor flat. If Thomas came Lucy and Paul would follow him around. Sometimes he gave them rides in his wheelbarrow, or pushed them both together on the swing, all squashed up in the wooden box with their legs sticking out through the holes at the front. Their favourite place was the common, and they would lie on their stomachs looking into the pond and poking it with sticks. Lucy was always hoping David would come and find her there, but he never did.

She hadn't had a chance to try out George's recipe

for removing keys from doors because she knew Aunt Sarah would be up and down those stairs, but she felt frustrated that she was frittering her holidays away by doing nothing about it. She still didn't know what her escape plan was going to be, but she couldn't do anything until she had been inside the father's flat and looked for the record of her birth.

One cold rainy day in August, when it was too wet to go out, Lucy and Paul sat at the kitchen table playing with his farm set.

"One, two, three hens," said Lucy. She counted out the little wooden pieces and made clucking sounds.

"One, two, three hens, cluck, cluck, cluck," repeated Paul, counting off his thumb and two fingers.

"See? There's some more here."

"Four, five," said Paul. Then using his fingers he counted up to ten.

"Clever boy!"

Aunt Sarah had gone out into the lobby and locked the kitchen door. The children could hear her trundling up the stairs pulling the vacuum cleaner behind her, puffing and grumbling to herself. Then down she came again. The vacuum bag needed changing. She unlocked the door, pulling the machine into the kitchen.

"Fetch me a new hoover bag from the cupboard," she grunted, already out of breath before she had even started her cleaning work.

Lucy burrowed in the back of the cupboard and found a clean bag. Sarah sat down for a moment to catch her breath, and then took out the old bag and inserted the clean one.

"Take this out to the bin please," she said handing the full bag to Lucy.

Trying not to breathe in the dust, Lucy took the bag and ran out through the back door and round the back of the wing to the bin. When she returned Sarah was washing her hands and muttering to herself. Sitting down while she dried them she took some deep breaths and then, making a huge effort, she heaved herself up, grabbed the hoover and left the kitchen, shutting the door behind her.

There was no locking sound.

Lucy stood with her ear to the door and listened as the vacuum cleaner clanked its way up the stairs once more. She tried the handle cautiously. The door opened. Lucy peeped round it and saw that the key was still in the lock. She craned her head towards the stairs, and could hear the father's front door being unlocked, opened, and shut.

She stepped out into the lobby and, holding her breath, she strained her ears for sounds. There was nothing except for the occasional clunk of furniture being moved out of the way. The blood pounded in Lucy's ears. She dashed back into the kitchen and grabbed Paul gently and gave him a hug.

"You stay here and play with the farm," she said. "I've got to go out for a minute. Be a good boy. I won't be long."

She crept into the lobby closing the kitchen door quietly. The stairs were wide and thickly covered in a rich crimson carpet. Lucy tiptoed onto the first step and then the second, and waited. She could hear the hoover getting into its stride. Despite the carpeting, some of the steps creaked. Stepping as lightly as she could to lessen the sound, she ran nimbly up the stairs onto a big square landing. The walls were panelled with dark brown wood, and red velvet curtains hung each side of a long stained glass window. Behind a highly-polished mahogany door the vacuum cleaner roared away. It stopped for a second. Lucy was poised to flee but there was a thud as though Aunt Sarah had given it a good kick, and it started again.

Checking around her Lucy could see that if she needed to hide the only place would be behind the curtains. To the right of the front door were the stairs to the second-floor flat, but there would be no point in hiding up there because Aunt Sarah would get back to the kitchen before Lucy and lock the door, and she'd have to knock to be let in.

The vacuum stopped again. Sarah said something crossly to herself. There was a clattering of dishes, and then a muffled trundling noise from somewhere behind the panelling to the right of the landing. Lucy recognised the sound of the dumb waiter. It went downwards, and she could faintly hear its familiar thump as it landed in the kitchen.

Just as she was wondering if she had time to run up the next flight of stairs to have a look, Lucy heard the vacuum being dragged across the floor. The door opened and she was rooted to the spot. Aunt Sarah's figure appeared side-on as she bent down to pick up her bag of brushes and dusters.

In a split second Lucy slipped behind a curtain and held her breath. Her mind raced. There was no way she could get back to the kitchen before Aunt Sarah. She didn't dare look round the edge of the curtain, and only hoped it would muffle the sound of the blood thumping away in her ears.

There was some more muttering and banging, and

the vacuum cleaner knocked against the stairs. It was going upwards.

Dizzy with relief Lucy peeped out and saw an ample behind proceeding up the next flight. There was a turning at the top, but Aunt Sarah didn't look down. She was hot and sweating and cross. With a final lug of the machine she moved out of sight onto the upper landing.

Darting over to the big mahogany door, Lucy put her eye to the keyhole, but could see nothing except light from a window and part of an armchair. She turned and ran down the stairs to the kitchen two steps at a time. Paul was crying. Shutting the door quickly behind her, she threw herself onto a chair and pulled him onto her lap.

When Sarah eventually came down with her equipment she realised she had forgotten to lock the door. She muttered something to herself, but the scene before her was peaceful, and she turned the key behind her with a puff of relief. The children seemed to be playing cheerfully with the farm set, and she didn't notice Lucy's burning face. She put the vacuum away, washed her hands, and put the kettle on.

"We'll all have a cup of tea and a biscuit as a treat," she gasped as she sat down heavily. "You've been such good children."

"Thank you, Aunt Sarah," said Lucy. "I'll make the tea. You have a rest." She put Paul down and started to bustle about with the mugs and the milk.

"I've said it before and I'll say it again," said Sarah. "You're a good girl. I've brought you up well."

"Lucy left me on my own," said Paul.

"I had to go to the bathroom."

"Well," said Sarah, "he's got to learn to be on his own sometimes. The father said so."

She sank back into her chair and closed her eyes, and added somewhat bitterly, "And his word is law."

CHAPTER NINETEEN

The rain stopped and the next day was fine and warm. Lucy and Paul went over to the common. They could see some of the children from the Drax and Copse communes playing far away over on the other side, near the backs of the houses where George lived. Perhaps Dorothy was there. Lucy searched for the mop of black curls, though she knew it was too far to tell one child from another. She was permanently anxious, but always hoping that Dorothy would reappear one day as cheerful and cocky as ever.

She and Paul stayed within their permitted area near the front of the house. They kicked a ball for a while, and then Lucy showed him how to do handstands. When he had mastered the skill of not collapsing as his feet left the ground they went through the bushes to the pond. They found suitable sticks and lay down on their stomachs to poke at the muddy water and disturb its interesting residents.

"See that? That's a water boatman."

"Where's his boat?" asked Paul.

"His feet. That's his boat. They keep him afloat."

"Hi, Lucy."

Lucy rolled over and looked up. A pair of wiry brown legs appeared, topped by scruffy blue shorts, and David pushed through the bushes with his bike. Lucy noticed that his knees were grazed and guessed that he'd probably fallen off doing tricks.

"Hello," she said. "I was looking to see if you were over there."

"Yes, I saw you." He leaned his bike up against a rhododendron and squatted down beside them.

"I wanted to tell you something," he said. "It's important."

He reached around to find a stick of his own, and started to poke at the water.

"I've heard something. The aunts were talking. I was hiding where Dorothy used to hide."

Lucy felt the sickness of fear at hearing Dorothy's name.

"I heard the aunts say that our Father Drax and your Father Copse..."

"Not *my* father, just *the* father," Lucy intercepted.

"Yes, I know you don't like it, but he is your father, so listen. Don't interrupt."

"But what about Dorothy?" Lucy was impatient. "Have you heard anything?"

David's eyes clouded over with despair. "Nothing." For a moment he forgot what he had come for. Lucy's anxiety turned to impatience.

"Well, what's the important thing you wanted to tell me?"

He swallowed. "This isn't to do with Dorothy. It's something quite different – about you."

Lucy sat upright and stared, and David continued.

"I heard that Father Drax and Father Copse are deadly enemies and rivals for the Holy Envoy's favour. They both want to be the Holy Envoy's deputy when this one retires."

"Oh," said Lucy, turning back to the pond. "Is that all?"

She wasn't particularly interested in what the father wanted, or what his enemies wanted, unless it meant he would be going away. It was Dorothy who was important, not the father.

"No, that's not all. There's going to be an election for the Deputy Envoy post, and whoever wins it will get the job. The Holy Leaders will have one vote each, and the Holy Envoy will have ten votes on top of that."

"Won't they notice over there that you've gone?" asked Lucy, waving her hand towards the other side of the common.

"I doubt it. There's no-one supervising. The aunts have all gone to a prayer meeting, and Matthew had to go to the dentist."

"I'm sick of prayer meetings," said Lucy, trying to catch a stickleback with her bare hands.

"I got a fish," said Paul as a silver streak slipped through his hands and escaped. He leaned too far after it and would have fallen in if Lucy hadn't grabbed his shirt.

"Careful, you silly boy! Aunt Sarah will be cross if you get wet." His rolled-up sleeves were already soaking.

"Listen to me," said David crossly, "and let me finish. You're being really annoying today."

He pushed his fair hair out of his eyes and lowered his voice. "What I wanted to tell you was not to trust anyone. I don't know what's going on, but there's something. They were saying that Father Drax wants to find out things about Father Copse that'll make him look bad to stop him from being elected. It's called discrediting him. And one of the things they said was that if you do something bad that could be used to discredit Father Copse."

"Me?" Lucy shot bolt upright, her eyes wide with astonishment.

"Yes. They said you're not as innocent as you look because you were seen talking to Dorothy, and if you can be lured into doing something to bring shame on Father Copse it would damage his chances in the election. Like when you had the guidance."

Lucy felt a rush of shock. Then she stood up, flushed and angry.

"Are you saying you deliberately sang those words to make me laugh just so I could be punished?" She hauled Paul to his feet.

"No, no, of course not, but it could well have put the idea in Father Drax's head, and if it did I'm really, really sorry." He grabbed her arm. "Please don't go. I was singing those words because Matthew dared me, that's all. It wasn't meant to make you laugh, and it was nothing to do with the fathers. I didn't even know they were rivals at that stage. Honest. I would never have done it if I'd known."

Lucy shook his hand off her arm

"It was you who told me not to trust anyone," she said. "How can I trust you? Come on, Paul."

She stalked off pulling a grumbling Paul behind her. David left his bike and ran after her.

"Why are you so unreasonable?" he almost wailed. "Why would I have warned you if you couldn't trust me?"

"To make me not trust someone else who really is my friend?"

Tears of despair filled Lucy's eyes. She had thought she had two friends as well as Thomas. Dorothy had gone, and now she couldn't be sure of David.

"Why does nothing happy ever happen?" she said sadly. "All I want to know is where they're hiding Dorothy. I don't care about Father Copse or Father Drax and their silly job." Holding Paul's hand firmly, she crossed over the road towards the house.

David sighed. It wasn't just that he felt permanently guilty that she'd had the guidance, it was that he had really been getting to like her. She spoke to him easily these days, and occasionally her face would light up so brightly that he could almost see inside her mind, but then someone or something would interrupt them, and the invisible wall would descend again and it was as though she wasn't there. Now that she was being irrational he wasn't so sure that he liked her after all.

He fished his bike out of the bushes and rode sadly back over the bumpy grass until he found the path. Dorothy was somewhere. She had been right about needing a friend he could trust in an emergency, but he needed that friend to trust him too.

Lucy and Paul went through the front gate, turned left under the laurel arch into the driveway, and past the garage into the back garden. Thomas was there, cutting the lawn with the ride-on mower. He gave Paul a ride and Lucy pushed herself slowly back and forth on the swing. She wondered if she should tell Thomas what David had said just so that he could say "What rubbish!" and put her mind at rest. She wished she knew how to run away without waiting for the birth record. All the possible problems jiggled about in her mind – how to find food, where to sleep, how to keep Paul with her, and most worrying of all, how to avoid the infiltrated police.

"What's troubling you, young lady?" asked Thomas,

handing Paul over to her and popping a fruit gum in her mouth at the same time. "Have you been having any climbing adventures lately?"

Lucy looked at him for a moment, loving his kind face and gentle smile.

"No. I've stopped that. I was really scared the tenant would complain about me, but she didn't. I'm not risking it again."

"Very wise," said Thomas. "You have the wisdom of a Queen Solomon."

He pulled a very wise and serious face and Lucy laughed. Thomas could be funny sometimes. It was good to be able to laugh. Aunt Sarah was never funny, and the father was just terrifying.

"Thomas," she said. "Do the fathers ever quarrel?"

"We're all human," he said. "Everyone falls out with someone now and then. But I've not heard that the fathers quarrel. It wouldn't be appropriate. They're supposed to set us all a good example. What made you ask?"

"Someone told me that Father Drax and Father Copse are rivals because they both want the same job."

"Who told you that?"

Lucy hesitated. It would not be fair on David to say his name. She fell back on one of Aunt Sarah's expressions.

"A little bird."

Thomas laughed.

"And you can't tell me who the little bird is?"

"Not really," said Lucy.

Thomas looked disappointed.

"Can't you tell a friend a secret?" he asked, popping another sweet in her mouth.

Lucy didn't want to hurt his feelings. It might seem as if she didn't trust him. On the other hand he might say something to David if he knew, and she didn't want to get David into trouble.

"I'll have to ask her permission before I can tell you," she said deviously, "because she told me in confidence."

"How soon can you ask her?"

"It'll have to be when school begins."

"OK. But just be very careful who you trust, in school or anywhere else."

"Yes," said Lucy. "I will."

CHAPTER TWENTY

It was the last day of the summer holidays. There were workmen in the drive when Thomas arrived.

"Morning!" he called as he changed out of his tidy jacket and hung it on the hook inside the garage. "What are you up to?"

"Fixing the gate. The automatic gear ain't working properly. Too slow."

Thomas watched them for a while. It was a beautiful day, and the morning sun warmed him gently. The children would be playing in the garden today, though it was supposed to rain later. He must try and chat to Lucy to see if she had any useful information for him. Drax was getting on his nerves, always on at him to find a way of discrediting Copse. Soon it would be too late because the interviewing had already started. As Thomas turned towards the back garden a plan started to form in his head.

Aunt Sarah had acknowledged the last day of the holidays by making a cake. Lucy lifted the lid of the cake tin and she and Paul pushed their noses in to sniff the delicious smell of chocolate. Sarah clattered noisily down the stairs with her equipment, and the children hastily put the lid back. The key turned in the lock and when she came in both children were looking out of the back door, watching a magpie strut about the lawn.

"One for sorrow," said Aunt Sarah. "But if you blink, you'll have seen it twice and that makes two. Two for joy." They both blinked.

Sarah was in a good mood. The father was going abroad for a few days, to be interviewed in the palace of the Holy Envoy.

Lucy had come into the kitchen when he was giving Aunt Sarah final instructions. She was to clean his flat and the stairs daily. That was daft. What was the point of doing it daily when he wasn't there to dirty it? There was to be no contact with Drax House, and he wanted a full report on the children's behaviour when he came back. Ok. Well he had that every week anyway. He'd handed Sarah a key, saying: "Top flat. For emergency only." She had bowed her head submissively and dropped it into her apron pocket.

Now Aunt Sarah was smiling to herself which was most unusual, and both Paul and Lucy felt their hearts lift. While she was putting her cleaning tools away Lucy ran out to the swing and Paul ambled off to look for stones to decorate his garden. The sun was shining, and the air was hot and filled with the sweet scent of cut grass.

Sarah breathed deeply. Tomorrow would be Thursday, and by early Friday morning the father would be gone until Monday. It felt like a holiday.

She put the vacuum bag in the bin and went round the side of the garage to check the rat poison. Immediately she saw that the wire barricade had been removed and the sheet of hardboard had disappeared. It had been there yesterday. As she squeezed into the gap between the garage and the garden wall she looked up and saw that the little wooden roof had gone. Looking down she saw that the plastic pipe containing the rat poison had gone too. She searched up and down the length of the gap, but there was no sign of it. Her heart began to thump. Emerging into the garden she called to Lucy.

"Why did you move the barrier?"

Lucy jumped down from the swing and ran over.

"What barrier?" She looked down the side of the garage. "I haven't moved any barrier."

"What did you do with the bit of pipe that was here?"

"I didn't do anything. What pipe?"

"Where's Paul?" Sarah's voice was sharp with anxiety. Lucy pointed.

"Over there. Doing his garden."

Sarah ran, gasping and clutching at her chest.

Hidden by a shrub Paul was kneeling happily in front of his garden with the piping in his two hands, dribbling out a fine line of blue granules in loops and twists all around his pansies. He looked up at Sarah and smiled.

"I'm making a pretty pattern," he said.

Sarah snatched the pipe out of his hands. His smile vanished and he started to yell.

"It's mine, mine!"

Holding the pipe in one hand, she yanked him away from the flowerbed with the other. Lucy looked on in silent astonishment. Paul screamed.

Thomas came up behind them.

"What's going on?" he said. Then he saw the blue granules. "Holy Magnifico! What's happened?" He lifted Paul in his arms and took him over to a bench and sat him on his lap. Waiting for a gap in the howling he gently asked, "Did you eat any of it?"

Paul renewed his howls. Thomas tried again.

"Did you eat any of the blue stuff?"

"No," wailed Paul, tears streaming down his face.

"Did you touch any of it with your hands?"

"No. It came out of the pipe."

"That's good," said Thomas. "Stop crying now. Everything's alright."

The sobs subsided and after a few hiccups Paul climbed down.

"It's mine," he said.

Sarah plonked herself down on the bench next to Thomas clutching at her chest and panting. Gradually her breathing eased. She pulled a duster out of her apron pocket and wiped the sweat off her face.

"What is it?" asked Lucy. "That blue stuff."

Sarah glared.

"Don't you act all innocent with me, Miss. It must have been you who moved the barricade. Paul couldn't have shifted it."

"What barricade?"

Sarah's face was purple.

"You know perfectly well what I'm talking about," she said furiously. "Always playing around by the garage and climbing things and touching things, and hiding in corners and bushes, and pretending you're praying when you're not."

Lucy didn't dare say any more.

"I'm sure Lucy wouldn't have moved the barricade," said Thomas soothingly. "Perhaps the workmen thought it was spare wood and used it for something." Taking a piece of flat stone he scooped all the blue crystals off the flowerbed into a plastic bag and thrust the bit of piping in after it.

"There. I'll get rid of this safely, and no harm done."

151

Trembling, Sarah gathered herself up and, grabbing Paul by the hand, led him off to the safety of the kitchen. Lucy stood forlornly watching them go in, and then went into her special hidey-hole under the spotted bush.

They missed the Wednesday prayer meeting that evening. The three of them sat down at the table for tea, but neither Sarah nor Lucy could eat any of the chocolate cake. Paul enjoyed it immensely.

CHAPTER TWENTY-ONE

The following day was Thursday, the first day of the autumn term.

"The aunts said you tried to kill your little brother," said one of the girls from Drax House.

"Don't talk such stupid rubbish," snapped Lucy. "Anyway, I haven't got a brother."

"Of course you've got a brother. All Father Copse's children are your brothers or sisters. How can you be so ignorant?"

"No they're not. Some of them are discards."

"The aunts said you tried to poison him with rat poison. I'm going to tell them you said they talk stupid rubbish." The girl laughed and ran off.

Lucy was tense as she walked home. If the girl reported her to the aunts she would be punished. But why had she said that about killing her brother? Someone was making up stories about her. Perhaps David was right. Perhaps Father Drax did want to make her look bad. It was a nasty feeling. And Aunt Sarah would have told her if Paul was her brother.

"What's the matter, misery guts?" shouted George, but she ignored him.

He jumped down from the gate and grabbed her arm.

"What's the matter?"

Lucy stopped and looked at him.

"I'm afraid," she said.

"What of?"

"I don't know."

Her eyes filled with tears and he let her go.

In the house Aunt Sarah was preparing food. The father would be gone first thing tomorrow. She had no intention of cleaning the stairs or his flat until the Monday morning just before he came home. Her stern countenance softened as Lucy came in.

"There. I've made you a nice tea," she said.

"Thank you," murmured Lucy.

"I know you wouldn't have moved the barricade," said Sarah. "It's just I was so frightened for Paul. I got in a panic and acted unreasonably."

"Yes," said Lucy. "I understand."

She went to her room and sat on the bed until Sarah called her.

"It's only right I should ask your forgiveness."

Lucy patted Sarah's hand.

"It's alright," she said. "Who did move it?

"It must have been one of the workmen. I found the sheet of hardboard propped up against the fence by the gate."

"In school they say I tried to kill Paul," said Lucy bleakly.

Sarah's face flushed scarlet with anger. It was that Drax House lot. She knew without being told. Who had passed on such evil gossip? Something was up and she didn't know what. She had to calm down before she could speak.

"Just ignore them," she said lamely in the end. "They'll think of something else to lie about soon."

"But how did they know?" wailed Lucy. "It was only us there."

"Maybe the workmen saw something," said Aunt Sarah, "and made five out of two and two. Oh dear," she sighed, "what have I done with my false accusations? It must be all my fault. I'll go over to the Copse House commune tomorrow and get the aunts there to spread the word and put it right."

"They're saying Paul's my brother."

"We are all brother and sisters in the eyes of the Magnifico." Sarah gave a scornful sniff. "Even that Drax House lot."

Father Copse was sitting upright at his desk, slowly sipping his wine. The sound system was switched off. He couldn't be bothered to listen to silly women talking their usual rubbish. All they seemed to think about was clothes, or the colour of their hair. There were far more important things on his mind. He was troubled by a rumour.

Early tomorrow he was supposed to be flying out for his interview for the Deputy Envoy post, and now he was wondering if he should go. He had had a sense of danger for weeks. There had been nothing he could put his finger on until today when an anonymous caller on his office phone had whispered, almost inaudibly, "Watch Drax. He's after the red-headed one." Later, at a lawyers' conference, a man he had never met before had approached him giving the infiltrators' hand signal. He had muttered "Watch your back. Drax is after you," and walked straight on past.

The father cast his mind over the women in the Copse House commune. There was one redhead, but

155

she had been there for years and was almost ready for disposal. As for Claudia in the top-floor flat, Drax could never have seen her, or even known about her, unless of course he had his spies at work. He shrugged. The women upstairs were secure. No-one could reach them.

More pressing were his financial problems. If the Holy Envoy discovered that he was in debt there was no hope that he would be appointed as his deputy. He fetched his files, as he did most evenings, and looked at his accounts.

He would happily be rid of the expense of keeping the redhead, but not to Drax. If only he could bring himself to get rid of the other woman – the real woman. She had already served her true purpose by providing him with children, and he might avoid a lot of difficulty if she were disposed of. But he couldn't do it.

In the end he decided to fly tomorrow as planned and sort things out when he got back. After all, if the interview was successful he could forget about Drax and money problems, and concentrate on winning the woman over. He had every hope of getting the job because Drax's commune had suffered two casualties this year – that boy John with the twitch, and the girl Dorothy who had absconded. It all reflected badly on Drax. His own embarrassment over Lucy seemed small in comparison, especially as he had pleased the Magnifico by dealing with her so firmly at the time. If he didn't get the deputy post he'd just have to be ruthless and dispose of a couple of kitchen aunts. He'd think up some justification. As for his woman upstairs – his Belinda? The ring of pain pressed into his head and suddenly he had a brilliant idea. Suppose he just kept her hair? She could go then. The good doctors could take her away.

He was unaware that at that moment Claudia was carefully, but unsuccessfully, investigating every nook and cranny, every bit of furniture, and every scrap of carpet, curtain, and cushion, for bugging devices. She had climbed a chair and was tapping the ceiling.

"If we could only find a hollow sound," she whispered, rustling a tissue in front of her face, "we could break into the attic and find our way out through the roof."

"I've tried that. I've been trying everything for years," Maria said softly, "but you never know, I might have missed a bit."

She fetched a chair and started tapping.

CHAPTER TWENTY-TWO

On the Thursday afternoon, a rumour started to circulate through the school in whispers. Someone had heard that Dorothy had been moved from one place to another, but still no-one knew where she was.

"Perhaps she's in the upper rooms," David said quietly to Matthew as they waited to cross the junction after school. "I'll have to try and reach her. You must help me."

"We'd probably be wasting our time." Matthew replied. "More likely they've sent her to another commune. That'd be easier than keeping her upstairs with everyone nosing around."

"Surely the aunts must know. Do you think they'd tell us if we asked?"

Matthew laughed. "Not likely! Forget it for now. Wait and see if anything happens overnight."

"We've got to listen," muttered David. "The aunts are sure to let something slip." He was just wondering if he dared tell Matthew about the secret listening place in the linen cupboard when the lights turned green, and they pedalled hard up the High Street one after the other.

"I tell you what," said Matthew as soon as they reached Drax House. "I'll go to the kitchen and offer to help them lay the table for supper. I might hear something while they're gossiping, and I'll earn some good marks for being helpful at the same time."

"Gosh thanks! You're a true friend!"

Matthew dashed off to put his bike away, and David followed more slowly. There was an hour still to go before supper – enough time to get to the linen cupboard and listen for himself, provided nobody saw him. He had been there almost every evening since Dorothy had left but had heard nothing useful except for when she'd been caught and then, yesterday, that she was to be moved.

Now, yet again, he crept up the stairs to the walk-in cupboard above the kitchen. He looked around but there was no-one in sight. The door closed quietly behind him and he stood in complete darkness. He felt for the light switch and looked quickly around at the slatted wooden shelves that ran down both sides of the room. They were piled high with sheets and pillow cases, and blankets and towels, and everything was as normal. He pulled again at the light switch and his disembodied self was plunged into a pitch black pit. Was this what the black hole had felt like when the world began, he wondered, almost expecting to be whisked and swirled up into a suction of nothingness. He felt his way along the right-hand shelves until he reached the end, and then dropped down and rolled under.

He lay in the corner with his ear pressed close to the floor. Voices floated up from the kitchen below, sometimes clearly and sometimes fading away or disappearing altogether. The aunts were discussing the supper menu. Not very interesting, and he hated macaroni cheese. Once or twice he recognised Matthew's voice, mingling with the clatter of plates and cutlery, and he laughed to himself. Good old Matthew, he thought, a true friend. He waited.

Suddenly, the door opened. A beam of light streamed in from the landing, and then someone pulled the light switch and came in. David held his breath. He could feel his heart thudding. A pair of sensible lace-up shoes marched up the narrow gangway and stopped almost opposite his face. For what seemed like a billion years the owner of the shoes shifted or sorted the piles of sheets above David's head, and tutted and sighed. At one point the piles separated and light pierced its way down through the slats. David instinctively pressed his silver-blond head back against the wall.

The shoes moved back and forth. A towel fell to the floor, and was followed by a pair of plump arms. As they swooped down to pick up the towel, David could just see the side of the laundry aunt's head and shoulders. If she had twisted slightly to the right she would have looked straight into his eyes. How could she not have heard his heart beating? The voices in the kitchen below continued unheard, deadened by the pounding of blood in his ears.

Then, as suddenly as they had come in, the shoes turned back towards the door and the laundry aunt gave a loud sigh of satisfaction as she switched off the light. "Good job done!" she said aloud to herself. The door closed behind her.

David didn't dare move in case she came back in. As he waited he breathed deeply, trying to calm his taut nerves. His first thought was to how get out of there without being seen, but then he remembered why he had come. He tried to focus once again on the sounds from below.

"Father Copse is going to be away for the whole weekend," commented one voice. "Sarah won't know she's born!"

There was laughter, and someone said, "I know. I heard. But we shouldn't laugh because it's not going to be funny. Something's going to happen there tomorrow night."

David tensed. The voice faded briefly and then returned, and he caught, "Father Drax's men are going to do it. He wants the redhead." There was a clattering of pots and pans and a distant murmur of voices.

His heart beat faster and he thought of Lucy. She might be in danger. He would have to warn her that something was planned for tomorrow night. He listened a while longer, and caught 'old woman', and then nothing more than the meaningless chatter of the aunts as they moved back and forth. He hoped that Matthew had managed to pick up any important bits he had missed.

Just as he was about to roll out from under the shelf he caught Dorothy's name and then his own. He froze. There was something about the 'disposal cells'. Every pore in his body was alert.

"If he guesses she's there he'll try and get at her. Matthew's been given instructions not to let him out of his sight."

A current of shock ran through David's body. Matthew! He couldn't move. Was this a nightmare, or was it real? A red hot hammer thumped in his head. He desperately tried to remember whether he had told Matthew any of Dorothy's secrets, even inadvertently. With horror he recalled that less than an hour or so ago he had nearly told him about the linen cupboard.

Suddenly someone shouted, "You've forgotten to put in the potatoes!" and sounds of universal panic wafted upwards.

David pulled himself together and rolled out of his

hiding place. He stood up silently and tiptoed through the blackness to the door, testing each floorboard for possible creaks. As soon as he was out on the landing he glanced around, but reminded himself that Matthew didn't know where he was. As he hurried down the stairs Lucy's and Dorothy's faces swam before his eyes.

In the hall Matthew was standing, looking anxious and uncertain. A wave of relief passed over his face when David appeared. In a flash it was replaced by the cheerfully open expression that made everyone his friend.

"Where were you, you lazy devil?" he asked, affectionately. "I've been working hard on your behalf while you've been idling away upstairs." He linked his arm through David's. "I've nothing to report, I'm afraid. Only the gabbling of a bunch of old women."

David didn't pull his arm away. "Had a headache so I lay down. It's gone now." He tried to sound natural. "I've been thinking about what you said. You're right. It's best to leave things be for a while."

"Good lad!" said Matthew, slapping him on the back.

An aunt appeared, and banged the brass gong that was suspended just outside the dining room door. Children poured in from every direction, and they went in to supper. Matthew stayed by David's side all evening. Later, as they lay in their dormitory beds, David listened to Matthew's breathing through most of the night and knew that he was awake.

CHAPTER TWENTY-THREE

The Holy Leaders had held several meetings with the
fathers to discuss what should be done about Dorothy.
They didn't take things lightly. Next week she would be
sixteen and in the normal course of things she would
have been allocated to a father in marriage. After all, she
was a beautiful girl and highly intelligent, and would
make excellent material for the breeding rooms. The
trouble was none of the fathers wanted the responsibility.
As her biological father and the father of her commune,
Drax had been given an opportunity to express his views.
He was furious with her. "Just like her mother!" he had
spluttered. "Let her go the same way."

One of the Holy Leaders had gently reprimanded
him. They had wanted his views but not his emotion.
"There is no room for feelings in such a serious matter,"
he had said. "We must be objective." As a result of his
outburst Father Drax was not allowed to vote. Even so,
the result was unanimous. If no-one was prepared to
take on Dorothy as a wife in the breeding rooms, the
only alternative was disposal.

Soft voices swished and swam round Dorothy's head
but she couldn't hear what they said. This couldn't be
real. She shook herself but the nightmare didn't go away.
Here were the aunts she'd known all her life. Tears were

falling down Aunt Bertha's cheeks. "Stop that now," said someone gently. "It's the Magnifico's will. Blessed be his holy purpose."

Unfamiliar loose black trousers had been tied with a cord round her waist, and now a long black tunic was being pulled down over her head.

"Where am I?"

No-one answered. There was no need. She looked around the sparsely furnished cell and knew where she was. It was something that had happened to others. It had happened to her mother, but she had never really believed it could happen to her.

"You may be here for a few days yet," said an aunt. "The *Holy Vision* is on the table if you want something to read. We'll bring you your supper later."

Supper! As if she could eat!

The aunts left and locked the door behind them. Dorothy looked around her. There was a table, a chair, and a sort of camp bed. She lay down on the bed. Five months of freedom passed before her eyes like a documentary film. Had it been worth it? There was Tom who'd looked after her for weeks. He had shown her the safest railway arches to sleep under, the best restaurant bins for food, the most confusing side roads for avoiding pursuers, how to use money and a mobile phone, and how to beg and to kiss. That had surely been worth it. But Tom had said he had to go away for a while and that he'd contact a friend who would look after her and find her a proper job.

That was when things went wrong. The friend got her an interview in a small hotel and left her there on her own in a smart little lounge to wait for the proprietor. A girl with dreamy eyes brought her a drink, put it gently down on the coffee table next to a potted plant, and floated away. A few minutes later another girl looked in. She was more alert and smiled at Dorothy.

"Drink up," she said.

Dorothy sniffed the drink, and wondered what alcohol smelled like.

"You'll be glad of it if you're new to all this," said the girl with a wink. "It'll help you relax. Be quick about it before the old cow comes or I'll get into trouble."

Dorothy was beginning to feel uncomfortable. All she wanted was a job, not a drink. She didn't want to sound rude so she just nodded and waited till the girl had left, and then hastily poured it into the potted plant.

She was leaning back in her chair with the empty glass in her hand when a smartly-dressed middle-aged woman appeared in the doorway.

"Ah, good!" she commented. "They gave you a drink. We like to look after people." She sat herself down opposite Dorothy and seemed to be waiting for something.

"Oh well, I haven't got all day," she said at last. "Let's get straight to the point. Are you experienced?"

Dorothy gazed at her blankly. "I've got no experience at all of hotel work," she said, "but I'm a quick learner."

"Well, I don't normally take girls off the street. You'd have to have a health check."

What on earth was she talking about? Suddenly a horrible sick feeling had grabbed at Dorothy's stomach. She'd heard of places like this. One of the girls under the railway arches had told her about them. Next time she saw Tom she'd have to warn him about his friend.

"There's been a mistake." She stood up. "I have to go." Thank goodness she hadn't touched the drink. She hurried through the hall and was out in the street before the woman had time to get out of her chair. Tom couldn't possibly have known what his friend was like. She'd have to tell him as soon as he got back from wherever it was.

Outside, the friend was leaning against the wall talking on his mobile phone. Dorothy started to run and he ran after her. "Hey, wait!" He caught her arm, and she shook it off. With her fist curled into a hard little ball she turned and punched his nose and ran. She was a fast runner but when she looked back over her shoulder there he was, just yards behind, with blood all over his face. Then she did the most stupid thing she'd ever done in her life. She ran into a policeman.

CHAPTER TWENTY-FOUR

"Maria!" Claudia called softly, on the Friday morning. "Eureka! At least I hope it's eureka."

She stood in a corner of the living room moving her feet up and down. The floor creaked beneath the rug.

"Let's look," she whispered.

"He's gone," laughed Maria. "There's no need to whisper while he's away."

They rolled back the rug and the underlay, and revealed the floorboard. It was split several inches down from a nail at one corner. On their hands and knees they prised the wood away from the nail with the knives from their meal tray, and wrenched it up with their hands, splitting it full length. In the next board a corner nail was loose. That came out easily with the use of a fork. Digging around the remaining nails with the knives and the fork they loosened all three until the board came up quite easily. Working intensely, they repeated the process until they had lifted four boards.

The joists underneath were firm and in good condition and spaced about eighteen inches apart. Pipes and electric wires ran along the gap.

"We'll never get through those," said Claudia. "We'll have to do some more."

They worked hard all morning. By midday they had

managed to force up five more floorboards with good clear gaps between the joists.

"I won't be able to squeeze through there," said Maria, "but you might."

Lying on their stomachs and stretching down with knives in their hands, they tried to reach the lath and plaster ceiling below, but the space was too deep. Maria jumped up and fetched a broom. She banged the handle down onto the plaster. It was hard and solid. However fiercely she banged, it had no effect. They gazed down into the space and racked their brains for a tool of some sort.

"Water!" announced Maria suddenly. "A flood!" She ran to the bathroom and filled a large plastic bowl with hot water, and carried it to the living room.

"We'll do this all day and all night if we have to," she said, pouring the water through the joists. "We'll pour and pour, and bang with the broom handle, and it'll get soggy and collapse. His cleaner won't come up till Monday. We've got two days. We'll never have this chance again." Her parents' faces swam before her eyes and filled her with an energy she'd never known before.

"My father's going to be so angry with me," puffed Claudia, as she thumped away with the broom handle. "He told me not to walk home alone if I had to work late. I was supposed to ring him for a lift, but I'd been there all day in that stuffy library writing my dissertation. The outside air seemed so fresh and sharp and I just needed to stretch my legs. And, you know, you never think it could happen to you."

"No. We all think we're invincible till it happens!" Maria grunted as she poured another bowlful into the gap. "But he'll be over the moon to find you! Of course he won't be angry – or if he is it'll be because of the relief."

On that same Friday morning Lucy dragged herself reluctantly to school. She kept to herself in the playground and tried to avoid the Drax House children.

"Murderer," whispered a girl, passing in the corridor. Lucy flushed scarlet.

"Liar!" she retorted angrily, but immediately wished she hadn't. Any response to insult usually led to further taunts. In the past she would have run her fingers along her reminder and that would have kept her calm, but she couldn't bear to touch it these days. She was angrier with herself than with the girl, for losing her self-control. Linking David's warning that she was to be Copse's downfall, together with the rat poison incident, had made her jumpy.

After school David followed her down the steps.

"Meet me on the common as soon as you get home," he muttered, scarcely moving his lips as Matthew loomed up behind him.

Lucy pretended she hadn't heard and marched off, over at the lights and up South Hill. George was not in his usual post and she hurried past his house. She had always liked David, but now she wasn't sure if she could trust him. Perhaps she shouldn't meet him. How could she know that he wasn't trying to frighten her with false information.

Thomas usually came on a Friday. He would know what to do. When she reached number 3 Mortimor Road she went straight round the back into the garden, but he wasn't there. She waited a little, and in the end she decided she'd go on the common and listen to what David had to say, but she wouldn't have to believe it. Checking that Aunt Sarah wasn't watching, she hastily crossed back over the road and disappeared into the bushes surrounding the pond. David would know where to look for her. She waited for what seemed like an eternity.

Back in Drax House David was racking his brain for some means of escape, when Matthew told him to wait for him in the hall while he just popped in to Senior Aunt Sonia's office.

"I only want to ask her about the badge on my new blazer. I'll be back in a tick."

You have to report to her more like, thought David bitterly. As soon as the office door closed behind Matthew, he ran. Less than ten minutes later he was cycling over the grass towards the pond. He chained the bike to the base of a bush and slipped through the foliage. Lucy was just about to leave.

"Sorry I took so long. Nobody saw me," he said. "I hope."

He crouched down by the side of the pond and pulled Lucy down next to him.

"Listen," he said. "I've got two things to tell you, and you mustn't be unreasonable." His piercing blue eyes looked urgently into hers.

"I'm listening."

"The first thing is I heard the aunts say Dorothy's been taken to the disposal cells. I know where they are. They're in the underground passage behind Drax House. It's where they put people before they take them away to be disposed of."

Lucy caught her breath, and her heart seemed to stop beating.

"I don't believe you! It can't be true! They wouldn't really, actually, do it. Not to someone who's only fifteen!"

"You've got to believe me!" he insisted. "They even dispose of babies if they're not likely to be any use to the Holy Cause – at least that's what I've heard. And anyway, it must be just as horrible for someone of fifty as fifteen."

Lucy's mouth was dry. She had to swallow hard before she could speak.

"If she is there, is there any way we could get her out?"

"I'm going to try. I know how to get there from the outside. They think we don't know but we all do, all us kids. You go up that narrow road the other side of Drax House. There's an entrance there into the woods behind the house, and if you go through the woods back towards the house, the passage is on the left just before you reach the garden fence."

Lucy forgot her doubts.

"I'll come with you!" she whispered, her mind immediately working on the problem of getting out through all Aunt Sarah's locks and bolts at night. "I can get out through the cellar!"

"No. I can't go yet. There's a problem. The entrance to the passageway is locked with a padlock and I don't know the code to open it. All I know is it's six numbers. I'll just have to keep eavesdropping – that is if I can get back into the linen cupboard without being caught."

"Can't you ask some of your friends if they know it?"

"No. You can't trust anyone, even your friends. Some of them are training as infiltrators, but I don't know which ones. I only definitely know of one. They report back to the aunts on everything we do or say, and the aunts report to the Holy Leaders."

The thought of Thomas jumped into her head. He

had been grooming her to be an infiltrator, and it had made her feel useful – important. Now the whole idea horrified her. She was shocked at her own naïvity. Holy Magnifico! They might even have asked her to spy on David and Dorothy! Or perhaps David was spying on her at this very moment.

David shook himself. "Well, sitting here isn't helping Dorothy. I simply have to find that code." He looked at her anxiously. "Do you trust me?"

Lucy had a question. "If you don't know which ones are infiltrators, why did you risk singing those words in assembly? You could have been heard by a child infiltrator. One of the boys that dared you could have been one."

"It was the risk that was exciting. I've had the guidance cane so often that I don't care about that anymore. But you could be right. Now I think it might have been deliberate, and guess who the infiltrator was! Sitting right next to me. It must have been something to do with trying to get you into trouble."

The significance sank in and Lucy gasped. "Holy Mag! Matthew! He's your friend!"

"Exactly!" said David bitterly.

"OK. I'll trust you," whispered Lucy eventually. It was impossible to imagine how Dorothy must be feeling at this moment. "Well, at least it's something that we know where she is. If you only had the code!"

"The aunts might give me a clue. I'll just have to keep listening, but there isn't much time. She'll be sixteen on Tuesday. They won't keep her beyond that."

Lucy's throat constricted. She couldn't speak.

David stood up, "The second thing I came to tell you is that one of the aunts said that Father Drax wants the redhead. I don't know what that means. She said, 'They'll have to get into the house while Copse is away,' and then someone said 'what about the old woman?' That's all I heard, but I had to warn you. When is Father Copse away?"

Lucy tried to get her voice back.

"He's gone," she croaked. "He went this morning. He'll be back on Monday."

David looked down at her stricken face.

"Take Paul and get away from here before anything happens," he whispered. "If I can get back into the linen cupboard after tea, I'll keep listening. I'll let you know if I hear anything – if you're still here, that is."

He unchained his bike, and Lucy watched as he put in the code to the padlock. Then he left abruptly, and rode off over the common. As he approached the further side he did some practice twirls and swoops before disappearing down the little lane to South Hill.

Lucy's chest was tight with fear. They wouldn't keep Dorothy beyond Tuesday, and there was nothing she could do to help her. The father would be back on Monday. Today was Friday. If David was right, something was going to happen within the next two days. She had to warn Aunt Sarah, and she only hoped that she would believe her!

Maria poured and Claudia jabbed. The prospect of freedom lifted their spirits to an almighty high and filled them with energy. They laughed as they worked, mocking the idiocies of the Holy Leaders and Copse's absurd vanity. Their jokes seemed hilarious to them, and occasionally they would stop and collapse with stitches in their sides. Every now and then they swapped over tasks and Claudia would pour while Maria jabbed.

Their evening meal was sent up earlier than usual, and they stopped for a break. Maria flopped back in an armchair and pictured the blue front door of her parents' house, and the joy that would light up their faces as they opened it.

"Fifteen years!" she exclaimed. "I'm afraid to hope."

"We'll get there, don't worry," said Claudia. "If that Copse thinks I'm going be one of his wives he's got another think coming. Anyway, he must be about a thousand years old!"

"He's forty," laughed Maria.

"Yuk! Decrepit! I can't wait to see my boyfriend again. What a hunk!"

By the time they returned to their task the plaster was soggy, and after a few more buckets and jabs at the lath the ceiling below collapsed. Claudia squeezed her head and shoulders down through the beams and found herself looking into a luxurious living room. Maria peered through the space alongside her. They could see a leather armchair and a Persian rug which was now saturated with water and covered with chunks of wet plaster.

"Shall I try and get down?" asked Claudia.

"The trouble is you may not be able to get back up again."

"No, but I won't want to. I could ring for the police. He must have a phone there somewhere."

"But we don't know where we are."

"True! I suppose the police could trace the call – unless his phone is bugged and goes through to some headquarters or other."

"We have to be careful, even with the police," said Maria, "because they're heavily infiltrated with the Holy

Leaders' agents. If you could contact your father or your boyfriend first we'd be safer."

They pulled themselves back up and sat at the edge of the hole.

"If I can't get out of his flat through the door," said Claudia, "I'll simply jump out of the window."

Maria looked at her watch.

"My God! The day's gone in a flash. We've still got tomorrow. Let's have a break now and work out a strategy. I'm too tired to think at the moment."

"Me too," said Claudia.

CHAPTER TWENTY-FIVE

"Those banging noises have stopped at last," remarked Aunt Sarah. "They've been going on all day and goodness knows where they came from. Next door must have workmen in."

Lucy watched her as she put the tenants' meals into the dumb waiter and pressed the button that took it to the second floor. It was at least an hour before their usual eating time. Sarah was looking forward to an early night and a lie-in tomorrow morning. The dumb waiter whirred upwards, and she sat down to eat with the children.

She gave them the same food as the tenants. Lucy had never smelled anything so delicious in her life, but she couldn't swallow. She had to warn Aunt Sarah about the next two days and was certain she'd never believe her. She'd tell her not to talk rubbish and get on with her meal.

"Something's going to happen in this house before the father comes home." Lucy's voice was tense. "Within the next two days. Something bad."

"Who said that? One of the Drax House children I suppose."

"Yes. They heard the aunts talking about it."

Sarah was silent as she absorbed the information. A pain crept through her arm and chest and her head seemed to spin, just for a moment. Lucy looked curiously at her and was concerned. "Are you alright, Aunt Sarah? You've gone grey." Sarah nodded faintly, and Lucy pretended to eat.

The pain passed and Sarah's head cleared.

"Well, don't you take any notice of them." She was slightly breathless. "They're just trying to frighten you. There's too much gossiping in that commune."

Nevertheless Sarah was very worried indeed. She missed Martha who normally kept her in touch with what was going on. Tomorrow she would go to Copse House, ostensibly to ask after her bad back, but in reality to hear the latest rumours.

Lucy looked down at her plate. "Perhaps we should leave the father's house now, this very minute," she whispered.

"Nonsense," said Sarah, less forcefully than usual, "Pull yourself together."

When the meal was cleared up, and the table set out for the usual homework, Sarah pressed the down button and the dumb waiter appeared with the tenants' used plates. They'd forgotten to send back their knives.

"Never mind," said Sarah. "They'll come down with the breakfast things." She washed up and Lucy went into the garden to look for Thomas. He still hadn't come.

"What are you fidgeting about for?" asked Aunt Sarah sharply when she returned. "You've got your weekend homework to get on with."

"I was looking for Thomas. If he was here we might be safer."

Aunt Sarah snorted. "You'd be safer in a nest of snakes! Shut that back door, and I'll bolt it now. Let's hope that makes you feel better."

Lucy felt offended on Thomas's behalf, but said nothing.

Aunt Sarah put Paul into his pyjamas. Setting him down in her big chair with a book, she told Lucy to read him a story as soon as she finished her homework, and if he seemed bored he could do some drawing. She found some crayons and put them on the table with a large sheet of drawing paper. Lucy pretended briefly to look at her homework, but she could hardly make out the words. She squeezed into the chair next to Paul and found one of his favourite stories.

"Once upon a time there was a princess whose name was Beauty," she began. Her voice was shaky, and her ears were straining to listen for the slightest sound.

Paul sensed her distraction and took the book from her and studied the pictures.

"I can draw good pictures," he said. "And I can read words."

Aunt Sarah was far more anxious than she appeared. It was perfectly credible that Father Drax would take advantage of Father Copse's absence to damage his prospects. Her brow was furrowed as she pottered around the kitchen trying to think what he or his henchmen might do. The most obvious thing was that they might try and break in to get at the father's confidential files. In that case the children would be safe with her in the ground-floor flat. Nevertheless, she needed to check that all the upstairs windows were shut, and that the outer door to the lobby was locked and bolted.

She didn't want to frighten the children so she put her cleaning materials into the dumb waiter and pressed the button for the first floor, saying to Lucy, "I'll send these up now to save me carrying them, and then they'll all be ready for Monday morning." She dragged the vacuum cleaner out of the cupboard. "I might as well take this up at the same time. It'll be handy to have everything up there."

Before she went she disappeared down the hall, bolted the front door, top and bottom, and then popped into her bedroom to fetch her keys. Dropping them into her apron pocket she returned to the kitchen, fished one of them out again and unlocked the door to the lobby.

Lucy listened carefully. Aunt Sarah had locked her and Paul in, and was now testing the bolts on the outer door, sliding them in and out and in again. Then she started her usual grumbling journey up the stairs, clanking the vacuum cleaner behind her. She reached the top and pulled it up the last step with a thump. Lucy set Paul and the book down and went over to the door. She bent down and put her ear against it.

"What're you doing?" Paul asked, coming to join her.

They didn't see Thomas as he peeped through the kitchen window. Nor did Thomas see them.

Lucy put her finger to her lips and pressed her ear harder against the wood. A key turned on the first-floor landing. Sarah muttered something. Then the children heard her gasp.

"Save our souls!" she exclaimed loudly. "A flood!"

The vacuum thumped again. She must have dropped it, thought Lucy. Then there was a knocking sound as though it had fallen over, and a cry and a bang, and something, someone, came tumbling slowly and heavily down the stairs.

"Aunt Sarah," called Lucy.

A groan came from the lobby. Lucy called again. There was no answer.

"Aunt Sarah what's happened? Are you alright?"

179

With her ear still pressed to the door she could hear Aunt Sarah breathing heavily.

Paul stood next to Lucy, listening. She tried the door handle, but of course it was locked.

"Aunt Sarah," she called again, but there was still no answer. Aunt Sarah was trapped in the lobby and there was no way they could get at her.

Lucy knelt down and looked through the keyhole. All she could see was a bit of black metal. Then she realised she was looking at the key in the lock.

She jumped up and grabbed Paul's drawing paper from the table. He was too interested in keeping his ear to the door to object. Lucy made a quick mental review of George's written instructions. She pushed the paper under the door. It wasn't as big as a newspaper, but might do the trick if the key was heavy enough not to jump.

Scrabbling through the drawer next to the cooker she found a skewer. Then, on her knees, she started poking. The key fell with a heavy flop and she could feel its weight as she tugged the paper. She pulled it carefully towards her. It appeared from under the door, and she picked it up with an immense sense of achievement as well as relief. She mentally thanked George and his father who knew everything, and fervently hoped that he would get his reward in this world instead of the next.

She unlocked the door and peered out. Aunt Sarah lay at the bottom of the stairs. Lucy and Paul knelt beside her. The heavy breathing had stopped.

"Perhaps she's dead," whispered Lucy.

Paul gazed intently at the fallen body.

"Where's the fire of the melting flesh?"

Aunt Sarah groaned.

"Oh, thank goodness!" cried Lucy. The relief was overwhelming.

Aunt Sarah groaned again

"Help me up." Her voice was so faint they could only just hear her.

The children pulled at her arms and her shoulders and the back of her neck, but it was impossible to lift her. She lay still with her eyes closed, then rolled onto her side. With much gasping and grunting she managed to push herself up on one arm and onto her knees, and then onto the bottom stair, where she sat dazed with her back against the balustrade.

Lucy gathered her wits. She jumped to her feet.

"I'll phone for the good doctors."

"No!" gasped Sarah, "Don't! Don't trust them. I'll be alright in a minute." She managed to pull herself up and staggered to her feet. "I'll just go and lie down."

Clutching at the wall, with the children optimistically poised to catch her, she dragged herself through the kitchen, down the hall, and into her room. She collapsed onto her bed. Her face was screwed up and she grabbed at her arm. The children hovered anxiously at the bedside.

"Shall I get you some water, or shall I make some tea?" asked Lucy her eyes huge with concern.

"Just let me sleep," gasped Sarah, and closed her eyes. "It'll pass. I'll be better in a minute."

They took her dressing gown down from behind the door and laid it over her, and then closed the curtains.

"Lucy," she called faintly as they turned to leave the room. She squeezed her words out through the pain. "Whatever you do, don't call the good doctors. And don't stay here. Take Paul and run over to the Copse commune, and tell them what you told me today."

181

She feebly touched the circle of daffodils that hung from the chain at her neck. "And take this chain off. It's too tight."

Lucy gently eased the chain round until she found the fastener.

"Let me see you put it on. That's good. The chain is for you, and the circle of flowers is for Paul. Now go!"

The children tiptoed out and shut the door.

Paul was frightened. Lucy looked at the phone on the kitchen window sill. The good doctors' number was stuck on the wall to the side, and she mustn't ring them.

At last she knew in her heart that everything Dorothy had told her was true. The abductions were true, and the disposals were true, and it was true that they were carried out by the good doctors, and Aunt Sarah must have known about everything all along. When she said the red-headed girl was a tenant, she was lying!

If there was one person Lucy had trusted more than anyone in the world, it was Aunt Sarah. With her she had felt secure. She closed her eyes briefly and took deep breaths. Paul was anxiously stroking her hand, and she looked down at his upturned face. Her world might be shattered, but she would make sure his wasn't. She would never, ever let him down.

"I want you to remember all your life, that whatever happens, you can trust me." she said.

He nodded his head vigorously.

"Do you know what that means?"

"Yes. You'll look after me."

"That's right," she said, and hugged him tight.

Thomas was in the tree with his field glasses fixed on the first-floor window. He let them drop onto the cord round his neck, and spoke into his mobile phone.

"It's all clear," he said. "He's definitely gone, and the downstairs lot seem to be out too. I couldn't see anyone in the kitchen. The old lady must have taken the kids over to Copse House." He relaxed back into the tree, and rolled himself a cigarette.

Lucy's mind was working rapidly. If she took Paul to Copse House the aunts would call the good doctors who would say that Aunt Sarah was no further use to the Holy Cause and dispose of her. She decided that on this occasion Aunt Sarah must be disobeyed. Together, she and Paul would look after her when she woke, and help her get better. As soon as she was well again they would escape, and Lucy would pretend she was sixteen and find a job in the outside world, and look after Paul. But to find a job she would have to exist, and to exist she had to find Father Copse's record of her birth. She might have to change it to show she was sixteen, but she'd worry about that later. Never again would she have an opportunity like this.

"Come, Paul," she said, taking his hand and leading him to the lobby. "Let's go upstairs. We'll let Aunt Sarah have a sleep, and she might feel better when she wakes up."

They crept up the stairs. The vacuum cleaner lay halfway down and they left it where it was. The big mahogany door stood open. Lucy stopped to listen, but there wasn't a sound. "Come on," she whispered, and they stepped inside the father's flat.

CHAPTER TWENTY-SIX

Lucy and Paul entered the room tentatively. They looked around at the plush sofas and colourful rugs, and gold-framed paintings. It was very different from their own apartment on the ground floor with its sparse furniture and bare floorboards. Lucy tiptoed forward and touched a highly-polished dining table. She looked down onto it and could see her face. Paul let go of her hand and took a flying leap into a big leather armchair. He snuggled down inside it and gave Lucy a huge smile.

"Comfy," he said.

They saw the hole in the ceiling and stepped round white lumps on the carpet.

"It's all wet," said Paul, bending down to pat the carpet with his hand.

"That's what Aunt Sarah was saying before she fell. She said, 'It's a flood.'"

Lucy wandered up to the far end of the room and found the dumb waiter. She stretched over the sideboard and opened it up, and there was Aunt Sarah's cleaning box! "Look. We're right above our kitchen," she said.

She pulled the box out onto the sideboard. It was strange how the inside of the dumb waiter looked just the same here as it did in the kitchen even though it was in such a different world. It was just a big shelf with walls. Lucy shut the two little doors and checked the electric buttons on the wall next to it. There were up and down buttons just like in the kitchen. There was a passageway to her left leading towards the front of the house. Bedrooms, she guessed. She'd leave them till later.

David's warning was temporarily forgotten as they wandered round the room, touching the curtains and stroking the furniture, taking pleasure in the silky textures and smooth surfaces. In one corner stood a giant television set, and between the door and the fireplace there was a small table with a computer on it and a telephone. Lucy pressed a button next to the fire and the hearth filled with flames which lapped magically around and through a tasteful arrangement of logs. The warmth was immediate. Lucy rubbed her hands in front of it and then pressed the button again. The flames vanished. What an amazing luxury! The father must have come to some sort of arrangement with the Magnifico to be allowed to be comfortable. Imagine having something like this in the downstairs flat. She could just see herself and Paul sitting in front of it reading their books, and Aunt Sarah in her big chair working her way through her mending basket.

She looked around and spotted the desk under the window facing the big lime tree and suddenly remembered why they were here. If she wanted to find her existence there was work to be done, and the most obvious starting point was the desk.

It was a large desk made of some sort of red-coloured wood, with a leather top embossed with gold. Lucy pulled open the drawers. Her pulse quickened. There were notebooks and address books, and documents with figures and calculations. She turned over the pages and spread out the loose papers, but there was nothing that looked like birth records.

She found a key in the top drawer, and looked around for a keyhole to fit it into. It didn't fit any of the other drawers but – and Lucy held her breath – it slid easily into a cabinet nearby. The cabinet was full of files.

Hardly daring to hope, she checked the labels on the backs of the files – 'Bank', 'Car', 'Housekeeping', 'Commune', 'BWD'. The light outside was beginning to fade, and she took the 'Commune' file to the desk under the window. It was divided into sections headed 'Aunts', 'Mothers', 'Children'.

She went straight to the Children section. Most of the names were of children she knew from the Copse commune. Their details were set out like reports recorded in alphabetical order as at 30 September of each year. There was: *Adam, mother Diana, conduct good, non-academic, tendency to cry easily, unlikely to make strong father material, could be useful practical worker or craftsman;* and *Betty, mother Elizabeth, well-behaved so far, no sign of any particular talent, healthy.* And so on.

Lucy continued reading. She was so fascinated that for a while she forgot what she was looking for. Then she realised. Her own name wasn't there. It wasn't anywhere in the file. Nor was Paul's.

It seemed unlikely that they would come under Bank or Car. She took out the Housekeeping file. There were sections on gas, electricity, groceries, clothes and school, but again, no mention of her or Paul. She put the first two files back in the cupboard in the same order as they had been before.

The BWD file didn't look very promising, but she took it out and put it on the desk. Suddenly she felt the hair rise on the back of her neck, and she had an uncomfortable feeling that someone was watching her. Her heart started thumping. She looked round the room but, apart from Paul, who was busy tracing a bird pattern on the carpet with his finger, there was no-one else to be seen.

The hole in the ceiling was black and gaping but she could see nothing there. She peered out through the window. Her old friend, the lime tree, seemed sinister in the dusk. She closed the curtains.

David's warning about imminent danger was shouting loudly inside her head – but she couldn't leave yet. She had to find her name! Telling herself to stop imagining things she switched on the lights, went over to draw the curtains on the opposite window and returned to the desk.

An index in the BWD file set out categories, Births – Wives – Disposals. At the sight of 'Disposals' Lucy's skin prickled. There were nine entries. Seven were wives described as 'mistakes' or 'non-convertible' or 'incapacitated'. Two were children: *Stephen, mother Mary, aged four years, poor physical and mental health; Susan, mother Jane, aged eighteen months, blood disorder.*

Lucy was shaking as she shut the file. She sat down for a moment in an armchair near the desk and shut her eyes. Paul tapped her on the knee. She lifted her head and tried to smile, and remembered that she was still looking for who she was.

Stupid! She should have gone to the 'Births' section first. It contained a list of fifteen names under the headings, Child, Mother, Date of Birth, Weight, set out in chronological order. Lucy's eyes swept over the page. Two up from the bottom of the list was: *Paul, mother*

Belinda, formerly known as Maria. She checked the date of birth – three, nearly four years ago! Stars danced in front of her eyes, and she took deep breaths. 'Formerly known as'. That meant 'used to be known as'.

Lucy held her breath. She ran her finger up the page, and there she was! *Lucy, mother Maria…* Her heart pounded. She shut her eyes in case she was imagining things, and opened them again. There was the writing on the page! Maria, it said. She checked the date – fourteen years and nine months. Her legs turned to jelly and she dropped heavily down onto the father's leather office chair. It must be a mistake. She closed the file and had to force herself to open it up and check again. Supposing it wasn't there? But it was. And then the most amazing, beautiful, and exhilarating truth dawned on her – Paul was her brother. She had someone. He was hers.

Outside the house the automatic gates opened quietly. A large car purred up the drive and the gates closed behind it. Two men leaped out and a third was waiting for them by the lobby door. One of them immediately started to work on the lock, but the door wouldn't open. He swore under his breath. "The old lady's bolted it from the inside. Someone's tipped her off."

The front door too was bolted, and the back door was locked.

"Get the ram," barked the leader.

They lifted the ram out of the boot of the car. A man ran his hand over the lobby door. "The bolts will be just about here," he said.

Upstairs, Lucy called Paul to come and look. "That says who you are," she said excitedly, pointing at his name on the page. "You had a mother called Maria, and so did I. That means I'm your sister and you're my brother."

Paul stared. He could read his own name.

"Where is she?"

"She's somewhere." At least she hadn't been listed under Disposals. "We'll see if we can find her. Look! This is called the 'Wives' section. It says Maria has 'hair – dark brown, eyes – green, medium height'. You've got green eyes."

"So have you."

Lucy took out the Commune file again. "Perhaps this will tell us where she is." They looked through the Mothers and the Aunts sections, but there was no mention of a Maria, nor was there in the Household file. There was nothing to say where she was or what had happened to her.

They would just have to keep looking. Clutching the BWD file to her, Lucy started moving round the room again looking for anything that might contain files or notebooks. There was a small lamp on a table next to the fireplace. She pressed a switch in the wall and immediately switched it off again in panic as rustling sounds filled the room.

The children grabbed hold of each other in terror.

"Ghosties!" whispered Paul.

They crouched behind a giant armchair and held each other tight. Two faces peered cautiously through the hole in the ceiling in the middle of the room, and a woman whispered, "It sounded like children."

"I'm going down," whispered someone else.

"You'll never get through that space!"

There was shuffling and scraping, and gentle thumps of falling plaster. Lucy and Paul peeped round the side of

189

the armchair. Two legs emerged through the hole in the ceiling. Lucy clapped her hand over Paul's mouth before he could start screaming. The legs were followed by a body, and then a head with a mass of red hair. Two arms extended up into the hole and, one at a time, let go.

Claudia landed on the wet carpet. She jumped to her feet, rubbed her behind, and looked around. Paul gave a semi-smothered hiccup. Claudia tiptoed cautiously towards the armchair and looked behind it. Two pairs of green eyes looked fearfully up at her. For a second she said nothing. Then she burst out laughing.

"Two leprechauns!" she said. "Who are you?"

The children stood up slowly. Before they or she had a chance to say anything more there was a battering and smashing noise down in the lobby, and the rough sound of men's voices. It was followed by a clattering and swearing on the stairs as someone fell over the vacuum cleaner, and a loud crash as it was hurled over the banisters.

David's warning! Lucy was galvanised into action. She grabbed Paul and dragged him to the wall. Heaving him up onto a chair and onto the sideboard, she opened the dumb waiter, shoved him inside, and closed it. She quickly pressed a button and hoped it was the right one for the kitchen. The dumb waiter purred upwards to the floor above.

The desk pressed up against the curtains and left no room to hide. Lucy dashed across to the window opposite. The curtains there were big and heavy and velvet, and she disappeared into them. Claudia was standing stock still in the middle of the room when two men burst in.

"It's the redhead!" shouted one triumphantly. "The luck of the Devil!"

Claudia backed away and then sidestepped and darted forward towards the open door. As she did so a third man entered. The three of them grabbed her and threw her to the floor. One pulled a legnth of cord out of his pocket and quickly tied up her hands and feet, and then they dragged her out of the room.

On the way out one man turned to look back. "Holy Mag! There's been a flood!" he shouted.

"Never mind that now. Just get her out of here. Quick!"

Lucy could hear the thumps as they dragged Claudia's body down the stairs, bumping against each step one at a time. Then there was silence. David had been right. She should have taken Paul and left the house. Now it was too late. She didn't dare move.

Upstairs Maria had thrown the rug back over the hole in the floor as soon as she heard the men below. Lying with her ear pressed to the rug, she listened in horror as Claudia was taken away. She heard the man say, "Holy Mag! There's been a flood," and the dismissive response, and the distant thumping sound as Claudia was dragged down the stairs. In the ensuing silence the blue front door of her parents' house swam before her eyes and closed over their sorrowful faces. Then she heard a clicking sound and a small scared voice whispered, "Lucy?"

Maria jumped to her feet. The door of the dumb waiter had been pushed open slightly and a frightened little face peeped round it. She pulled Paul out gently and he started to cry.

"Hush," said Maria softly. "They'll hear us."

"I want Aunt Sarah," whimpered Paul. "I want Lucy."

CHAPTER TWENTY-SEVEN

The room was quiet except for the sound of someone breathing and a soft footfall over the carpet. There was a smell of cigarettes. Lucy held her breath and clenched her jaw to stop her teeth from chattering. The smell of cigarettes was coming nearer. Her legs started trembling uncontrollably, and suddenly the side of the curtain twitched and a hand shot in and grabbed her by the hair.

She nearly fainted, first with fright and then with relief. Her mouth was so dry she could hardly speak.

"Oh, Thomas!" Her voice was just a squeak. "Thank goodness it's you!" She threw her arms around his middle.

He grabbed her angrily by the shoulders.

"I told you not to poke your nose in things!" He shook her till her head rattled. "I've been watching you, you snooping, interfering little brat. You'd have been alright if you'd kept away. You've had it now!"

She was too shocked to move. This couldn't be Thomas! She had made a terrible mistake. It was a monster who looked like him. The blood drained from her face and her eyes were wide with fright. He caught hold of the back of her jumper and shoved her in front of him, down the stairs across the lobby, through the kitchen, and into the hall.

"You're not Thomas." Lucy's voice was a strangled choke. "The Magnifico is watching you."

"You little idiot! There's no such thing as the Magnifico. They're living in luxury and fooling the lot of you."

With one hand Thomas opened the door to the cellar, and with the other he threw her down the stairs.

"Get in there till I decide what to do with you. I've got more important things to think about while I'm here." He slammed the door after her and turned the key.

For a few moments Lucy lay dazed. Then, feeling around with her hand, she found the bottom step and pulled herself upright. Her brain felt numb. She rubbed her head. There was no nasty sticky feeling so she knew she wasn't bleeding. Her left shoulder and hip hurt but she hardly noticed the pain.

The true pain was inside her.

Thomas, the only person she'd really and truly trusted (other than Aunt Sarah of course), the man she'd once thought she'd like to marry – a traitor! She'd never trust anyone again except Paul. Even at this horrible moment there was a flash of joy as she remembered she had a brother. But somehow she had to get to Aunt Sarah to warn her. With a shaking arm she reached down and felt under the step for the plastic bag. It was still there, and the candle and matches were dry. Her fingers scarcely had the strength to hold a match let alone strike it, and she had to close her eyes and breathe deeply into the mouldy air for a moment. She had just managed to light the candle and was about to struggle to her feet when she heard feet and voices in the hall above her.

"The old lady's dead in her bed," said someone.

"Good. At least she's out of the way." Thomas's new voice, no longer kind and gentle, penetrated harshly through the cellar door. "Where's the boy?"

"Don't know."

"Well he's not a problem like the girl. He can't speak much."

For a moment Lucy wondered who the old lady was. Then she indignantly realised they meant Aunt Sarah. She wasn't old, just tired. Perhaps she was pretending to be dead so they wouldn't bother her. Holding the candle carefully upright in her left hand and feeling the wall with her right, she stumbled across the cellar.

Her escape apparatus was exactly as she had left it months ago. The strip of underlay was still there, and the crate, and the box on top of it. The underlay was wet and clammy under her knees. She pushed herself up and, giving the cover of the coal hole a good shove, she caught hold of the rim and looked over the edge. Outside it was not quite dark, but dark enough to blur a skimpy little figure as it emerged from the coal hole, flitted down the path, out through the gate, and across the road to the bushes by the pond.

Peering round the dense branches of a heavy rhododendron, Lucy could see that the high double gate to the left of the house was closed, but there was light and activity in the driveway. She darted back across the road and peeped through the diamond-shaped holes just above the crossbar.

It was as though she had seen it all before, only backwards. A splendid Mercedes with blacked-out windows stood in the drive facing the garage. The right-hand rear passenger door was wide open, and two men were emerging from the lobby dragging a wriggling, trussed up, red-headed bundle between them.

Claudia was struggling with all her strength and objecting as forcefully as she could, grunting into a gag which had been shoved into her mouth and halfway up her face.

"Let's give her a shot of tranquilliser," said one of the men.

"It's in the bag. I'll get it," said the other. As he dropped her, Thomas appeared.

"Just dump her there," he said. "Come upstairs both of you, and help me look for the key to the top-floor flat. Drax will give us a whopping great bonus if we can get both women at the same time. He might worm some useful information out of the older one and she can be disposed of afterwards."

The men dropped Claudia in a curled-up heap on the side path up against the house, and left her.

Lucy's mind raced. The key would not be upstairs. They were going to look for it in the wrong place. That would keep them occupied for a while. With her own ears she had heard the father say, "For the top flat," and with her own eyes she had seen Aunt Sarah drop the key into her apron pocket. Lucy had no intention of letting those men get hold of that key. Paul was in the top-floor flat. She would never let Traitor Thomas win this game!

She ran in a crouching position along the outside of the privet hedge to the front path, then into the garden and through the laurel arch that separated it from the driveway. The car loomed up in front of her. Darting up to the human bundle writhing on the ground she started pulling and tugging at the knotted cord behind Claudia's back. She loosened it quite easily and Claudia shook her hands free. She pulled the gag down from her face and they scrabbled together at the knot round her ankles. This was more difficult.

"Jump!" said Lucy pulling at her arm. Claudia shuffled till her back was against the house wall, and pushed herself up with her feet.

"Jump round there," whispered Lucy pointing to the laurels. "Keep working at the knot. I'm going to try and get the kitchen knife."

Claudia jumped with one hand against the house wall. She fell onto the ground on the other side of the laurel arch and grappled once more with the knot. Lucy bent low and crept towards the lobby door, past the car on one side and Aunt Sarah's bedroom window on the other. The curtains were still closed. She fervently hoped that Aunt Sarah wasn't dead.

She scuttled through the lobby and into the kitchen. Down from the father's flat came the sounds of grumbling and swearing, opening and banging of drawers, and shoving of furniture. Snatching the big knife out of the drawer next to the cooker, Lucy darted out again. As she shot through the door she heard footsteps on the stairs. She ran down the side path, through the arch into the front garden. Claudia was still struggling with the rope.

"Quick!" gasped Lucy, handing her the knife. "Cut it. They're coming."

She kept watch through the bushes as Claudia hacked at the cord and stood free but dazed. No-one emerged from the side door. Perhaps they were in the kitchen. Lucy's mind worked frantically. Grabbing Claudia's hand, she pulled her down the front path and out through the gate, and pointed across the road to the common.

"Follow that path till the end. It comes out in South Hill. Turn right and go to the third house down. Number 38. Tell George you're from Lucy. Tell them to send for the police – but not if they're infiltrated."

"What about you?"

Lucy gave Claudia a push.

"Go! Quick! George, number 38. Remember, not if they're infiltrated. His father will know."

"Come with me."

"I can't. I've got to get Paul. Quick! Run!" She gave Claudia another push, and vanished into the bushes.

Claudia ran.

Lucy nipped up the side path and slipped across behind the car into the gap between the garage and the garden wall. The rat no longer frightened her. Someone was moving around in the garage. Peering out from the gap she watched as a slight, hooded figure emerged with a hammer in his hands. He crouched low and tapped something into the front tyres and then darted round to the back of the car. Lucy could hear more tapping noises and then the rattling of a chain, the rustling of bushes in the front garden, and light footsteps running across the road.

Paul was her objective. She looked up at the garden wall that towered above her, but no way could she climb it. Passing through the gap she followed the wall round until she reached the lime tree. Crouching behind its trunk she could see the lights in the father's living room and the little barred windows above. Desperately she tried to think of a way to reach Paul. He might still be in the dumb waiter, half-suffocated and too scared to cry, and the tenant would never know he was there till she opened the door looking for her food and found him dead.

Suddenly there was a shout.

"She's gone!"

Lucy flattened her body and moved round the tree trunk until she could see at an angle down the side of the house. One of the men was standing beside the door holding the cord that had bound Claudia's wrists, and another was shouting into the lobby. They dashed about looking in the garage, under the car, and through the laurels to the front of the house. If they searched the garden Lucy would be found. Thomas knew where all the hiding places were.

She could slip out now through the back gate if she wanted to, but she had to get to Paul first, and for that she needed the key. Aunt Sarah always carried her keys everywhere with her. It must still be in her apron pocket.

Now the men were out in the street and Lucy knew they would be back any minute to search the garden. Lucy sidled along the garden wall and back through the gap to the front of the garage. She considered trying to get back into the house via the coal hole, but remembered the cellar door was locked on the outside, and there was no time to try George's key trick again.

A man appeared in the driveway and she ducked down behind the bonnet of the car. It was Thomas with a torch. She heard him move swiftly over to the bushes behind the garage. Peering round the side she could see the light from the torch searching behind the lime tree and over the flowerbeds into the shrubs. She nipped across the path, through the lobby and into the kitchen, and pressed the button for the dumb waiter in the hope that Paul might still be in it.

It seemed to take a thousand years to come purring down, and when it arrived it was empty.

Lucy dashed down the hall, past the cellar, and into Aunt Sarah's room.

Aunt Sarah lay on the bed just as Lucy and Paul had left her. Her eyes were closed and the dressing gown was still smoothed over her. She lay very, very still.

"Aunt Sarah?" whispered Lucy. There was no answer.

Lucy touched her face. It was just warm, but there was no breathing. She shook her a little but nothing happened. She laid her ear where she thought the heart was, but there was no sound or thump, and she knew in her own heart that the men were right – Aunt Sarah was dead. She touched the gold chain with the daffodil circle that now hung round her own neck, and her eyes filled with tears. But she had to move.

Pulling back the dressing gown she felt in Sarah's apron pocket and found her keys. There was no time to guess which was the right one. She covered Aunt Sarah up again, kissed her cheek and whispered, "Thank you for bringing me up. Goodbye." With the keys grasped firmly to stop them rattling, she tiptoed out into the kitchen. She stopped to listen before she ventured out into the lobby. There was someone on the stairs, and Thomas was talking outside.

"She'll have gone for the police. We haven't got much time. Find them keys quick or we'll have to go without them. He'll have left spares somewhere for the old lady in case of emergencies."

There was a murmur of voices.

"Check her room again. I'll check the kitchen."

Lucy pushed the keys into the dumb waiter and pressed the button for the second floor. She ran out of the kitchen into the hall. The front door wouldn't open and she realised it was bolted up at the top. Dashing back to the cellar she pulled the key out of the door, jumped inside, and felt in the dark for the keyhole.

Footsteps ran past towards Aunt Sarah's room. With shaking hands Lucy locked the cellar door from the inside and shuffled her bottom down the steps. She started stumbling towards the far end in the pitch dark

"No luck," shouted someone.

"OK. Let's go!"

Lucy could hear Thomas shouting up the stairs.

"No more time. Get out of here!"

"What about the brat?" called someone.

"Holy Mag!" said Thomas. "I forgot. She'll spill the beans if they find her. She'll have to come."

The handle turned on the cellar door.

"Where's the blasted key?"

"Just bash it in."

Within seconds the door had been smashed in and Lucy was being hauled out by the back of her jumper.

"Gag her. Hurry, damn you! Put her in the boot. We'll dispose of her later."

Something was stuffed into Lucy's mouth and a strip of cloth was wound around her head. Her hands were pulled behind her back and tied together with cord. She was hauled through the kitchen, her legs dragging, and thrown into the boot of the car. The lid slammed down and she was in total darkness.

Scrambling noises crunched on the gravel drive as one of the men climbed into the back seat.

"Shouldn't we set fire to the first floor? Destroy his records?" he shouted.

"No time," said Thomas. "Where's that idiot gone?"

"He went inside with the kerosene."

"He can chuck it into the ground floor. I'll tell him to hurry. You! Get the gate open."

There was some more scrambling in the gravel and a loud rattling of the gate, then a string of swear words that Lucy had never heard before.

"What's the hold-up?" called Thomas from the direction of the lobby.

"I can't open it. The automatic button's not working and someone's tied the gates together with a bicycle chain."

There was more rattling and swearing.

"We'll ram it then. Get in the car both of you."

"I've only fired the downstairs."

"It'll catch. Get in you fool, before the pigs get here."

Gravel crunched, car doors slammed, and the engine purred. The car reversed violently into the gate, and Lucy was hurled against the back of the boot. At the third attempt the car smashed its way through and out onto the road. There was a thump and it bumped over something.

The driver swore.

"God knows what that was!" he said.

"Never mind that. Just move!" shouted Thomas.

The car straightened up, bumped again, accelerated forward into top speed and hurtled down towards the main highway. After only a few yards it started to judder and swerve.

"It feels like a flat!" The driver's voice was sharp with panic.

"Just keep driving," yelled Thomas.

The driver rammed down on the accelerator. Every bone in Lucy's body jarred as the car lurched forward and sideways on its punctured tyres, but all she could think of was Paul. She'd promised to look after him for ever, and already he'd be wondering why she hadn't come for him. Police sirens wailed. The car screeched to a halt and its doors flew open. Lucy heard the men tumble out and run across the road to the common and, accidentally, she nearly thanked the Magnifico. Claudia had got there in time!

CHAPTER TWENTY-EIGHT

Lucy had promised him a reward and this was it – the most amazing adventure of his life. George stood with his father behind the police cordon watching the flashing lights, the torches sweeping over the common, and the chasing figures. His mother had told them not to come, to keep out of it. They'd done their bit, she said, by ringing the police and looking after Claudia. But they couldn't help themselves. A pair of busybodies, said his mother. He did sincerely hope that Lucy was alright and that she had managed to find Paul, but nevertheless it was very exciting.

Someone was caught in the bushes on the common. It was a boy. George moved along the cordon and watched as the captive was handcuffed and pushed into a police car. He ducked under the ribbon, ran down to the car, and peeped through the window.

A policeman was sitting in the back seat with David. He put his head out and glowered. "Get back over there behind the cordon," he said severely.

"That's Lucy's friend," said George. "You can't arrest him. Take those handcuffs off him. He won't have done anything wrong."

"Mind your own business and clear off."

George ran back to his father.

"That's Lucy's friend that they've put in the car."

"Is it?" said his father. "Look! They've caught another one."

A man was pinned down on the ground, far over beyond the pond. The scene was lit up as the torches flashed. The man was handcuffed and hauled to his feet, and pushed roughly over the grass to a waiting van.

The crowd was riveted. This was better than a film, thought George, but where was Lucy? He glanced back at the house and gave a shout.

"It's on fire!"

Smoke was pouring out of the further side of the house and tiny flames were licking through the edges of the front door. Suddenly the door to the police car burst open and David jumped out and ran.

The policeman leaped out after him, skidded on a pile of wet leaves and went flying. Within seconds David had reached the abandoned Mercedes and darted behind it. With his cuffed hands he pressed the catch of the boot and the lid flew up. Lucy's huge terrified eyes gazed up at him as he pulled down her gag.

"I saw them do it," he said, reaching into the boot and tugging at her.

For a moment she was too weak with relief to move. Then she managed to uncurl herself and sit up. Turning her back she presented her hands to be untied. Then she shook her wrists, and stepped out onto the road.

"Thanks," she whispered.

She glanced back along the road. A dark bundle lay directly in front of the gateway to the drive. "Holy Mag!" she muttered. "It looks like Matthew!"

For a second neither of them could move. Then she turned to look up at the house and gasped, "Paul!"

Just as the policeman caught up with David and grabbed him by the back of the neck, she slipped away and ran. The front door was burning. She dashed through the laurel archway and ran up the side path. As she passed Aunt Sarah's window she could see the curtains had gone and the room was in flames. Smoke was pouring from the kitchen window. She ran into the lobby. The kitchen door was open. Smoke was billowing through it, swept through by the draught from the window.

She ran up the stairs, past the mahogany door on the first floor, and up to the second landing. Just as she reached it the door opened and the tenant emerged, holding Paul with one hand and Aunt Sarah's keys in the other. Paul leaped forward and threw his arms round Lucy burying his face in her middle. She squeezed him to her quickly and then took his hand.

"Hurry! There's a fire."

They ran down one flight, only to be faced with a wall of smoke that made all three of them choke.

"In here," gasped Lucy, pushing them into the father's living room.

Slamming the mahogany door behind them, she rushed to the window and tried to reach the catch, but it was too high.

"I'll do it," said the tenant.

Stretching up she released it easily and pushed up the window. All three of them leaned out and looked at the ground below. It seemed a long way away. Quickly the tenant and Lucy fetched the big leather cushions from the couch and the armchairs and threw them out in as orderly a manner as they could manage. Paul tried to drag a cushion, but it was too heavy.

"Let me do it," said Lucy. "You take this." She handed him a cashmere shawl that was draped over the back of an armchair. "But don't throw yourself out with it."

The smoke was creeping under the door. They all looked out of the window again.

"You go first," the tenant said urgently to Lucy. "Curl up and roll over as soon as you hit the ground. I'll hold the little boy by his arms as low as possible and you must try and catch him."

Lucy took another look at the ground below. She put one leg over the sill, paused for a second, and suddenly pulled herself back into the room. The BWD file – on the floor behind the armchair! Dashing across the room she bent down behind the chair and snatched up the file.

"What on earth are you doing?" cried the tenant.

"It's to prove I exist."

She ran to the window and threw out the file, then flung her leg over the sill, twisted herself round, and dropped. She curled up and rolled as instructed, and landed comfortably. Jumping to her feet she steadied herself on the pile of cushions and held up her arms.

The tenant lifted Paul onto the sill and, grasping him by the wrists, she swung him over and dangled him for a second before she let go. He landed on Lucy and they both fell together on the thick soft leather.

Smoke was beginning to billow out through the window. The tenant was coughing. Lucy hastily moved Paul out of the way onto the grass. The tenant threw her legs over the sill. As she twisted round to face the room she inhaled a cloud of smoke, coughed, and fell. Lucy tried to break her fall but she landed awkwardly with one leg under her on the cushions and her head on the ground. Semi-conscious, she coughed and gasped for breath.

"Is your leg alright?" asked Lucy anxiously. The tenant coughed and coughed, and couldn't catch her breath.

Lucy grabbed Paul and one of the lighter cushions and ran to her hidey-hole under the bush with the spotted leaves. She plonked him down on the cushion and dashed back.

"I'm going to get help," she said. "I'll be as quick as I can."

The tenant had stopped coughing and was lying very still. Lucy quickly gathered up the scattered pages of the BWD file and the cashmere shawl. She ran back to Paul and threw the file down beside him.

"Don't move from here," she said, wrapping the shawl round his pyjamas and trying to sound as stern as Aunt Sarah. "I'm going to get someone to help the tenant, and you must not move or make a noise. Understand?"

Paul nodded.

She dashed out through the back gate and turned right along the alley, past the backs of two houses, down the side, and out onto the road. The crowd was still standing staring at the flames as firemen turned their powerful hoses on the front of the house.

"Get back behind the cordon!" shouted a policeman.

Lucy ignored him and ran towards a waiting ambulance.

"Quick!" she panted. "Round the back."

There were already firemen behind the house when the paramedics ran in with the stretcher. As they started shifting the tenant, Lucy backed off into the darkness.

She slipped out of sight into the hidey-hole with Paul and watched.

The paramedics went out the way they had come, through the back gate and down the alleyway. As they left Lucy heard one of them say, "What's happened to the little girl?"

"She must have gone back to the road," said the other.

The firemen were now on the lawn, their hoses thundering onto the first-floor flat.

"Come on," whispered Lucy.

Picking up the file, she took Paul's hand and, keeping behind the shrubs, they sidled along the wall to the back gate and out into the alley. Instead of turning right towards the access to the road, they turned left. They passed the wall of the father's house and reached the back gate of the house next door – the diplomat's house. It had looked empty when Lucy had seen it from the branches of the tree, and she hoped desperately that it still was.

She lifted the latch and they crept inside. In the light from the fire the neglected tennis lawn grew eerily tall and the flowerbeds were thick with weeds. They tiptoed furtively down an overgrown path to the rear of the house and, cupping their hands around their faces, looked in through the windows. There was nothing to be seen but the curtain linings.

The back door was locked. Lucy looked around her. On the step was a cast iron beetle with large antennae for removing gumboots. For a split second she hoped the Magnifico wasn't watching, and then remembered that he didn't exist. She picked up the beetle and, making Paul stand well back, she smashed the glass pane nearest the door handle. Gingerly putting her hand inside, she pulled put the key. They entered a lobby that led to the kitchen and silently shut the door behind them.

"We're safe now," whispered Lucy. They had escaped the fire of the melting flesh.

CHAPTER TWENTY-NINE

Just before midnight on the Friday night Father Copse received a coded message from the Holy Leaders. He was to leave the Holy Envoy's palace at once and withdraw his candidacy for the deputy's post. He was to go to the city centre where one of their agents would meet him and transfer him to a new identity with all necessary documentation and instructions. A flight had been arranged for the new identity, departing for Manchester in nine hours' time. From there he would be taken by car to run a commune in the north of England which had recently lost its father in a car accident.

All his life he had obeyed the Magnifico's instructions, delivered by the Holy Leaders, and there was no way he could disregard them. He withdrew his candidacy, took on his new identity as Father Arthur, and flew to Manchester on the Saturday morning.

Despite his adventure Paul was sleeping well. Lucy lay beside him in the king-sized bed. Everything was quiet apart from the distant voices of the firemen as they doused the remaining ashes of the father's house. She was still shaking inside as she went over the events of the day. It seemed centuries ago that David had met her by the pond and warned her, yet it was only today – that very afternoon. Since then she had been betrayed by a trusted friend, acquired a brother, and lost Aunt Sarah.

Lucy had taken Aunt Sarah for granted, had been afraid of her tongue and irritated by her homilies, and now she was ashamed. She stroked the gold circle of daffodils that hung from the chain on her neck and remembered the comfortable lap of years ago, and the face nuzzling into her hair – the kissing and cuddling, and the secret treats, and the soothing voice whispering 'my little darling'. And then she remembered that horrible day – the first day of school – when she had thrown her arms round Aunt Sarah's legs and asked to be cuddled. With tears falling down her fat cheeks Aunt Sarah had pushed her away. "No. It's not allowed. You're a big girl now."

Lucy turned away from Paul and buried her face in the pillow. She wept, not just for her own terrible hurt, but also for the sadness of poor Aunt Sarah who had owned nothing but the gold chain with the daffodil circle, and had not even been allowed to love.

A chink of light between the curtains told Lucy it was daytime. Her head hurt and her eyelids were so swollen she could hardly see through them. She snuggled a little further down into the bed. There was no need to get up.

Paul stirred beside her and opened his eyes.

"Getting-up time?" he asked.

Lucy climbed out of bed and went to the window. "It's Saturday," she said. Her voice sounded thick and heavy.

There was a gap in the heavily lined curtains, and she peeped out. The room overlooked the front garden and the main road. To the left she could see the remains of the father's house. It was still smoking in places and there were men climbing over the ruins.

Lucy carefully closed every bit of the curtains and went over to the door. She flicked the light switch but nothing happened.

Paul was bouncing on the bed when she returned.

"I think there's no electricity," she said. "It's like when Aunt Sarah has to light candles after a big storm."

Paul wasn't particularly interested.

"I'm hungry," he said.

They found a bathroom which was unlike anything they had seen before. The bath was made of beaten copper and stood like a great bowl in the middle of the marble floor. There was a mirror across one entire wall, from floor to ceiling. They stood in front of it and stared at themselves. For the first time in their lives they could see what they really looked like. The sight was a disappointment. Paul was still in his pyjamas and Lucy had slept in her day clothes, and they were both filthy, covered in soot and mud.

Downstairs they explored the kitchen. It was large and square with a giant wooden table in the centre and a big blue clock ticking away on the furthest wall. There were cupboards and yards of smooth worktops with mysterious gadgets lined up against mosaic wall tiles. In one corner stood a giant silver cupboard with two doors. Lucy opened the right-hand door. It was a refrigerator. A few bottles of wine lay on the wire trays inside, but there was nothing to eat. What was significant, Lucy realised, was that the light inside the fridge had come on. That meant at least there was power in the kitchen.

Paul had dragged over a chair and was looking at the gadgets.

"This is a pretty kettle," he said, lifting the lid. "All silvery."

Lucy tried the tap and after a few gurgles and splutters water started to flow, and there was a slight rumbling noise from the corner of the kitchen. The children opened a door and found a boiler churning away in good sized laundry room. A clothes airer like Aunt Sarah's hung from the ceiling, and the walls were lined with shelves full of towels, and sheets and blankets. A silver-coloured washing machine stood next to a matching tumble drier. An ironing board stood erected with the iron positioned ready for use.

If Aunt Sarah had had all these things, thought Lucy, her legs might not have got so swollen up.

Back in the kitchen the tap was still running.

"Look!" said Lucy. "Steam! That means we might be able to have a bath in warm water."

"I'm hungry."

Lucy opened the left-hand door of the huge silver cupboard, and both children stood staring. It was full of food. Paul poked it with his finger.

"It's cold," he said, withdrawing his finger quickly.

"It must be a freezer." Lucy looked at the carefully labelled shelves of vegetables, meat, fish, ready meals, puddings, ice creams, fruits, and fruit juices.

If Aunt Sarah had had a freezer she would not have had to go shopping every day. Lucy was astonished at the number of things that could have made Aunt Sarah's life easier, and they were all here right next door to her in the diplomat's house!

They took out a container of ice cream, a lemon cheesecake and a box of orange juice, and put them on the kitchen table. Aunt Sarah had taught them to eat decently at the table, so they found bowls and spoons and drinking glasses and laid them ready for their breakfast.

"We'll have to wait for them to melt," said Lucy. "Let's go up now and have our wash."

Upstairs they wandered through the bedrooms, opening cupboards and drawers. Just off the big front bedroom where they had slept, was a dressing room. It was lined with rails of women's clothes on one side, and men's on the other. There was nothing in the next room, other than a bed, a wardrobe, and an armchair, and a bathroom leading off it. Then there were three back rooms full of toys and games that neither of them had ever seen before. Judging from the contents of the chests of drawers and the wardrobes, the rooms belonged to a little girl of about three or four, a boy two or three years older, and another boy of about eleven or twelve.

Lucy had never seen any children or adults coming or going from this house, but then she wouldn't have if they were always abroad. Anyway, the father's instructions had always been to avoid social contact with non-followers. It struck Lucy that though she had occasionally seen a neighbour going in and out on the other side of the father's house, she didn't know who she was either.

She carefully selected clean clothes from the younger boy's room for Paul to wear after his bath. There was nothing big enough for her in the girl's room, so she decided she'd have to make do with the older boy's clothes until she had washed her own and Paul's. For once in her life she was glad she was skinny.

They went to the big marble bathroom. Lucy tried various knobs and taps in the shower but couldn't find how to make it work, so they filled the huge copper bath with lovely steaming hot water and laid thick white towels on a chair nearby, and had the only hot bath they had ever had in their lives. Lucy shampooed Paul's hair and then her own, and they laughed to see how different they looked with their hair full of bubbles. She rinsed their heads thoroughly, pulled out the plug, and reached for the towels.

Before they went downstairs again they admired themselves in the long wall mirror. Paul was immaculately dressed in trousers made of a fine cord material in rich navy blue, and a soft cable-knit sweater in cream-coloured cashmere. The trousers were a little long for him, but Lucy had tucked up the hems. She was dressed in jeans and a T-shirt, and they both wore trainers that they had taken, brand new, from their boxes.

"We'll have to be very careful not to get them dirty," said Lucy. "We'll have to put them back exactly as they were as soon as I've washed our clothes."

"I want them," said Paul, rubbing his hand gently over the soft cashmere.

"We're only borrowing them. We can't keep them."

"They're mine!" wailed Paul

"Stop your nonsense." Lucy realised she sounded just like Aunt Sarah and softened her tone. "Come on. Let's go and see if our food has melted."

They went downstairs and had ice cream for breakfast.

CHAPTER THIRTY

Very early on the Sunday morning Father Arthur was sitting in his office in the northern commune with his head in his hands.

He had watched the news on television, read the papers, and received texts from the Holy Leaders. So, his house had been burned to the ground. No need to guess who was to blame. With luck the one death would turn out to be Drax. The redhead had escaped and would have told everything she knew to the police by now, but so what? Perhaps she didn't know much. Even if she did Father Copse didn't exist anymore. More importantly, the woman – his woman – lay in a hospital bed surrounded by police waiting for her to wake up from a coma. It was annoying that Thomas had switched off his phone. There was a job that needed to be done and Thomas was the one person he could trust. He had to get a long, thick swatch of Belinda's hair.

Two hours later Thomas was still switched off. Father Arthur made himself a coffee. It was not as good as Sarah's but would have to do. The circle of pain was squeezing his head and it felt hot. The Magnifico was telling him to go down south and look for Thomas. In the bathroom he cut off his magnificent hair and then went over the whole of his head with his electric razor. His scalp felt quite sore but that was a small thing to be suffered for the sake of the Holy Cause. He looked at the pile of glossy black locks at the bottom of the bathroom bin. The sight of it hurt him more than his scalp. So sad! Such beautiful hair! But it would grow again. He cut off the bushy bits of his eyebrows until they looked almost elegant. There was no need to shave the bristle on his chin. It would perfect the disguise. He looked in the mirror and saw with a shock that he was no longer handsome. Indeed, had it been anyone else's face he would have said they were ugly. Depressing, but a temporary necessity. Even the faithful Sarah wouldn't recognise him.

In the corner of the office was a safe containing the commune's housekeeping budget for an entire month. He took out only half the money. After all, he couldn't let the children starve. He sent a coded text message to the Holy Leaders saying that the Magnifico had placed a crown of pain on his head and told him that Drax was responsible for the fire, and had given him direct orders to take money from the commune safe and go south where He had work for him to do.

In his predecessor's wardrobe he found a raincoat. It was short in the sleeves but would serve his purpose. He stuffed the money into the pockets, locked the safe up again, switched off his mobile phone, and stepped out of the commune door into a howling gale. The driving rain cooled his newly shaven head and he knew he was doing the right thing.

Down in the south the Holy Leaders had already sprung into action. They had a disposal infiltrator in the Mortimor Hospital waiting for a suitable opportunity to inject Maria before she woke up from her coma, and one

217

of their social workers had succeeded in taking David from the police station into care. He was now in the cells behind Drax House, and he and Dorothy would be disposed of as soon as the news story had died down. Public attention would be drawn away by a fabricated scandal to be created by journalist infiltrators faithful to the Holy Cause. As for Father Drax, he would be given a full opportunity to give his side of the story before any action was taken against him. It was important to be fair and objective in all matters.

Father Arthur reached the house after dark. The fire had been totally extinguished and the men had departed, leaving a cordon around the ruins. In the light from the streetlamp the garage stood solitary and blackened, its doors and its window still intact. He would sleep there like a tramp in his own backyard. But the house! Where were the signs of his old life in all this ash and rubble? The ground floor had been completely burned out and the flats above had collapsed into it. A scorched scrap of Persian carpet peeped up through lumps of plaster. He scrabbled away at some concrete and tugged at the corner of a picture frame, but it came away in his hands. And the woman? The most beautiful of all his possessions? His heart would surely break if he couldn't have her hair. As for his files and housekeeping records, there was no sign of them. Father Copse and his history had been wiped out by the flames.

He daren't hang about. Someone would see him. He sidled into the garage and shook out some of the sacks in the corner to the right of the door. Those could be shifted about a bit to make a mattress and he would cover himself with his raincoat. First he must find food.

He took some of the cash out of the raincoat pockets and draped it over the handlebars of the lawnmower. It slid to the floor, but he couldn't be bothered to pick it up. Later he would be glad of it, but for now the outside air was mild enough. Stuffing the money into his trouser pockets he set off for the High Street to find a shop that was open on a Sunday.

CHAPTER THIRTY-ONE

Paul and Lucy sat in front of a television set watching cartoons. They had found it in a small sitting room leading off the kitchen. The screen flickered and darted colourfully onto the walls of the room and the closed curtains. Paul was enthralled. He sat buried in the soft cushions of a velvet-covered armchair, his eyes fixed on the magic of the screen.

Lucy's eyes too were fixed on the screen, but her mind was elsewhere. She was glad that Aunt Sarah had outwitted the fire of the melting flesh by dying before it reached her. Now her soul was safe. She may well have been stern and unsmiling and over-focused on the hereafter, but Lucy knew in her heart that she had done her best for them. David's warning had come true and had been dealt with for now, but there was still Dorothy, and tomorrow was Monday – only one day to go before she was sixteen. Lucy shivered. She wished she could think of some way to break a padlock.

Saturday and Sunday had been spent playing with toys in the upstairs rooms and watching television, and they had tried the various foods that they had managed to defrost, but all the time their own predicament as well as Dorothy's had been preying on Lucy's mind. On the Saturday a man had come to the front door and rung the bell and called "Hello!" through the letter box, and she and Paul had hidden in the hall cupboard. Then a voice had said "Don't bother. The neighbour says they're in the States." The man had gone away but Lucy didn't feel safe. She knew they couldn't stay here for ever. The diplomat's family might come back any time. The broken pane in the back door would immediately alert the owners that there had been a break-in. They would call the police, the house would be searched, and she and Paul would be found.

She left Paul for a moment and found a brush and pan, and carefully swept up the broken glass inside and outside the back door. Aunt Sarah would not want her to leave a mess. With a tea cloth wrapped round her fingers she managed to pull the remaining shards out from the sides of the pane and dropped them in the pan. There was nowhere safe to put them so she wrapped them all up in the cloth, tied it in a knot, and dropped them into the kitchen bin.

She stood back and admired her work. The door looked so much tidier, and if that man called again and checked around the back he might not notice that the bottom pane had no glass. She wondered if David had heard anything about Dorothy. If he'd been with the police all this time he must have told them everything and they would have rescued her by now. The thought made her feel a lot better. Even so, she couldn't stop worrying that something might have gone wrong.

Sitting down again with Paul in front of the television she tried to visualise the route to the outside entrance of the underground passage through which Dorothy would pass on the way to disposal.

When she was small Lucy had been to Drax House with Aunt Sarah many times, but there had been no social visits for a few years now because Aunt Sarah thought the fathers might have fallen out. She remembered playing in the large garden at the back of the house, and they had occasionally had picnics in the woodland beyond the garden fence. She knew about the entrance from the side road into the woodland because sometimes they had gone in that way for their picnics. As she pictured Dorothy's route out of the underground passage she realised that the side road would provide easy access to a waiting van, and nausea swept over her as she pictured poor Dorothy's body being bundled into it.

Her attention was caught by a change on the television screen. The cartoons had finished and were now being followed by advertisements. Paul objected to the disappearance of the cartoon characters and Lucy pressed various buttons on the remote control to find some more. A man's head appeared and she caught the words, "and now to the news where you are." For a second Lucy wondered how on earth the man could have known where she and Paul were. Then she realised this must be the local news.

Paul climbed out of his chair and wandered around the room, while she watched with interest. There was an item about hooligans in the High Street just beyond the Magnifico's school, and she recognised the shops. She waited eagerly for further familiar scenes. There was something about objections to planning permission for a new supermarket. Suddenly she was riveted.

The man was talking about a failure to identify the body of the individual who had died in Friday night's fire at 3 Mortimor Road. Examination of the site had established that the cause of the fire was arson. The owner was still abroad and could not be contacted. A woman who had allegedly been abducted by the owner had been returned to her family, and police were still waiting at the hospital bedside of another woman, believed to have been a resident, who remained in a coma. A young girl and boy were understood to have resided at the house and were missing. The public was asked to report any possible sightings to the police. A man caught at the scene was still being questioned. A fourteen year old boy, found on the common while the fire was in progress, had been detained for questioning, but had disappeared while in the care of an individual claiming to be a social worker.

Lucy's heart sank right down into the bottom of her stomach. The story was followed by something about council tax, and then the weather, but she heard none of it. If the fourteen year old boy was David, why would he have been released to a social worker? If anyone could have given information to the police it would have been David. She had no doubt that it was he who had hammered the nails into the tyres, and who had chained up the gate. He must have seen the whole thing from the bushes on the common – the perfect witness.

The news item buzzed around in Lucy's head. If the social worker was an infiltrator, David would not be safe. In fact he would be in great danger. He was probably in the cells at this moment, awaiting disposal along with Dorothy. She would have to do something! Her eyes were fixed on Paul as he pottered gently in and out of the furniture. How could she make a rescue bid with a little boy to look after? She couldn't leave him here on his own. Her mind reached out in all directions, seeking suggestions.

Paul was the least of the obstacles. Without the code

she would never break through the padlock. She tried to visualise the contents of Thomas's toolbox. He had once sawed through a chain with a special tool, but it had been noisy and so heavy that she knew she wouldn't have the strength to use it. She remembered a time when he had locked himself out of the garage. He had poked the keyhole with a piece of bent coat hanger wire while holding the lock down with a piece of metal. That seemed simple, but it might not work on a coded padlock. Even so, it was the only thing she could think of. She would have to get to the garage and find Thomas's toolbox.

Lucy lifted the blind on the back door and peeped through into the back garden. It was already dark outside. If she could find the cartoons again perhaps she could leave Paul on his own, just long enough to find something in the garage – anything that might be useful to her.

"Paul," she said, as the cartoon channel reappeared, "I've got to go out for a few minutes. You're not to move from that chair till I get back."

She wondered for a moment whether to tell him the Magnifico would be watching him if he moved, but felt sick at the thought.

Paul was absorbed in the bright dancing colours.

"Did you hear me, Paul? You are not to move till I get back."

Paul nodded his head, his eyes still fixed on the screen.

Dorothy lay on the bed in a heap. The key turned in the lock and two kitchen aunts appeared. One of them guarded the door while the other one put a tray on the table.

"Eat up," she said. "We made something especially nice for you." She stepped over to the bed and took Dorothy's hand in hers. "It'll be days yet. Perhaps they'll give you time to repent and let you come back to us, you never know."

"And even if they don't," the aunt at the door said kindly, "you'll be better off than in other countries where they get stoned to death or shot. You'll just feel a tiny prick in your arm and you'll go to sleep. No more worries."

Everything went black and when Dorothy came to, the aunts had left.

She slid off the bed and went over to the table. Never ever would she be able to eat another morsel. What was the point? It made her feel sick to look at it. She covered the tray over with the table napkin and shoved it away next to the copy of the *Holy Vision*. Of course, as the aunt had said, they might give her a chance to repent. She brightened a little at the thought. And the fact was now that she had experience of some of the nastiness in the outside world, the Magnifico's world had a lot to be said for it. An orderly existence where everyone knew their place without protest or disturbance must surely be a good thing. If she followed the rules she'd be safe, even if she was stuck in the kitchens or the breeding rooms for the rest of her life. She opened up the *Holy Vision* and started to read. She'd have to know her stuff if she was to put forward a convincing plea.

After a while she closed the book. It was so boring and, anyway, it had been dinned into them so often at school she more or less knew it by heart. As she sat back thinking how best to convince the Holy Leaders that she had reformed, she heard heavy footsteps coming down the corridor from Drax House. She put her ear to the door. There were men's voices. Her heart seemed to stop. Was this it? Then she heard a key being inserted in a lock, but it wasn't the lock to her door. She waited. Someone was being settled into the cell next to hers.

"That's it, mate," said a voice. She recognised the commune caretaker's deep growl. "Good luck, that's all I can say." The door clanged and the footsteps faded away up the corridor.

There was absolute silence. Then, through the thickness of two doors, very faintly, she heard a muffled voice call, "Dorothy! Are you there?"

"David, I'm here," she yelled at the top of her voice. Holy Mag! She mustn't do that. They'd hear her up in Drax House if she wasn't careful. The sudden joy in her heart turned to horror. How did they catch him? She would never plead for forgiveness and leave David to face his fate alone.

Lucy let herself out via the back door in case someone happened to be passing the front of the house. She ran along the back alley and into the father's garden. Her eyes quickly became used to the dark. The sight of the rubble and ruined walls was a shock, but she had no time to linger.

Following her old route she crept silently behind the shrubs, along the garden wall round to where the garage still stood. She went down the gap between the garage and the wall and came out in front of the doors. For a moment she stopped to look around. All that remained of the high laurel hedge with its arch through to the front garden was a collection of black branches twisted like great pieces of charcoal. The big double gate with its diamond-shaped holes was totally wrecked, leaving the gravel driveway open to the world.

The doors to the garage were slightly open and Lucy slipped inside. She felt on the window sill to the right for Thomas's torch. It was still there. Stepping around the gardening equipment, tins of paint, and an old bike, she crossed over to the shelves at the far end. The toolbox was in its proper position on the middle shelf. She shone the torch into it trying to keep the light as low as possible and took out a screwdriver and the awl. There were gadgets and other tools on the shelves and on the floor, but there was nothing that looked as though it would help her pick a lock or break open a padlock. She wondered if long nails would do the trick. At the thought of nails she remembered David and the tyres, and noticed that the hammer was missing.

As she turned to leave she caught her foot in a pile of cloth and nearly fell. She shone the torch on it, and saw it was a man's raincoat. Thomas never wore a raincoat. He had his old gardening anorak and the tidy jacket that he wore when he arrived for work. Picking up the raincoat and draping it neatly over the handle of the lawnmower Lucy made her way round various objects towards the door. The torch might be useful, she thought. It surely wouldn't count as stealing. After all, it was Thomas and his friends who had burned down her so-called home. When she reached the door she shone the torch over the window sill in case there was anything useful. There was a jam jar full of small screws and dead flies, and another with dried-up paint brushes, but nothing interesting. In the corner between the window and the door, just under the hooks where Thomas hung his anorak, were the sacks that she and Paul used to hide under when they played hide-and-seek. They weren't in their usual tidy pile. Somebody had been in and rumpled them up.

At that moment Lucy heard someone approaching along the main road outside. She quickly switched off the torch and stood holding her breath waiting for the footsteps to go past. Instead they turned into the driveway and crunched through the gravel. There was no time to hide. She grabbed Thomas's anorak and, pulling it over her head, dropped down into the corner on top of the sacks just as the towering figure of a bald-headed man appeared in the doorway, a plastic carrier bag dangling from his hand.

Dropping the bag by the door, he came towards the corner where Lucy crouched, kicked against a tin of paint, and then seemed to be feeling along the window sill. He muttered some swear words. Lucy guessed he was looking for the torch. She pressed her face down into the sacks and held her breath as he stumbled away towards the further end of the garage. He knocked into the lawnmower and swore again. For a moment he was silent and Lucy guessed he had discovered the neatly folded raincoat. She heard him shaking it out and then quickly making his way back towards the door. Lucy lifted a tiny corner of the anorak with her finger and peeped out. She could see him standing just inside the doorway, pulling on the raincoat. Then his feet crunched hastily down the gravel drive and she heard him hurrying away, almost at a run.

She waited until the footsteps had died away before she dared to pull the anorak away from her head. Sitting bolt upright on the sacks, she listened. A few cars went by, but no pedestrians. Rain started to patter heavily on the garage roof.

Panic swept over Lucy as she remembered Paul. She had no idea how long she had been there. Clutching the torch, she jumped to her feet, and looked round the door. She could see Thomas's hammer and a handful of nails lying near the wrecked double gates, but she daren't leave Paul any longer, and she left them where they were.

The rain was pelting down. Lucy hurriedly put on the anorak and pulled up the hood. The plastic bag lay on the floor where the man had dropped it. She shoved the torch, screwdriver and awl into it and ran, with visions of Paul lying injured or dead from some terrible accident. Almost tripping over the bottom of the anorak she dashed across the lawn and out via the rear alleyway into the diplomat's garden. Brushing against weeds and tall grass, she ran down the overgrown path and in through the back door, and straight to the little sitting room off the kitchen. The cartoon characters were still jumping about on the screen, and Paul was asleep in the armchair. Lucy nearly collapsed with relief.

Taking the anorak off in the kitchen, she shook it outside to get rid of the drips. She draped it over the back of a chair and, feeling some bits and pieces in the pockets, she took them out and laid them on the table. There was a biro, matches, tobacco and cigarette papers, and a tiny notebook. Her nice new borrowed trainers were soaked, and she put them in the laundry room. Then she shut the back door, pulled down the blind, fished the torch out of the plastic bag, and stood it in the centre of the table. Her eyes were so used to the darkness that the sudden light made her blink.

She emptied the bag onto the table. Apart from the screwdriver and awl, there was a bottle of milk, two wrapped sandwiches, an apple and a banana, and a Mars Bar.

In the side room Paul was stirring and snuffling.

229

"Come on, lazybones," said Lucy, snuggling down next to him for a minute. "It's time for tea. And you've been such a good boy, there's something really nice."

Shoving the contents of the anorak pockets up one end of the table, she set out the plates and mugs, and divided the plastic bag picnic into two equal shares. She hung the bag on the knob of a chair back to dry, and then they sat down and started with the Mars Bar.

CHAPTER THIRTY-TWO

Later, in the dark on the Sunday night, Father Arthur was prowling round the outside of Copse House looking for Thomas. It was possible he might be here, helping in the kitchen. His shift in the hospital should have ended long ago, so why hadn't he switched his phone back on? The lights had been off in his terraced cottage, and no-one had answered the door.

Through the dining room window Father Arthur could see the aunts, who used to be his, laying a long table ready for the children's supper. There was no sign of Sarah, nor of Thomas. He waited till the children started trooping in for their meal. They stood at their places like young sentries and bowed their heads in prayer, thanking the Magnifico for his generosity. At a signal from one of the aunts they all sat down and waited in silence as the meal was served. Fifteen children, all his plus a few discards, but Lucy and Paul were not among them.

He needed somewhere to sit comfortably and think, and at the moment he had nowhere to go. The garage was out because it was obvious that someone else had been there and had seen his mackintosh. It might have been Thomas, but on the other hand it could have been one of Drax's men snooping around – or a lingering fire officer. He couldn't take the risk of going back there, and he was hungry. Creeping away from the window, he made his way back to the main road and, looking up and down in both directions, set off to find the nearest bed and breakfast. No-one would recognise him with his shaven head and stubbly chin. Tomorrow he would go into the woods behind Drax House and wait. Thomas occasionally worked in Drax's gardens, and he might be able to catch his attention.

With the light of the torch Paul and Lucy found themselves some clean pyjamas in the children's bedrooms, and made themselves ready for bed before going downstairs to watch more television. Lucy settled Paul down in the armchair, and went to the kitchen to clear up their supper plates. She washed and dried them and put them away, just as Aunt Sarah would have wanted her to do. Then she looked at the bits and pieces from the anorak pockets.

There was nothing very interesting, though the biro might be handy. The notebook was too small to be much use, and the writing in it was just numbers next to names. One name jumped out at her. 'Sarah' it said, and there was Aunt Sarah's telephone number. Lucy had often answered the phone when it rang, and would recite the number politely before saying, "Father Copse's private residence."

Lucy ran her eye down the list. There was Drax House, and 'Father Drax private' and, the good doctors, all followed by their phone numbers. Apart from that there was nothing familiar. At the end of the list were some capital letters, but all they said was 'DRAX'. There was nothing Lucy could make use of. She didn't even have a phone. She put the biro on the worktop and threw the notebook in the bin along with the lighter and the cigarettes. On second thoughts she retrieved the notebook. There were a few empty pages in it, and it might come in handy. She put it next to the biro.

As for the plastic bag that had contained their supper, that was just what Lucy needed for the BWD file. If she had been carrying it on a night like tonight it would have been absolutely soaked, and her existence might have been washed away. It was important to keep it clean and dry. But however much she organised things for the time being, it was all pointless if she didn't know how to reach the disposal cells. She sat down at the table and picked up the notebook again and stared at the figures. The problem of the code buzzed round and round in her mind.

Paul wandered round the room, humming.

"Shush!" said Lucy. "I'm trying to think."

He climbed onto the chair opposite her and sat quietly until he was bored. Then he began to chant quietly to himself.

"A, B, C," he sang, "A is for apple, B is for boy, C is for cat." He repeated: "A is for apple, B is for boy…"

"Shush," said Lucy again.

She looked up. He was counting the letters on his fingers as he sang.

"You don't need to count A,B,C on your fingers," she laughed. "That's for when you count numbers, one, two, three."

"One, two, three," sang Paul, counting on his fingers.

"That's right. Clever boy!"

Paul looked pleased. Lucy tore a clean page out of the notebook and fetched the biro.

"There now! See if you can draw me a tiny little picture while I'm thinking," she said.

There was silence for a little while as Paul drew his picture. Then he began again. "C is for cat. C is for cat." He stopped, and Lucy looked up. He was counting on his fingers. Then he repeated, "C is for cat," and plonked a thumb and two fingers flat on the table with the remaining two curled under his hand.

"Let's see your picture," said Lucy. He scrambled down from his chair and came to stand by her side. Lucy studied the piece of paper carefully and managed to stop herself from saying, "What is it?"

"It's you and me," said Paul.

Light dawned. "Of course! I can see exactly what it is. That big circle is the gold chain – that's me – and that little circle with the flowers is you."

"Yes. We hold each other safe."

They watched the 'news where you are' again. There was another request for the public to report any sightings of a girl who looked about eleven or twelve (what a cheek!) with a boy of three or four, but there was nothing really new, and no mention of David and the social worker.

Later, as she lay in bed, Lucy's mind searched for a way to get into the Drax cells. It was hard without really knowing what the actual entrance looked like. Perhaps she could dig a hole. If she went and had a look tomorrow some idea might come to her. She just hoped it wouldn't be too late for Dorothy, but she couldn't take Paul with her on a night like this. The screwdriver or the awl might not be enough to break a padlock, but they would do for scratching out some earth or poking into a keyhole. If it weren't for the certainty that George's parents would feel obliged to hand her over to the police or a social worker, she would have asked them how to break a padlock. She regretted now that she hadn't taken the hammer and nails – she might have been able to bash it open. It would be too risky to go back for them now in case that man reappeared.

As for getting to Drax House in daytime, that could be awkward because she would have to walk past the school, and she might be recognised in the street unless she could think of a disguise. She wouldn't be able to leave Paul behind, and people would notice two children walking about in school hours. On the other hand, she couldn't leave it too late because if the primary school had come out, George might be sitting on his gate. The best time to go would be just before three.

Paul fell asleep almost immediately that night, but Lucy lay awake, her mind going round and round. Once she and Paul reached the shops no-one would notice them, but further on it would be risky. Drax House was on the left beyond the High Street and they would have to pass in front of it, as well as in front of Copse House which was on the opposite side of the road. If they managed to reach the narrow road that ran along the further side of Drax House they would be out of sight and safe. The entrance to the woodland was only a few hundred yards up that road. She could guess from David's description where the opening to the passageway into the Drax House cells would be, and then the only remaining problem would be how to get in.

In the end she decided she would have to cross that bridge when she came to it. Maybe she would be able to call out quietly to David, or even Dorothy, and they might have some ideas about the code or how to use the tools. Just as she was falling asleep she remembered the notebook and all those numbers. But none of them had six figures, and David had said the code was a six-digit number. The odd one out was DRAX which didn't have a number at all, and was only four letters. Why would Thomas have written DRAX, when he'd already put in the Drax House phone number and the private residence? She would have another look at it in the morning. Suddenly something clicked in her head. Her heart beat rapidly. Paul and his fingers! Now she was wide awake and she crept out of bed and down the stairs. She couldn't wait till tomorrow.

CHAPTER THIRTY-THREE

Paul was objecting loudly. "I don't want to!" he wailed, as Lucy struggled to pull some tights up his sturdy legs. "It's for girls."

"No, it's not. It's a disguise for boys," she said firmly. "So no-one can recognise you. It's like playing dressing up."

On the bed she had laid out a skirt taken from the little girl's room, a jumper, an outdoor jacket made of cream-coloured fake fur, a woolly hat to hide Paul's curls, and some suede leather boots.

"You might be a bit hot as it's only September," she said. "But the fur will hide the shape of your body, and the boots will hide the shape of your legs, and of course, the hat will hide your head. So there's no Paul left for anyone to see."

For herself she had the jeans she had worn yesterday, with a jumper, some clean trainers, a warm navy jacket, and a baker boy cap, all taken from the older boy's room. When she had finished they looked at themselves in the floor-length mirror next to the wardrobe. She pulled the woolly hat further down on Paul's face.

"See, no-one would ever guess it's you!" she exclaimed. "It's like being invisible."

Paul didn't look happy.

"Now," said Lucy, "the only thing wrong with me is

my hair." It was too long and heavy to go under the cap, even if she wound her pigtail round her head.

In the kitchen she found some long pointed scissors in the knife drawer. Her plait was too thick to cut through, so she pulled off the elastic band and shook her head vigorously. Soft brown hair sprung up around her face and over her shoulders in a mass of curls. Bending over the bin she hacked it off in bits until it was short enough to get the scissors near the scalp. She ran her fingers all over her head and cut away the lumpy bits until it felt like a furry ball. They studied themselves in the mirror again. Lucy was satisfied. She looked exactly like a boy, especially when she put on the cap.

"Paul and Lucy have disappeared," said Paul. "We're invisible."

Lucy pulled the blinds up slightly to let the daylight in, so that she could study the little notebook yet again. She sat down at the table and turned the pages.

Paul distracted her for a moment.

"It's too hot," he said, pulling off his woolly hat.

"Yes, it is hot. I won't be long." It was quarter to three. "We'll go soon," she said. "Be quiet now for a little while. I just want to double-check this."

She picked up the scrap of paper with Paul's drawing and turned it over. On the back she wrote: $D = 4; R = 18; A = 1; X = 24$. She set the numbers side by side: 418124. Yes, there were six digits, no mistake.

"Paul! You might be a genius," she breathed. "Only might be, but it's worth a try. Come on. Let's go. We're going to get some fresh air."

She burrowed among some shopping bags hanging on a hook in one of the kitchen cupboards, and found a canvas shoulder bag. The BWD file, wrapped up in the plastic bag, went in first, and then the screwdriver, the awl, and the torch. The notebook and the scrap of paper with Paul's drawing went in her pocket.

"Right! Off we go!" she said. "And if anyone stops us on the way, don't speak. OK? I'll do all the talking. You are not to say a word. Not a word."

They turned right out of the back gate into the alleyway, passed the father's house and two more houses, and then turned right again towards the main road. As they emerged onto the pavement they bumped straight into the woman who lived on the other side of the father's house. She stopped and looked at Lucy suspiciously.

"What have you two been doing round the back there? I hope you've not been up to mischief, and why aren't you at school, young man?"

Lucy thought quickly.

"We're looking for our cat."

The woman did not seem convinced.

"Oh yes?" She sounded very slightly disbelieving. "And what does your cat look like?"

"He's ginger. His name is Marma, short for Marmalade."

The woman stood with her hands on her hips.

"You should be in school, not looking for cats. What's your name and where do you live?"

"I'm George, and this is my sister, Elizabeth."

Paul started to hum.

"We live over there, number 38 South Hill," said Lucy hastily. "I was allowed a short break. I'm going back to school now as soon as I've taken Elizabeth home," she said, waving her hand towards the other side of the common.

The humming grew louder.

She smiled nervously at the woman and hoped she couldn't see that she was shaking inside.

"Goodbye!" she said. "Come along, Elizabeth." She stepped away firmly pulling Paul with her. They crossed the road and made their way as fast as they could over the common. The woman stood staring after them, trying to think where she'd seen them before.

On the common nobody took any notice of the young lad pulling his little sister along by the hand. Lucy kept her eyes open for suspicious characters, but it was a cold, windy day, and there was no-one around other than two joggers and a woman with a dog. As they approached the backs of the houses on South Hill they could see a drunk sleeping against a tree near the path, a bottle in his hand, and a couple of empty cans on the ground beside him. They tiptoed past. He opened one eye and shouted "Oy!" and they took to their heels and ran.

As soon as they reached South Hill they slowed to a sedate walk down the hill towards the junction. The headmaster was just coming down the school steps on the other side of the road as they passed. He glanced over at them, but showed no sign of recognition. Lucy watched him waddle round to the side of the building where he kept his car. He was probably going home for a really big tea and a nap, she thought.

Once in the High Street they blended into the crowd, tagging along behind pushchairs and toddlers whenever they could. The most nerve-wracking bit was walking between the two sets of big bay windows that stared at them from Drax House and Copse House. Lucy tried to assume a confident and purposeful air, as though she were on her way to take a message to her grandmother, or some such thing. She briefly wondered if she had a grandmother somewhere in the world. When they reached the side road on the left just past Drax House, she heaved a sigh of relief. There was no-one in sight. They found the opening into the woodland three hundred yards up, and disappeared inside.

Almost immediately Lucy was struck by doubt. There was no real reason to suppose that David was in the Drax cells. It was only panic that had made her think he was. He might be living comfortably in the home of a kind foster mother at this very moment. As for poor Dorothy, it was unlikely the Holy Leaders would have kept her there for long once the police had caught whoever it was on the common. Lucy tried not to visualise the sickening consequences if she and Paul were too late.

In the woods Paul held tightly onto her hand, and looked around him at the trees and the undergrowth with eyes wide open.

"Where's the gingerbread house?" he whispered.

"It's alright," said Lucy. "There's no gingerbread house here. You're safe with me." She tried to sound confident, but her voice shook slightly.

They approached the back of Drax House through the trees and paused when they reached the edge of the wood. To the left, among the brambles and stinging nettles, she could just see part of an iron-barred grating set into the ground. Beyond it there were more brambles, and several yards further on was the high wooden fence to the back garden.

The fence was so high that it seemed unlikely to Lucy that anyone in the house would see them approaching, especially if they crouched very low. She was not sure whether to leave Paul where he was and to go on her own to the grating, or to take him with her.

"Will you wait here while I go into those prickly bushes?" she asked him. "I'll be very quick."

He clung even harder onto her hand.

"I like prickly bushes," he insisted.

They crept forward quietly, trying to trample down the worst of the prickles. By the time they reached the grating Paul's borrowed tights above the suede boots were full of snags and holes. Lying on their stomachs they looked down into a steep passageway that disappeared into darkness in the direction of Drax House. They put their ears to the metal bars. There wasn't a sound. Lucy whispered, "Dorothy? David?" down into the void, but there was no reply. Paul put his face onto the bars and started to hum. Lucy called again as loudly as she dared, but no-one called back.

The grating was chained. Lucy reached through the bars, and pulled a heavy piece of chain and a large padlock towards her. It was different from the padlock on David's bike. There were six little wheels with numbers on it, and she guessed that they were for the code. She pulled Paul's drawing out of her pocket and studied the numbers on the other side. Closing her eyes she almost said a prayer to the Magnifico, but stopped herself just in time. She turned the little wheels until the numbers matched those on her piece of paper and waited for the hoop to jump up. Nothing happened. She felt sick with disappointment.

"Let me see," said Paul, reaching for the padlock. She passed it over to him, too dejected to think what to do next. Paul turned it over in his hand. It was heavy, and he dropped it back onto the metal bars with a clang.

"Shush!" whispered Lucy hoarsely. "They'll hear us in the house. Come on. Let's go back."

As she spoke the padlock gave a little click. She picked it up and the metal hoop swung round. They both looked at in disbelief.

"It's worked. You've done it!"

When they'd recovered from their astonishment Lucy tugged at the grating. She gave a little groan. "Now we've got to try to lift this thing."

It took them a while to unwind the chain because it was long and heavy and had been twisted round the rods of the grating several times. As soon as they had managed to get it all out onto the ground they started pulling at the rods, but the edges of the grating were blocked up with mud washed in by yesterday's rain, and it wouldn't budge. Lucy took the screwdriver and awl out of the canvas bag. She handed the awl to Paul.

"Poke the earth out along the edges with this. And be careful. Don't poke yourself with it," she said, starting to dig out the mud with the screwdriver.

The two of them scratched and poked until the rim was clear. Lucy grabbed the grating again and pulled upwards. It moved slightly. It was a lot bigger than the grating over the coal hole in the father's cellar, and much heavier. She found a thick piece of wood and handed it to Paul.

"When I lift the metal you must try and push this under it, just here, so I can get a grip," she said. "But you mustn't push your fingers under with it."

Paul stood poised ready for action. Lucy grabbed the outer bars and pulled up with all her strength.

"Quick! Now!" she gasped, and Paul shoved the wood between the grating and the rim.

"Good boy," panted Lucy. "Well done."

Bit by bit they built up the leverage with some larger pieces of wood and a couple of logs they found among the trees, until Lucy was able to give one gigantic pull upwards and the grating stood upright on its hinges. She pushed it backwards, and the entrance to the passage was fully open.

"Phew!" she puffed, straightening her back and shaking her arms. "Thank goodness for that. Now we must hurry. That took absolutely ages!"

CHAPTER THIRTY-FOUR

Father Arthur's bed and breakfast was comfortable. He'd had a good lie-in followed by a hearty meal of bacon and eggs, toast, and coffee. The landlady had served him, and he'd given her his smile. He heard her whisper, "…gives me the creeps," when she went back into her kitchen. A couple of elderly residents were seated quietly at the window table, and he wondered which one she was talking about.

It was an overcast, miserable day and he didn't intend leaving the house until late afternoon. The woods behind Drax House would be dark and gloomy and he would be able to wait hidden in the bushes until the light had faded enough for him to start prowling. The September evenings were still long, but dusk would fall early on a dismal day like this.

He sat in the residents' lounge, and watched television. There was no rush. On the local news there was something about Claudia's abduction, but nothing about Maria or the Holy Cause. It looked as though neither she nor the man who had been caught on the common had talked. At five o'clock he had a cup of tea and told the landlady he'd be back later, and left the house. Within half an hour he was in the side road beyond Drax House. He checked that there was no-one to see him, and then he turned sharply left into the woods.

Before finding himself a good place to hide in comfort he decided to have a quick look at the back of Drax House to see if there was any sign of Thomas. He made his way through the undergrowth towards the fence. The brambles had already been trampled down to make a path, and he guessed that someone had passed this way in the last few days, presumably fetching a sinner for disposal. He moved cautiously because he had no wish to meet any of Drax's henchmen. As he drew nearer the fence he could see that the grating to the disposal passageway was open. He realised with surprise that they must be about to bring someone out. That was not normally done while it was still daylight – it was too big a risk.

Taking the torch out of the canvas bag Lucy shone it onto stone stairs that led down into the darkness. She lowered herself into the hole and Paul scrambled after her. There were ten steps. They were a good width and were not worn or sloping. It would not be difficult, thought Lucy, for a big man to carry up a body for disposal. The passageway was about seven foot high. There were stone slabs on the floor, and the walls and ceiling were lined with timber. Lucy was surprised at how clean it was. She had expected something like the coal cellar in the father's house.

She held tightly on to Paul's hand and, gathering confidence, they moved silently along the passage following the light from the torch. Every now and then alcoves had been built into the walls, some with hooks holding what looked like dark cloaks, and others with shelves for coils of rope, and torches, and handcuffs, and rolled-up blankets or sleeping bags.

They came to a slight bend and then a fork in the

passageway. They took the right-hand fork and, almost immediately, a glimmer of light appeared several yards ahead. Lucy switched off the torch as they tiptoed towards the light. It filtered through a grille in a door at the end of the passage. Lucy had to stand on tiptoe to peep in. Paul pulled at her leg whining softly, "Let me see, let me see." There was nothing to see, just a small dimly lit room with a table and chair, and a dark bundle of something on a bed in the furthest corner. Lucy picked Paul up with difficulty, and he pressed his face to the bars.

"It's a lady," he said.

Lucy dropped him with a thump.

Dorothy lay on the bed, a heap of black clothes. It was all her fault. If she hadn't run away David would never have been in the cell next door. He'd be having a laugh with Matthew and planning some stupid joke. She wondered what the time was. If it was evening they'd be up on the common with their bikes, showing off to the girls, with their whole lives in front of them. She'd know when it was evening because the kitchen aunts would come with yet another unwanted meal, like a sort of clock. Her ears strained for footsteps, but there was nothing.

Suddenly she heard whispering and a soft thump. It didn't come from the direction of Drax House.

Dorothy's heart jumped into her mouth and she sat up. There were people in the disposal passageway. So they'd come for her at last. Had they come for David too? She crawled off the bed and stood up shakily, facing the passageway. Then she pulled herself up, put her shoulders back and held her head up straight. "Be proud," she said to herself.

Lucy peered through the grille again and, sure enough, the dark bundle in the corner had stood up and was staring towards her, its face a ghastly white.

"Dorothy!" she whispered through the bars. "It's alright. It's Lucy – and Paul." She started burrowing in the canvas bag. "I've got a screwdriver and something pointy to try and break open the lock."

"I think there's a key." Dorothy's voice shook. "Look! Over there behind you."

The torch lit up an alcove about three feet behind Lucy, well out of reach of the cell door.

"That's it. On that hook just above that pile of handcuffs."

Lucy grabbed the key and with shaking hands pushed it in the lock. Nothing happened.

"Let me try," said Dorothy urgently, pushing her hand through the grille and snatching the key.

She pushed and pulled at the door. Suddenly it flew open, and she leaped out into the passageway.

"David's in the next cell! How can we get at him?"

"There was a fork in the passageway. He's probably up there. Quick! We'll have to go back. I know where it is." Lucy gave her a push. "You run! Take Paul and just keep going straight. I'll get David."

But Paul had already entered the cell and was inspecting it. A single light bulb dangled over the table, and the corners of the room were dark. There were no interesting-looking books or magazines, or drawing paper. He climbed onto the bed and jumped up and down.

Lucy followed him in and grabbed him. "Shush!" she hissed. "We've got to hurry. You can't play now."

As she spoke they heard footsteps approaching down the corridor from the direction of Drax House.

"Someone's coming!" Lucy called quietly to Dorothy. "Quick! Come back in and look as though nothing's happened. Paul, hurry! Get under the bed."

They shut the door to the passageway swiftly and silently, and Paul and Lucy disappeared under the bed. Dorothy threw herself on top of it, dissolving once more into a bundle of black cloth.

A key turned in the lock and two kitchen aunts appeared in the doorway. One placed a tray on the table. The other remained firmly on the threshold, ready to pounce at the slightest sign of movement. Dorothy lay languishing in a heap on the bed. Lucy could just see the aunts' feet. Good, strong, sensible shoes. Paul too could see the shoes from his corner under the bed. They reminded him of Aunt Sarah. He started to hum very quietly. Lucy's heart froze. Then he began his chant.

"I can see you. I can hear you." His voice rose in a crescendo. "I can watch your every action."

The aunts stood stock still. They looked at Dorothy who lay silent and expressionless on the bed. The chant was repeated, louder and louder, and then broke into a wail. Dorothy's lips didn't move. With a look of absolute terror on their faces the aunts screamed and ran. They left the door wide open with the key still in the lock and another key dangling from it. Lucy scrambled out, ran to the door and pulled out both keys. Dorothy's eyes were tight shut. She couldn't move.

"Come on!" said Lucy, shaking her. "Get up. Look! There are two keys. One might be David's. Quick! Before they come back."

She hauled Paul out from under the bed.

"You sang that beautifully," she said, "but we never want to hear it again."

Dorothy gathered her wits. She leaped to her feet and dashed out to the lobby.

"David!" she called with her eye to the peephole in the door of the next cell.

Lucy's hands were shaking so hard she nearly dropped the keys. The second one worked. Dorothy dragged David out by his sleeve and pushed him into her own cell. Lucy locked the door from the inside and they dashed across into the passageway, their hearts thumping and their ears buzzing.

CHAPTER THIRTY-FIVE

Keeping his huge frame as low to the ground as he could, Father Arthur approached the passageway and listened. He knew it well because in his youth he had often assisted in carrying the sinners out, handcuffed beneath dark cloaks or wrapped in blankets, with balaclavas hiding the gags over their mouths. Sometimes they had been sedated with syringes and pushed into sleeping bags and thrown over powerful shoulders. Big strong men like himself were expected to volunteer for the task of bringing them out. He had enjoyed the undercover adventure of it all, and was briefly envious of the strong young men who had taken over from him.

Leaning down past the grating he could hear no sign of movement. He quietly descended the stone stairs and, keeping one hand on the wall to his left, he moved carefully along, ready to back into one of the many alcoves at the first sign of activity. He rounded the bend just before the path forked and thought he could hear sounds coming from the right.

Torchlight wavered in the distance and there was a rustle of whispering voices. He moved a little nearer and stopped again to listen. The whispering grew louder. It sounded like children's voices. So it wasn't a disposal after all. It was children, children playing in the woods no doubt, whose adventures had taken them into forbidden territory. It was a pity because he had nothing against children as long as they weren't his responsibility and didn't cost him anything, but they would have to be stopped before they talked to their parents or to half the neighbourhood. The last thing the Holy Leaders would want would be children playing in the disposal passageway.

He drew himself back into a deep alcove. There was a shelf piled with coils of rope and blankets at shoulder level, so he had to stoop, and he knocked his head against a row of hooks as he settled himself in. Muttering a swear word followed by a hasty prayer, he felt around in the darkness and pulled a big black cloak over himself, and waited.

With trembling fingers Dorothy hurriedly locked the cell door from the outside. Lucy put the keys in her canvas bag, grabbed Paul's hand, and shone the torch down the passage. Then they ran.

Lucy and Paul were ahead, with David immediately behind. Dorothy came last, but she was tall and had no problem seeing the torchlight over the heads in front of her. It was impossible for any of the older ones to run very fast because of Paul, and they could have screamed with the slowness of it.

"You go first," said Lucy, pulling aside to let the others pass. "We're holding you up."

"No, go on, quick!" David pushed them on. The blood was pounding in their ears. If the disposal officers reached the passageway entrance from the outside before they did, they would be trapped from both directions – ahead and behind.

They ran on. Suddenly Lucy found herself flat

on the floor, pinned to the ground. She had let go of Paul's hand and the torch had gone flying. It flickered and went out. For a few seconds the passage was pitch dark, and then the torch flickered on again. She could see Paul pressed up against the wall to her left, a look of astonishment on his face. Her immediate thought was that his fake fur coat would have softened any blow, and then gasping and grunting noises told her that David was struggling with someone just behind her.

She screwed her head sideways to see that an enormous foot was pressed into the small of her back. David was trying to shout Run! Run! but his voice came out in a strangled cry. His arm was held by a massive hand in a grip like a vice. It belonged to a monster with a shining bald head who, at that moment, was twisting round and stretching with his free arm to reach a coil of cord from a shelf in the wall. With the foot firmly on the middle of her back Lucy was unable to move. The monster pulled David round and bent down to tie his wrists behind his back. As he did so a sharp set of teeth sank into his ankle. He cursed and shook Paul off, trying to give him a good kick as he went. Paul nipped neatly out of his way.

"You can't reach me," he shouted. "I'm invisible."

Lucy took her chance and rolled sideways and tried to scramble to her feet, only to be kicked down and stamped on again. Dorothy stood stock still and silent in the darkness behind them, holding a cloak and a long piece of cord in her hands. Her heart thumped and she held her breath. The man bent once more to tie David's hands, muttering incoherently. As he leaned forward Dorothy threw the cloak over his head and pulled it back under his chin. He staggered backwards, grabbing at his head, and fell. David jumped away from him and Lucy sprang to her feet. Dorothy had dropped the cord and was struggling to hold the cloak in place by twisting it behind the man's neck, while his powerful hands tugged at the cloth and he somehow managed to wriggle himself up onto his knees.

David snatched the cord up off the floor and tied it round one thick wrist. He was not strong enough to pull the hand away fully, but the other hand instinctively released its grip on the cloth and shot across in front of the neck to try and seize the cord.

Dorothy pulled the cloak down harder over the floundering head. With difficulty Lucy hung on to the two writhing wrists. She was flung from side to side as David tied them as close together as he could. There was not much time. Every second that passed could bring the disposal squad closer to them. For good measure Dorothy wound another rope firmly round the mighty neck to hold the cloak in place, and tied it in a knot at the back well away from the fettered hands.

She felt in the pockets of the monster's raincoat. They were stuffed with money, but she only took the mobile phone.

"I'm going to phone the police to tell them where you are," she hissed close to his ear through the layers of cloth. "And I shall tell them who you are too. I saw your face when you turned. I'd know you anywhere you disgusting pervert, even without the hair."

Lucy picked up the torch and they ran as fast as Paul's legs would permit towards the entrance to the passage.

"If you hear anyone coming," puffed Dorothy, "hide in one of these alcoves."

As they approached the light from the entrance Lucy

switched off the torch. They hurled themselves up the steps and into what was left of the daylight.

"Give me the code, quick!" said Dorothy.

She stood to one side with the mobile phone and gave the police the code and hasty details of where to find the underground passageway, while David and Lucy closed the grating and scrabbled for the chain and the padlock.

"He's called Father Copse, but he's shaved off his hair," Dorothy was saying.

David grabbed her arm and shouted into the phone. "His house burned down on Friday night. In Mortimor Road."

Meanwhile Lucy had managed to twist the chain round the rods and locked the padlock.

"He'll know the code," she said breathlessly, "but at least it'll hold him up for a couple of minutes."

Dorothy threw down the phone.

"Ugh! I can't bear to touch his horrible stuff," she said, wiping her hands on a piece of grass. "Gross!" She was trembling and her face was a deathly white against the black of her clothes.

"How do you know it was the police and not an infiltrator?" asked Lucy.

"I don't, but whoever they were, we don't want them to know where we are. Come on. Let's go!"

They ran, tripping and stumbling over the brambles and nettles, into the wood. The sound of a car engine from the direction of the side road made them stop for a second to listen. There was a slamming of doors followed by voices. With a final spurt they veered away, raced across a small stretch of bare ground towards the undergrowth, and threw themselves down behind the roots and twisted branches of a low growing willow. They held their breath and watched as two men hastened across the rough ground towards the grating and started working on the padlock. One of them switched on a torch shaped like a lantern, and then they lifted the grating and disappeared down the stone steps. David darted over and pulled down the grating as silently as he could. He carefully and quietly pulled part of the chain round one of the steel rods, clicked the padlock into place, and ran back to the others.

"They might have heard that, but it'll confuse them," he said. "It'll give us a few extra seconds to get away. Let's go!"

"We can't go to the side road," whispered Dorothy. "There might be a driver waiting for them."

"The quickest way to the High Street would be to cut down through the Drax House garden," said David.

"Yes. There's that narrow side path." said Dorothy, her voice shaking. "It's a risk but there are lots of bushes. They're more likely to search for us in the woods. It won't occur to them we'd dare go through the garden."

They hastened towards a small back gate in the fencing, opened it cautiously, and stepped inside onto a concrete path. It curved and twisted between shrubs and flowerbeds on the right-hand side of the garden all the way down to the main road.

It was still daylight but the sky was heavy and grey.

"There are lights on in the house," whispered Dorothy. "If they look out of the window the garden will seem dark to them. Keep low and go slowly. Any quick movement might catch their attention."

She took Paul's hand and pulled him over to her right side, so that her black clothing blocked out his cream-coloured fake fur jacket. They slipped silently down the path with pounding hearts, sometimes hidden from the house by shrubs, and sometimes totally exposed.

As they passed the kitchen area one of the aunts came out to put something in the bin. The children froze and held their breath, fully visible to anyone who cared to look. Someone called from inside the house and the aunt went in and shut the door. They scuttled behind the next set of bushes and then out the other side. There was a light on in the dining room, and as they passed the window they could see the Drax House children filing in for their supper and bowing their heads in prayer.

"Poor fools!" muttered Dorothy.

The nearer they drew to the High Street the harder it was not to run. They could almost feel the Magnifico's horrible breath on their necks.

Aunt Bertha had been sent upstairs. The others were fed up with her constant crying, and now they were all in a tizzy because of the wailing spirits in the cells.

"Pull yourselves together," Aunt Sonia had snapped. "There's no such thing as a wailing spirit. The men have gone to investigate and there will be a simple scientific explanation." She had turned to Bertha. "And you – go to your room and stay there till you can control your emotions."

Now Bertha sat in the dark by the window. She didn't care about wailing spirits. All she could think of was Dorothy, David and John, and the others that she had helped raise from babyhood only to see them go the same way. She hoped the Magnifico in His mercy would forgive her, but however hard she tried she could not accept the purpose with a joyous heart. She raised her swollen eyes to the window and gazed out into the darkness. Something flickered in the garden. What a misery life was. If only some of the glories of the next world could be spared for the here and now. Whatever it was flickered again, and she leaned forward, suddenly alert.

She could just make out the shapes of the shrubs, but nothing moved. It must have been some sort of reflection from the lights downstairs. Then, sure enough, something flashed through the gap between one shrub and another and disappeared. Bertha knew that head of hair. She would have known it anywhere. Ash blond they called it – just like his mother's. She couldn't breathe. A ghost? She tried to clear the muzziness in her head. They couldn't have done it already – there wasn't time.

She strained her eyes and the darkness yielded slightly. The flicker reappeared with a shape below it this time, and other shapes before it and behind it. With her hand to her throat, Bertha watched the intermittent procession. She held her breath until it reached the gate and vanished.

The aunts were in a huddle in the kitchen, whispering about the wailing spirit. As the door opened it squeaked and they clutched each other in fright. It was only Bertha. Then they looked again and gaped at the joy in her face. She beamed at them but said nothing. Going over to the table she picked up the potato peeler and quietly got on with her work. How great was the Magnifico in His goodness and mercy!

"Look casual," whispered Dorothy, trying to keep the panic out of her voice.

She straightened her back as though she had all the confidence in the world. Nobody grabbed them. They stepped out through a little wooden gate onto the pavement and turned off to the right. Their strength dissolved immediately. Now their teeth started to chatter and their legs were like jellies. They couldn't have run if they tried. As they merged with the throng of evening shoppers two wailing police cars wove their way through the traffic. One halted directly in front of Drax House, and the other passed it and turned left up the side road.

The children turned their backs on the police cars and moved away down the hill.

"Where do we go next?" said David.

"You can come back with us." Lucy's voice was shaking. "Come on. It's not far. Just over the common." But it seemed very far, an eternity of forcing one foot after another, yet hardly moving. They stumbled rather than walked, and at one point Dorothy nearly fell as someone rushed past her towards the Underground station. When at last they reached the wide open space of the common their legs regained some strength and speeded up, and although they couldn't help looking behind them and around them constantly, the sense of suppressed panic subsided a little.

As they approached the bushes around the pond, something glittered.

"Stop!" whispered Lucy. "There's somebody there."

The leaves rustled in the wind and parted for a second. Their hearts stood still.

"Who's there?" called David hoarsely. There was no reply. He stepped forward. "Phew! It's nobody. It's only my bike." Now they could see the shiny handlebars glinting through the leaves. "Leave it," he said, and they hurried on.

CHAPTER THIRTY-SIX

Dorothy lay in the copper bath, a neat little radio playing music on the stool next to her, and a soft fluffy bath robe waiting for her to slip into it. A scented candle cast a gentle light too faint to be seen through the Austrian blind that draped the frosted glass of the window. On the floor in a far corner of the bathroom lay a bundle of shapeless black clothes.

She closed her eyes and tried to let the warmth of the water wash away the terror. Don't panic, she told herself. Everything's going to be alright now.

Downstairs Paul lay asleep on the sofa in the television room in a snug pair of pyjamas taken from the little boy's room. Thanks to David's interpretation of the symbols on the washing machine in the laundry room, the fake fur coat and the rest of the disguise outfit were twirling around on the wool cycle. With shaking hands Lucy was laying the kitchen table with pretty plates and glasses that she'd found in a sideboard in the dining room. David made a silent inspection of the freezer. He took out four frozen pizzas and put them in the oven, pressing what he hoped was the right button. The television was just a floating murmur of voices as Lucy listened out for the music that would herald the news. The regional news would be another hour yet, but she didn't want to miss it.

Although they had the electric power there was still no lighting, and they ate in silence by torchlight.

The pizzas were edible but no-one, except Paul, could taste a thing. David, moving mechanically, put the plates in the sink, and Lucy scooped out the ice cream into bowls. When they had finished doing their best to eat they cleared up, and Lucy fetched a jigsaw puzzle from upstairs. She and Paul sat in the torchlight at the kitchen table, and quietly put it together.

"I bit the monster's leg," remarked Paul.

"So you did!" said Lucy, as calmly as she could. "You were very helpful. I'm proud of you. He's gone now and he'll never come back, so we're safe."

Her hands were still trembling as she pressed the jigsaw pieces into place.

Dorothy and David were huddled silent and ashen-faced on the sofa in the television room. The screen flickered in front of their faces, but they didn't see it. All they saw was the disposal cells. Outside the wind blew up. A shrub brushed against the window, and they clutched at each other.

"It's only the wind," whispered David.

Dorothy closed her eyes and breathed deeply. If only her heart would stop thumping she might be able to think properly.

The jigsaw was completed and put away, and Paul and Lucy joined the others in the television room. Lucy turned the sound up slightly. "It'll be the news in about fifteen minutes," she said quietly, "so it's important that we listen out for it."

The others nodded. Nobody spoke, until Lucy remembered something horrible. "What about Matthew?" she whispered.

"Dead," said David. "Serve him right."

Dorothy was roused from her semi-stupor. "What on earth?"

"I'll explain it all sometime. He was an infiltrator! My so-called best mate!" He stood up and paced around angrily.

Lucy's stomach lurched. "I felt the car bump over him."

"What are you talking about?" Dorothy was sitting up straight.

"He was following me. These men caught Lucy and put her in the boot, and it backed right over Matthew."

"Holy Mag!" exclaimed Dorothy. "What have I missed?"

"Please don't use that expression. It makes me feel sick. Anyway, I locked him in a cupboard because I couldn't get rid of him and, obviously, he got out. The aunts would have guessed where I was. They knew something was going to happen at Father Copse's house."

"Save our souls! And everyone really liked him!"

"That's why they chose him, I suppose."

"What with him and Thomas I don't see how we can ever trust anyone again," said Lucy.

"We can't," said Dorothy, taking a deep breath. "We'll have to face the fact that we can only trust ourselves." She glanced at the television. "Come on, David. Sit down. It's nearly time. They might tell us something on the news."

They sat subdued, squashed together on the sofa, and waited.

Suddenly they sat up straight. The national news was announcing a police siege outside a religious commune suspected of having connections with an alleged abduction and a recent fire at a London property. Drax House and the cordon round it appeared on the screen, and both Dorothy and David gasped as they recognised the caretaker and Senior Aunt Sonia being escorted to a police car.

There was a fuller story on the local news. Three men had been brought out of a tunnel at the back of a religious commune known as Drax House, and various members of the household had been taken into custody. The whereabouts of the so-called Father Drax who ran the commune were unknown. One of the men in the tunnel was believed to be the owner of the house in Mortimor Road that had burned down on Friday night.

A picture of the remains of Father Copse's house appeared briefly on the screen.

The public was asked to report any sightings of a stout elderly woman with two children, a girl and a boy aged about eleven and three respectively, who had gone missing from the burned-out house. A next-door neighbour had been unable to help, other than to say the girl always wore her hair in a long plait. She had described the family as keeping themselves to themselves. The body found at the scene of the fire had still not been identified. Another body, found in the road outside the house, had been identified as a teenage resident of Drax House.

The children were absolutely riveted. The Magnifico's world seemed to be collapsing before their very eyes.

Later that night, as he clambered into the big bed, Paul whispered, "We're safe now, aren't we, Lucy?"

"Of course we are," she said. "I expect the monster man is in prison by now, all tied up in chains."

Paul stroked the gold chain that lay round Lucy's neck, and gently fingered the circle of daffodils until he fell asleep.

CHAPTER THIRTY-SEVEN

The children spent the next few days quietly, apart from a couple of scares. Once somebody knocked on the door and went away. Then two men looked around the garden at the back of the house. They didn't seem to notice the missing pane in the back door, and they too went away. Occasional peeps through the upstairs curtains showed that the visits of officialdom to the site of the fire were diminishing, and they began to relax. Their appetites returned and David worked out how to use the microwave.

"We've been here nearly a week," said Dorothy. "We'll have to think about what to do next. We can't stay here for ever. Supposing the people come back?"

Where could they go? The same thought ran through all their minds. The outside world was daunting, and they would never find anywhere as luxurious as this, so they might as well try and unwind for one more night – or perhaps two.

"I've got a friend," said Dorothy slowly. "His name is Tom. He helped me before and if we can find him he might help us again. He went away but he should be back by now. I think I'll know where to find him."

Their spirits lifted a little. "We'll have to tidy up here before we go," said Lucy. "It's bad enough that we've used their stuff, without leaving a mess."

"Well, at least we've got no baggage to weigh us down," said David. "All we have to do is get on our feet and walk. Easy!"

"What about your bike?" asked Lucy. "It could be useful for carrying stuff."

"It's a nice bike," said Dorothy. "Almost new."

"Yeah, but I don't want it. I don't want anything they've given me. Someone can find it and keep it."

"It's a shame," said Lucy. "I always wanted a bike. It seems such a waste."

Dorothy agreed. "Perhaps we could sell it and get some money."

"Tell you what," said Lucy. "That's if you don't mind, David. When it gets dark I'll nip across the road and fetch it, and we can clean it up and think about it. If you really and truly don't want it I could find a use for it."

"I'll fetch it," said David. "Someone might recognise you, even if you have turned into a boy."

"You'll have to watch out for the nosy neighbour."

Later that evening they gave the bike a good wipe down in the kitchen, and it gleamed in the torchlight.

"Are you really sure you don't want it?" asked Lucy.

Dorothy turned on her sharply.

"What would you want it for?" she asked. The old panic grabbed at her. "You're not going somewhere without us, are you?"

"No! Of course not! I don't even know how to ride a bike. It's a friend who helped me, and I said he'd have a reward in due course. I didn't have anything for him so it was an empty promise, and now I've had time to think about things I feel really bad about that."

Lucy turned to David. "You've met him. He's George, the one on the gate who said about nutters."

"I remember him. He was right. They're worse than nutters. He can have it if you like."

Lucy studied the bike a bit doubtfully.

"It might be much too big for him. I think he's only ten. He's still at the primary school."

"That's alright," said David. "All he has to do is lower the saddle and the handlebars, just here."

"His father will know how to do that. He can do everything."

"Right then," said David.

"I can't imagine what would have happened to me, and to Paul, and even the tenant, if George hadn't shown me how to get a key out from the other side of the door so we could find my existence record and escape."

They were silent for a moment. Then Dorothy said, "And if you hadn't escaped, you couldn't have rescued David and me."

The enormity of their gratitude to George began to sink in. Lucy took Thomas's biro out of her bag and tore a page from the little notebook. She wrote: *For George, his reward from Lucy and her friends. You saved our lives. Thank you for ever.* Using a piece of ribbon she found in the kitchen drawer, she tied the message to the handlebars.

"Aren't you afraid to go out again?" asked Dorothy anxiously. "We'll come with you. Or why don't you wait till tomorrow? I don't want you to go. It's such a risk."

"I'll be less noticeable on my own, and I'd rather do it tonight while it's dark and get it over with. I don't think I'll ever be as scared as I was in the Drax House garden. I'll be about twenty minutes," she said, pulling the baker boy hat firmly down over her curls. "Ten minutes there, and ten minutes back."

She wheeled the bike out along the back alley and

down to the road. There was no-one in sight. It was dark, and on the common she was afraid. Supposing that drunk had come back, or, even worse, supposing the monster had escaped from the police? If only she could cycle. It must be a wonderful sensation to be mobile and free, and able to escape if someone chased you.

It was late-night shopping in the High Street and there were still quite a few people about when she emerged from the lane onto South Hill. Down at the bottom of the hill the tube station was disgorging its late commuters. Lucy hoped they wouldn't see anything suspicious about someone who looked like a boy pushing a bike when he should have been at home having his supper. No-one took any notice of her as they made their weary way up the hill. The pavement cleared and she was relieved. Then, suddenly, a group of youths burst out of the Underground and swaggered up the hill towards her.

She tried to cross the road but there was no gap in the late rush hour traffic, and the gang was upon her before she could duck into a front garden. Somebody grabbed the handlebars of the bike, and another boy pulled off her cap and threw it up into the air.

"Where d'ja think y're goin', Curly locks?" sniggered one of them. "Nice bike you got there. It'd just suit my young brother."

"Look! He's tied a pretty ribbon to his handlebars!" jeered another, and they all laughed as he pulled it off. The little note fluttered to the ground. The boy leaned over and grabbed Lucy by a tuft of hair. "Let's see if we can tie up his girly curly locks with ribbon and make him look sweet!" he cried, to approving guffaws and whistles.

Lucy jerked her head away. For once her quick mind

was numb. The skin on her face was tight and a vice squeezed her throat.

At that moment there was a shout from the bottom of the hill and a joint cry of triumph, and a gang of youths with shaven heads came pounding up the pavement towards them. Within seconds Lucy found herself standing alone as they swept past on each side of her and her adversaries disappeared into the distance.

Leaning the bike against a wall she picked up her cap and put it on her head. She waited for her legs to steady themselves, looked around for the scrap of paper and the ribbon, and then shakily carried on the few more yards to George's house. Everything went smoothly. The gate opened quietly. There was a light on in the hall and in the front room. The curtain was closed, but she could hear the sound of the television. She propped the bike up against the wall inside the porch. The paper with its message was screwed up tightly in her hand. She smoothed it out. It was muddy, but still readable. With fingers as clumsy as frozen sausages she tied it to the handlebar. Then she rang the bell and ran silently down the path, up the hill to the lane and onto the common. Reckoning that she could run faster than all the drunks and monsters in the world, she took a deep breath and flew over the common, crossed the road, and reached the alley out of breath and gasping with relief.

There was no mention of the commune on the national news that night. The children were disappointed.

"I hope they're not going to forget about it," said Lucy anxiously when it finished.

"I suppose it just means there's nothing new to report yet." Dorothy was anxious too. It would be helpful to have some sort of information before they decided what to do next.   "Perhaps there'll be something on the local news."

She was right. When the local news came on they sat straight backed, all ears. The woman who had been rescued from the fire at number 3 Mortimor Road was showing signs of emerging from her coma. A spokesman for the Mortimor Hospital explained that the process could take some time, and a full recovery was not yet imminent.

"Of course! The tenant! I'd forgotten all about her," exclaimed Lucy. "How could I?"

"Holy Mag! I mean Holy Bag!" cried David. "So had I, and all this time I've known where she is, and it went right out of my mind!"

The others stared. "You know where she is and you never said?" exclaimed Dorothy.

"How could I have not remembered!" David groaned. "It was the caretaker – the fake social worker – he was telling the kitchen aunts all about it when he brought me in. He said she's in a private room off Ward 14 at the Mortimor, and they're going to try and dispose of her before she comes round. And that was ages ago. Anything could have happened since then."

The children digested the information. "Well, at least we know it's not happened yet," said Lucy, "or she wouldn't just be coming out of a coma."

"We'll have to do something before they get at her!" announced Dorothy. "It's too late to do anything tonight. Let's work out a plan for tomorrow. We'll just have to keep our fingers crossed it's not too late."

The pain had gone from Father Arthur's head and it was filled with a glorious light. Of course he had been hurt that his own children had betrayed him – children by whom he had always done his holy duty – but now he could see it was all part of the purpose. The Magnifico had been good to him. He had been chosen.

These fools had asked if he wanted a lawyer. Why on earth would he want a lawyer? They were talking about the non-followers' law, not the Magnifico's law. Their law had no relevance to him other than that it was the way he had earned his living, and now he would never need to earn his living again. He would be housed, clothed and fed, and it would cost him nothing for the rest of his life. They'd wanted him to make a statement. Why should he make a statement when he wasn't subject to their law? They'd wanted to know if he was guilty or not guilty. He couldn't even be bothered to respond.

He no longer needed the comfort of the woman's hair, for the Magnifico had smiled upon him and had lifted away his burdens. No more wives, no more children, no more Drax. In a cell for the rest of his life he would be free. All he would need would be a copy of the *Holy Vision*. He would let his beard grow long and preach to convert his fellow inmates. The food wouldn't be as good as Sarah's, but that was a small sacrifice to make. From now on he was a martyr for the Holy Cause, on the path to glory.

He stood up and put his mouth to the grille in the door and lifted his eyes towards Paradise. "Praise be to the Magnifico!" he thundered. "Beware the fire of the burning flesh!"

"Shurrup!" came a voice from the next-door cell.

CHAPTER THIRTY-EIGHT

Paul had slept well snuggled up against Lucy's side while she lay staring into the blackness of the night, listening for the slightest sound. The three older children had hardly slept at all. Now, in the light of day, their nightmares had been pushed aside and were replaced by a jittery cheerfulness.

"I think we're all going to have to face the fact that we'll have nightmares for the rest of our lives," Dorothy announced at breakfast, trying her best to sound matter-of-fact. "We'll just have to accept that. But we must be positive and remember it's a small sacrifice to make for the good that has come out of all this."

"You sound like Senior Aunt Sonia," said David with a nervous laugh.

Dorothy continued as though she was giving a lecture. "Not only have we managed to escape, but also we've managed to destroy the commune and perhaps the Magnifico with it. That's a considerable achievement!"

"A considerable achievement," echoed Paul.

David nodded his head vigorously. "That's what we'll always have to remember," he said, "whenever we think scary thoughts. We achieved something good."

Lucy said nothing. The only one who seemed genuinely unshaken was Paul.

After breakfast they cleared up and tried to eliminate all signs of their stay.

"We don't want the owners to be able to trace us by finding our clothes or Lucy's hair in the bin," said David. "They might get a police dog to take up the scent. We'll have to look for a rubbish bin somewhere between here and the hospital."

Dorothy was doubtful. "There won't be one big enough," she said. "Not for everything."

"We could take a black bag to the bushes just inside the father's back gate when we go past," suggested Lucy. "If anyone finds it they'll think I cut my hair off there, and that we changed our clothes there. They'll never guess we were in this house, and if we empty the bag the rain will wash our scent away."

So that was agreed. There was nothing they could do about stolen food and stolen clothes, but they cleaned the bathroom and the kitchen, made the beds, and put any rubbish and the contents of the kitchen bin into a black plastic bin liner.

"Ugh!" grunted Dorothy, as she shoved her black disposal cell clothes into the bag. "I'll never wear black ever again. They said it would help me make my peace with the Magnifico when I went before His Almighty Throne of Judgment!" She shivered and washed her hands thoroughly at the sink. "It makes me feel dirty just to touch it. And why me? They let David keep his own clothes."

Lucy was staring at Dorothy's bare wrists, a look of horror on her face.

"What's the matter?"

"Your reminder!" croaked Lucy.

Dorothy twisted her right wrist round and flicked

273

off the drops of water. "Don't look so shocked," she laughed. "It's gone."

David came over, and both he and Lucy stared at the naked wrist as all sorts of warnings and threats and visions of the fire of the melting flesh raised their ghastly heads.

Dorothy's laughter stopped abruptly. "I know what you're thinking," she said quietly, "because I was terrified too. But it's alright. You get used to it."

"How did you get it off?" whispered Lucy.

"That boy Tom. He took me to a jeweller's shop and they cut it off. They said it was gold and gave us money for it, and Tom bought me a mobile phone. I didn't have anyone I could ring, so I lent it to him when he went away."

"Wow!" said David in a hushed voice. "It's as though you really are free!"

Dorothy dried her hands. "We'll get yours cut off too as soon as we can." She looked at Lucy. "By the way, where did you get that chain?"

"Aunt Sarah gave it us. My bit's the chain and the circle is Paul's."

"Can I try it on?"

Lucy unclipped the chain and handed it over. Dorothy held it up against her own neck. She stepped into the hall and looked in the mirror. "It's really pretty. I love these tiny flowers." She returned to the kitchen and passed it back to Lucy. As she did so it slipped out of her hand. All four children stared as the chain lay sadly on the floor and the ring of flowers rolled under the table. Then Paul began to scream.

The others jumped and looked around in panic. There was no-one there. Paul threw himself down on the floor and shrieked. Lucy was frightened.

"Paul, stop it!" she cried, and tried to haul him up. "They'll hear you outside. What on earth's the matter?" He clung to her and in between his sobs he gabbled incoherently.

"It's something to do with the necklace," said David, bending to pick up the chain.

He grovelled under the table and found the pendant. Paul held his breath in mid-scream as he watched him thread the two pieces together and fasten them round Lucy's neck. His hysterics ended as quickly as they had begun.

The three older children were shaken. Lucy wiped his face and sat down, and pulled him onto her lap. "It's alright," she murmured into his ear. "We're safe."

Dorothy was the first to recover. "Right," she said briskly. "Episode over. Now let's get a move on." She pulled down her sleeves, and set about the remaining tasks of clearing up.

When the place was reasonably clean and tidy they went through the wardrobes and found what they needed in order to carry out their plan.

"Wow! You look fantastic. At least thirty!" said Lucy admiringly. Dorothy applied a second coat of lipstick and checked her mascara. She stood tall and slim in front of the mirror and tried to flatten her shining black curls with her hands.

"Don't spoil your hair," said Lucy. "It looks absolutely lovely."

Dorothy turned round to study herself from all angles in the mirror. She was beautifully dressed in a red woollen suit from the walk-in wardrobe off the big bedroom, and had found a plentiful supply of make-up in the dressing table drawer.

"I don't think I'd be able to walk far in high heels,"

she said, sorting through a pile of shoes at the bottom of the wardrobe, "especially if we have to make a run for it."

She found an elegant red pair with low-heels and a big silver buckle in front.

"These match my jacket, and they fit." She gazed at them in admiration. "I just love these shoes," she laughed, standing up to have a final look in the wardrobe mirror. "They make me feel happy just to look at them."

Downstairs in the hall she leafed nervously through the local phone directory, and found the number of the Mortimor Road Hospital. The others stood by, deeply impressed, as she rang to enquire about visiting times.

"Three till four, and seven till eight. Thank you so much," she said, deepening her voice to what she hoped was a mature pitch.

"Right, guys!" She put the phone back in its cradle. "We'll aim for three o'clock. That means leaving here at ten to three. It's only up the road."

David spluttered a little laugh. "Guys! Where did you get that from? We're not guys."

"It's how people speak these days," said Dorothy, a little haughtily. "It's modern. It's American."

At half past two they all gathered in the kitchen for final instructions. Paul had refused to wear his invisibility disguise. He was back in the blue cord trousers and cream-coloured cashmere jumper. Lucy had found him a weatherproof jacket with a quilted lining.

"You'll have to wear the woolly hat to hide your hair," she said. "If Thomas is still around he'd recognise you."

She pulled the hat firmly over his brown curls.

"Now, you have to pretend that you're Dorothy's

little boy, so you'll hold her hand, not mine, and I'll pretend I'm David's brother and walk a little way behind you."

"You're my sister. You're not a brother."

"I know, but it's my disguise."

They checked that they had left the place tidy. Apart from the clothes that they were wearing and the black bin liner, the only thing they took from the house was the canvas bag. It contained the keys from the cell, and the awl and the screwdriver, which Lucy thought they should keep in case they came in handy. Most important of all, the bag contained the BWD file, carefully wrapped in plastic.

They looked each other over. Lucy pulled on her baker boy hat and slung the canvas bag across her chest. She hoped she looked like someone's brother. David had found a navy anorak upstairs, and he pulled the hood up over his head.

"Final instructions," said David, authoritatively. "Dorothy knows the way to the hospital, so we follow her and Paul. People will be on the lookout for a three year old boy with an eleven or twelve year old girl, not a mother with her child. Lucy and I will be Dorothy's two other boys. I'll be older than Lucy because I'm yards taller, and we'll be walking along behind looking like two surly teenagers."

"Don't look too surly," said Dorothy. "We want to look as respectable as possible, or the hospital might not let us in. I just hope I look old enough to have a great big boy who looks sixteen even though he's only fourteen."

"Perhaps you were a child bride." Lucy put her hand to her mouth. "Sorry!" she said. "Inappropriate joke!"

"Now let's recap what happens in the hospital,"

said David. "We walk in as casually as possible, Dorothy and Paul in front. If anyone asks we say we're visiting a friend. There'll be signs to Ward 14, and the room is sure to be guarded. The police won't want to let us in, but we say we've come to identify the patient. If the guard's outside the room, I'll be the one to create a diversion."

The others nodded.

"I'll have to think about how to do that at the time," he said. "Once we're in the room Lucy will do the infiltrators' secret hand signal, and if no-one responds we'll know they're not infiltrators."

For what seemed like the hundredth time, Lucy practised the gesture that Thomas had taught her.

"Don't make it too obvious." David was a perfectionist. "It's got to be subtle or they'll say, what's going on?"

She tried again.

"Good! That's perfect," exclaimed Dorothy. "No-one would notice it unless they're looking out for it, and then they'd signal back and give themselves away."

They set off at ten to three. As they left via the back gate, a car drove up at the front.

"Holy Mag! Sorry. Holy Bag!" exclaimed Dorothy as they hurried along the alleyway. "Maybe we only just made it!"

As they were passing the back of Father Copse's house, Lucy peeped in through the back gate. There was no-one in sight. She dashed in and emptied out the black bin liner behind the bush with the yellow and green spotted leaves. The leather cushion and the cashmere shawl were still there. It was only ten days since Lucy had thrown them in there, but it seemed like a thousand years.

"They'll not find that for a while!" she whispered triumphantly as she joined the others. "By the time they do it'll have all been soaked through, and it'll smell of mould. That was my hidey-hole and no-one ever found me there – except Thomas of course. He always knew where I was."

CHAPTER THIRTY-NINE

The hospital foyer was small and old-fashioned, and was full of people arriving for visiting time. A map had been pinned up on a board to tell everyone where to go. The children studied it carefully. 'You are here', it said next to a large arrow. They were to go up the central stairs, and Ward 14 was on the first floor.

"Come along, children," ordered Dorothy, in her newly acquired mature voice. "Follow me please, you boys. Look sharp!"

They trooped nervously up the stairs together with the other visitors, expecting to be shouted at any minute, and trying their best to look cool, calm and collected. At the top an arrow indicated that Ward 14 was on the left. They pushed through some double doors into a long corridor bustling with nurses, orderlies, trollies, and the patients' friends and relations. The far end was quiet and they could see a security guard outside a closed door.

"Don't jump back!" hissed Dorothy, as their first instinct was to do exactly that. "We've got to look as though we're meant to be here."

"But how will we get in?" whispered David.

"You now have to create your diversion." She thought for a moment. "All we have to do is get him to move away from the door long enough for us to slip into the room. Let's think."

They moved slowly along the corridor looking into the various rooms as though they were searching for a particular person. Patients were sitting up or lying flat with tubes coming out of their arms and noses, while their visitors perched on the edge of the bed or on the arms of the one and only chair. Paul wrinkled his nose at the smell of disinfectant and ran his fingers along the green and cream painted walls. He would have painted prettier colours than that.

"I've got it!" said Dorothy quietly. "David, when we reach the guard you must suddenly rush off down the corridor whooping, as though you're a badly-behaved boy playing a stupid game. He's bound to move after you to tell you to be quiet, and we'll get into the room while his back is turned."

David absorbed Dorothy's instructions.

"OK," he said, breathing in deeply. "I just hope he's not one of those so-called social workers, that's all."

"We'll have to take the risk. Come on, Lucy. You go in front and open the door and jump in like greased lightning, and Paul and I will follow. David will have to get in if he can."

The little family continued nonchalantly down the corridor, peering into the side-rooms all the way along as they approached the guard. He was standing very upright staring at the opposite wall, deep in his own thoughts. As they reached him David let out a piercing hoot and twirled around in a circle waving his arms about, and then danced madly down the corridor. The guard shouted and leaned forward to catch him. Lucy opened the door and nipped inside, followed quickly by Dorothy and Paul.

The tenant lay very still, a mass of tubes. A policeman sat on one side of her bed, and a policewoman on the other. Lucy gave the secret hand signal. Neither officer responded to it, but they both jumped to their feet and the woman pulled a phone out of her pocket.

"We've come to identify her," said Dorothy in her deep grown-up voice, waving her hand towards the bed. The policewoman spoke into her phone and the security guard appeared in the doorway holding David by the scruff of his neck.

"We saw it on the news." Dorothy's carefully mature voice disappeared and was replaced by a young girl's anxious treble. "Lucy here knows her."

The police officers were immediately interested. The woman studied Lucy in her boy's clothes and baker boy hat. No point frightening them. Hearts and minds and all that.

"Hello," she said. "My name is Edna and this is Bill. Are you able to help us?"

The children relaxed slightly, and Lucy nodded.

"What's your name, love?" Edna asked Dorothy.

"I'm Dorothy and this is Paul, and that over there is David."

"Well, Dorothy, you sit in that visitor's chair and Paul can sit on your lap, while Lucy tells us what she knows."

Edna moved round the bed and sat next to Bill, so she could study the children's faces carefully. Bill had a notebook and pencil in his hand. He looked at Lucy.

"Are you a boy or a girl?" he asked.

"I'm a girl. I'm in disguise." Lucy pulled off her baker boy cap and threw it on the window sill. Her curls sprang up around her face.

"Name?"

"I'm Lucy."

"Lucy what?"

"I don't like my surname, I'm just Lucy. And can you please tell that man to let David go?"

Bill nodded at the guard and he released him. The room seemed very full.

"David can't identify her, so he could stay outside with the guard if you think it's too crowded in here," said Lucy. "He might be useful out there in case one of the nutters comes."

"Nutters?" Edna smiled at David. "Would you prefer to stay outside with Walter?" she asked. David nodded. Walter placed a firm hand on his shoulder and steered him out of the room.

Edna turned to Lucy. "Now love, tell us if you can identify this lady, and how."

Lucy stepped up to the side of the bed and looked sadly down into the pale, beautiful face.

"She's the tenant," she said. "She and Paul and I escaped from the fire."

Bill was scribbling down her words. Light began to dawn on the officers' faces, and Edna spoke again into her phone.

"I think we've got the missing children from Mortimor Road, a girl and a boy."

"What's the patient's name?" asked Bill.

"I just called her the tenant. She lived on the top flat and never came down. I think she was locked in. Behind bars like a lunatic. I never saw her properly till the fire."

"Do you know where the owner of the house is?"

"Yes," Dorothy chipped in, bitterly. "We left him tied up in the secret passage behind Drax House, and we saw on the news that the police have got him now."

Lucy studied the tenant's face. It reminded her of

someone, but she couldn't think who. She wanted to stroke the shining waves of dark brown hair.

"She looks so pretty and peaceful," she said, "but we've come to rescue her. Somewhere in this hospital there are infiltrators, and they want to kill her before she wakes up. David heard them talking."

"What do you mean?" asked Bill. "Can you explain clearly, please."

Before Lucy could answer, the door opened. A male nurse appeared, his sandy hair peeping out from the edge of a round green cap, and his face smooth with compassion. The faintest possible smell of cigarettes wafted in with him. In his left hand was an enamel dish containing a syringe, partly covered by a piece of white gauze. He nodded at the police officers and signalled with his right hand as he entered, but neither of them responded.

"I've been instructed to give her an injection," he said in hushed tones, hardly glancing at the children. "I wonder if you would all mind leaving the room for a moment."

The officers stood up and moved towards the door gesturing to the children to follow them. Paul gave an excited squeak and darted away from Dorothy. He wrapped his arms joyfully round the nurse's leg and smiled up at its owner. Lucy drew in a deep breath. She leaned over, and struck the enamel dish out of the nurse's hand. The syringe went flying.

"It's him! Stop him," she yelled as the nurse made for the door. She reached the doorway just after him. Walter was halfway down the corridor speaking to David who was slouching at the far end near the double doors, his hoodie pulled down over his face.

"David! It's Thomas! Catch him," screamed Lucy, as Thomas sidestepped Walter and started to run towards the double doors.

David threw back his hood and dashed forward. Thomas twisted round only to find Walter bearing down on him from the other direction. He turned again towards the doors, shoving David with his left hand. David staggered for a second then took a flying leap and wrapped his arms round Thomas's legs, bringing him to the ground. Walter knelt astride his back and had his wrists in handcuffs in two seconds.

"Do you play rugby?" he asked David, as he rose to his feet.

"No."

"Well you ought to!"

Lucy drew David back into the room. Her teeth were chattering. He went over towards the window and sat, white-faced and shaking, on the arm of the visitor's chair.

Edna was on the phone again.

"You're not ringing for social workers are you?" asked David standing up quickly. "Because if you are, we'll have to go."

"No," said Bill. "It's just to get someone to take the nurse away."

Lucy stepped over to where the syringe lay on the floor.

"It's full of poison," she said. "Full of lethal injection." She bent to pick it up, and Bill pulled her back.

"Don't touch it. We'll need it for analysis and fingerprints."

She went to stand by Dorothy who had completely lost her air of sophistication, and was clutching onto Paul as though his and her lives depended on it.

"Were you actually living at number 3 Mortimor Road when the fire broke out," Edna asked Lucy, "or were you just visiting?"

"I was living there, in the downstairs flat, with Paul and Aunt Sarah. She died just before they set the house on fire. I think she had a heart attack because she fell down the stairs and was holding her chest."

Bill's pen moved rapidly.

"Was she your only family?"

"She wasn't my real aunt. Paul is my family."

"Who are you, Lucy?"

"I don't know. But I do exist," she said.

She rummaged in the canvas bag that still hung across her chest.

"I'm here in the record." She produced the plastic bag with the BWD file, and laid it on the bed.

She opened the file and turned to the births section.

"See? There I am. And there's Paul. Our mother is called Maria, but we don't know who she is or where she is. Father Drax is sure to have a file showing David and Dorothy and who their mothers are. You must look in his office, not just in Drax House, but in his private residence as well. It's right next to Drax House. If he's like Father Copse he'll have kept all his records near his desk at home."

Outside in the corridor there was a scuffling sound. Lucy dashed to the door and peeped out. Another police officer had arrived, and Walter was handing Thomas over. Lucy felt ill just looking at him. As he was marched away he turned round. His eyes pierced right through her. Evil rays, she thought. Just like the first Holy Envoy.

"We've got your photo on record," he hissed. "We'll get you for this!"

CHAPTER FORTY

Peace reigned in the hospital room for a little while. Dorothy sat in the visitor's chair with Paul on her lap, while Lucy and David perched on the wooden arms each side of her. Edna was out in the corridor talking on her phone, and Bill sat in silence with his pencil and notepad on his lap, thinking out his next line of questioning.

A nurse came in and the children watched suspiciously for the hand signal, but there was none. She picked up the medical record at the end of the bed.

"According to this she last stirred half an hour ago," she said.

"Yes," said Bill. "She half-opened her eyes and her lips moved, but that was it. Nothing since."

"Well, it's progress." The nurse felt the tenant's pulse. She checked the various tubes and fiddled with some knobs.

She turned to the children.

"What are you doing here? She's not supposed to have visitors."

"It's alright," said Bill. "They're helping us."

"I'll be back in half an hour," said the nurse, and left the room.

Lucy picked Paul up onto the side of the bed.

"My goodness, you're heavy!" she puffed. "Come and say hello to the tenant."

Paul looked down at the peaceful face.

"Sleeping Beauty," he said.

Lucy smiled.

"Perhaps if you give her a kiss she'll wake up."

He kissed the tip of her nose, but nothing happened.

"She said that perhaps she was my mummy."

"I expect she was lonely," said Lucy, "living up there all on her own except for the lady with the red hair."

She lifted him down and they settled back on the chair with Dorothy. Bill was writing. Lucy could sense that Dorothy and David were getting anxious. Edna was still out in the corridor. Perhaps she was ringing for a social worker.

It was time for them to be going. They had identified the tenant as best they could, and had saved her from disposal which was what they had really come for. Lucy stood up quietly and took her BWD file off the bed, wrapped it up in the plastic, and put it back into the canvas bag. As she slipped the bag across her chest she turned to face the others and tilted her head slightly towards the door. David nodded almost imperceptibly.

At that moment Edna returned. She sat down by the bed, and Bill looked up at her enquiringly.

"Right! That's organised," she said. "I've arranged for someone to come and take you all to a safe place, and you'll be able to stay there until this is all sorted. You've been very helpful so far, but we'll need to ask you lots more questions, and you'll have to make formal statements."

The children stared at her.

"We don't want to be kept in a safe place," said Dorothy, just about managing to keep the panic out of her voice. "We'll only be safe looking after ourselves.

We'll answer questions if you tell us when to come, and where, but we won't be taken away. We don't trust anyone."

David and Lucy nodded.

"We only trust each other," said David.

"Well, I'm afraid you have no choice."

As she spoke there was a murmur from the bed. Both officers leaned over the tenant. Her lips were moving slightly and her eyelids fluttered. Edna pressed a bell and a nurse arrived almost immediately. While the three adults hovered over the bed the children quietly moved towards the open door.

"Goodbye for now," said David quietly to Walter, as they slipped past. "They don't need us anymore."

"Goodbye then. Good rugby, that!"

The children had almost reached the double doors when a voice shouted.

"Come back! Stop them!"

For a split second Dorothy and David paused. Walter came thundering towards them and grabbed them by the arm, just as Lucy and Paul pushed through the double doors.

"Lucy, Paul! Come back!" called Edna from the doorway of the room. Bill emerged and tore down the corridor, through the doors, and onto the stairs.

"Got you!" he said, as they wriggled under his grip.

"It's for your own safety," said Edna as they were hauled back into the room.

The nurse was still by the bed, and turned crossly to the children.

"See what you've done? She needs peace and quiet, not some great hullabaloo. Now she's gone back into her shell. You shouldn't be here if you're just going to make a nuisance of yourselves."

The children stood disconsolately over by the window as Walter remained firmly in the doorway, and the two police officers settled themselves back in their chairs. The nurse fussed about for a while checking equipment, and writing something on the record at the end of the bed. She gazed down into the tenant's face.

"Happy dreams," she said. "I'm going off shift soon. See you tomorrow."

As she spoke the tenant's lips began to move. The nurse turned back and all three adults leaped to attention once more. The children looked towards the door where Walter stood with his arms folded. There was no hope of escape now.

"What is she saying?" whispered the nurse.

The tenant's eyes opened. Her lips were still moving almost inaudibly. Lucy had a good look out of the window to see if there was any possibility of jumping out, but they were high up, and without the father's soft leather cushions it was unlikely they would land safely. Dorothy was looking out too, and shook her head slightly at Lucy.

"I'm going off shift now," called Walter from the doorway. "My replacement's come. It's Fred. Got to rush."

"Bye," said Edna, without taking her eyes off the tenant. "See you!"

He went out and shut the door.

The voice on the bed rose into a definite murmur. The tenant moved her head slightly and looked around. The sound became clearer.

"Lucy, Paul, Lucy, come back, Lucy, Paul, Lucy," she said. "Lucy, Paul, Lucy, come back."

"She must have heard you shouting," the nurse said to Edna. "It's sparked her off, so you've done some good there! This might be all she needed."

"She's probably thinking of the fire," said Lucy. "We had to leave her behind when the paramedics came. We knew she'd be alright with them."

The tenant closed her eyes and there was silence for a while. The nurse made some more notes on the record sheet and prepared to leave. "That'll be it for a while, I expect," she said.

There was a movement on the bed. The tenant's eyes opened and tried to focus on the three faces hovering over her. "Where are they?" she said. Her voice was low and husky. "Lucy, Paul?"

Lucy picked up Paul and sat him on the edge of the bed.

"Put him down. Get away from the bed, both of you," snapped the nurse.

Lucy ignored her.

"Here we are," she said soothingly. "This is Paul, and I'm Lucy."

The tenant turned her head slowly towards them, and looked into their faces.

"Hello," she whispered.

Paul started to hum. The nurse pulled Lucy away and plonked Paul down on the floor.

"I told you to get back!" she said crossly. "Now, all four of you, get out. You can wait outside. Police or no police, the patient comes first."

"And don't you dare move from there," called Edna after them.

The tenant closed her eyes and turned her head away, and the children hurried out of the room. Fred was standing by the door. Dorothy looked up at him and smiled.

"We've been told to leave," she said. "Someone's

coming to take us to a safe place, and we're going to wait for him down in the foyer."

"S'long," said Fred.

They walked calmly though the double doors, down the stairs and across the foyer. As they left the main entrance behind them they passed two police officers on their way in.

Back in the hospital room the tenant stirred again. Voices floated and faded, and floated back again. Warm and comfortable. Was she dead? Was this heaven? Then nothing. Just sleep. They came again, the voices. This was nice. Perhaps her mother was here somewhere, and her father. Could she see the blue front door? No. She couldn't because her eyes wouldn't open. Too much of an effort. She felt safe. Then, nothing but darkness. Sleep. Voices again, louder this time. She'd heard those names – Lucy, Paul. She could see a baby, pink and pretty, and then another one. The names were important, but she couldn't place them. Never mind. This was very pleasant. She breathed deeply, once, twice, and again. With each breath a mist lifted slightly. Now she remembered her own name – Maria. Her pulse quickened. There was a fire. Two children. She lifted her head slightly.

"Where have they gone?"

The three adults had no need to bend forward to hear what she said because her voice was clear. Bill started writing.

"Where are my children?" She tried to move. "They were here just now."

"Can you tell us your name, love?" said Edna gently.

"I'm Maria. Where are Paul and Lucy?"

"They're outside with the guard. I'll fetch them for you, Maria."

There was a knock on the door and two police officers entered with Fred just behind them.

"They've gone," said Fred. He sounded embarrassed. "They said they were being fetched."

CHAPTER FORTY-ONE

From behind his newspaper Father Drax had his eye on the main entrance to the hospital. He needed to catch Thomas when he came out, and he wished he'd hurry up. The shift must have finished at least twenty minutes ago. He was fed up with this damp bench and did consider sitting on his briefcase, but decided against it. It might crush it out of shape, and it had been very expensive. All his documents were in that case – his bank accounts and different pin numbers and aliases and passports, as well as all his children's birth records.

The hat was pressing into his forehead. It was much too small for him. He wasn't used to hats, but the brim was fairly wide and it hid his yellow hair. If it weren't for his hair no-one would recognise him now – not after more than a week of sleeping under those filthy railway arches. This was the first time he'd dared to come back to the area in daylight since his commune was raided, and he hoped he just looked like a very tall tramp. He stooped his shoulders to make himself shorter, and bowed his head. Thomas would get him away somehow so that he could lead a normal life, but first he must help him find those two treacherous brats of his. He'd stop their mouths for ever – especially the girl. She'd started it, and she'd ruined everything for him – her own father!

A police car pulled up outside the gates and he

buried his face in the sports page as two officers walked purposefully towards the main entrance. He peeped out sideways as they went up the steps, and then he swore quietly to himself. As cool as four cucumbers his son and daughter, plus a couple of Copse's kids, sauntered down the steps, past the police officers, and out through the gates. There was no need for Thomas now. Pulling the hat down even tighter he stood up, picked up the briefcase, and followed the children, throwing his newspaper in the bin as he went. It had his face on an inside page but no-one would recognise him in this get-up. Even so, he took the paper out again and crumpled up the middle bit and then put it back in the bin.

"We'll go along the Southcote Road first," said Dorothy, "and pick up some food."

They followed her down a side street to a long road that ran behind the hospital, full of market stalls. Some of the traders were beginning to pack up. Dorothy picked up a fallen apple and popped it into Lucy's canvas bag. A few yards later on she found a small bunch of bruised bananas.

"We've got quite a long walk in front of us," she said. "I'm going to take you to where I hid when I ran away from Drax House. It's under a railway arch, and lots of people like us go there, and they can light fires and keep warm and cook things. The police will be looking for us near the hospital, so they won't guess we've gone so far. Maybe that boy called Tom will be there, and he'll help us."

A tiny flame flickered in her heart as she thought of Tom.

They trudged along pavements for over an hour.

For a while they followed the Thames, but they felt too exposed, and turned in towards the back streets. Paul was exhausted and was dragging on Lucy's hand, whining. They came to a small triangular playground with swings, some dreary bushes, a bit of grass, and public conveniences. There was nobody else about. Dorothy shoved her hand into a rubbish bin and groped around, and pulled out two cardboard coffee cups.

"We'll stay here for a little while," she said, sitting down on a bench. "Here, Lucy, take Paul into the lavatories." She handed her a cardboard cup. "Wash this really thoroughly till you've got rid of all the germs, and then make sure you both have a good drink of water because we might not get another chance for a while."

When she and Paul returned Dorothy dished out the bananas, and they all had a couple of bites of the apple. Huddled together on the bench, they tried to work out a plan of action, but without much success.

Dorothy's spirits rose as she thought of Tom.

"Once we've had a good night's sleep, we'll be fine." She smiled as she remembered the laughter in his voice and his cheery acceptance of life under the railway arches.

"I'm too tired to think," said Lucy. "They've caught Thomas, and Father Copse, so the only one left is Father Drax. I suppose the Holy Leaders will see that he gets away safely."

"I'm not so sure about that," said Dorothy slowly. "It may be that they want to get rid of him so they can pretend he's nothing to do with them. They might even try to dispose of him unless he's got the sense to escape."

The children sat in silence, recovering their strength. Paul leaned on Lucy and fell asleep. It was nearly dark.

"I'll have to carry him piggyback," said Dorothy, "otherwise we'll never get there. It's only about another mile."

They woke Paul up and made him stand on the bench behind Dorothy. She pulled his hands round to the front of her shoulders, and wrapped his legs round her waist.

"Holy Bag! He weighs a ton!" Her legs buckled momentarily, and she straightened herself up. "Right, now we're going to have to try to follow the railway line."

Trains thundered past overhead as they plodded on slowly through dimly lit back streets.

"Is it here?" asked Lucy nervously, as they reached a railway arch seething with dark figures.

"No, not that one," whispered Dorothy. "Come away from there. That's a bad one. Keep going."

She put Paul down.

"I can't carry him any longer. It's not much further."

David and Lucy each took a hand and pulled him along as best they could. Then they linked their palms and sat him on their hands with his arms clutching their shoulders.

"You're too tall," said Lucy. "We're lopsided."

"It's you. You're too short," said David.

For a moment the strain left their faces and they looked at each other and laughed.

Every few hundred yards they stopped and changed sides.

"Paul, you'll have to walk now," groaned Lucy eventually. Her arm felt as though it was about to drop off. "You must try to be big and strong."

They put him down, and all four children trudged

on, too tired to complain. A wind blew up and it started to rain. David pulled up his hood. Big cold drops fell on Lucy's head.

"I left my cap in the hospital."

"Never mind," said Dorothy, pointing to a flickering glow two hundred yards ahead. "Look, there it is."

At last they came to an arch where a fire was burning and a delicious smell of sausages wafted out towards them.

"Let's see if Tom's there," said Dorothy quietly.

They stepped somewhat fearfully into a great black cave, lit fitfully by the leaping red, yellow and orange flames of the fire.

"That's Tom!" whispered Dorothy. She pointed at a young bearded man in a brightly-coloured cap propped up away from the fire against the right-hand wall of the arch.

Stepping over a body to reach him, she said softly, "Hello, Tom. It's Dorothy."

He looked up with glazed eyes. His arm crept round the shoulders of a woman leaning next to him. Her head flopped sideways, and he muttered, and his eyes rolled up till only the whites were showing.

"You won't get nothing out of him, love," laughed someone. "He's been stoned for days."

Dorothy's heart sank. She stepped back to the others. Trying to keep the shock and disappointment out of her voice, she said quietly, "He's very tired. Come on. Let's go in the farthest corner out of the way, and try to sleep for a while."

No-one took any notice of them as they snuggled down together, and despite their hunger and the mouth-watering sausage smell that washed over them from the fire, they slept the sleep of exhaustion.

When they woke dawn was casting a faint grey light into the entrance of the archway. The fire had gone out and sleeping bodies lay around the embers. Dorothy stood up and stretched. Tom and his woman friend were wrapped around each other, their faces a ghastly white against the black of the wall. A syringe lay on the floor beside them.

Dorothy tried to push away the dull ache of misery inside her. Living in a commune made you pretty naive about the outside world but, even so, she felt embarrassed that she had believed in Tom. And she was ashamed that she had brought the others here. It had seemed so friendly, even cosy, when she had been here with Tom all those weeks ago. Now it just seemed sordid. Well, at least it had given them shelter for the night, and they could leave now, before everyone woke up. There was nothing to keep them. She breathed deeply, trying to quell her nausea, but the air was full of dust and ash, and the delicious whiff of sausages had settled into the sickening smell of grease.

Ok. So she too had been betrayed by a friend. Too bad. It was time to pull herself together. She looked down at her nice red skirt. It was dusty and crumpled. She brushed it down briskly with her hands and fluffed up her hair, and glanced over to the further side of the fire. In the dim light she could just distinguish some of the sleeping shapes and features. She breathed in sharply.

"David," she whispered. "Look who's over there, beyond the fire to the left."

She pulled at his arm and he stood up. In the dim light from the mouth of the archway he could just make out the curled-up shape of a very tall man with thick golden blond hair. His head rested on a black briefcase, and his face was relaxed in sleep.

"He's followed us," murmured David.

"Or perhaps he's hiding from the Holy Leaders. Whatever it is, let's go!"

CHAPTER FORTY-TWO

The children crept out into the street. As they left Father Drax lifted his head and then clambered stiffly to his feet. He picked up his briefcase and looked around for his hat – his disguise. It wasn't on the ground. There it was two feet away, adorning the medusa-like locks of a sleeping youth. Nits? No thanks! Never mind the hat. Clutching the briefcase he stepped over several bodies. Then, keeping well back, he followed the children as they hurried up the street.

After a few hundred yards Dorothy slowed down.

"At least he didn't see us," she said. "I've got to find a phone. We don't need money to phone the police."

They half-ran along the back streets looking for a public telephone. There wasn't a soul to be seen in the early morning light apart from one sleeping body in a doorway. They sidestepped past it quietly, and it didn't stir.

The first phone was vandalised and it took them some time to find another.

"No wonder people use mobile phones," grumbled Dorothy.

At last they found a phone outside a pub, and it actually worked. The children sat on the pavement next to the booth. It took Dorothy some time to get through to the right person and to make herself understood. David and Lucy were desperate to move on. Paul's attention was caught by a cyclist, and then, far away at the bottom of the street, by a tall man with fair hair.

"Yellow hair," he said. "Father Drax had yellow hair." David and Lucy followed his gaze, but, apart from the cyclist who was coming up towards them, there was no-one to be seen.

"His hair's not yellow," said Lucy. "It's his cycling mackintosh."

Dorothy was giving directions to the railway arch.

"He's tall and blond," she said finally. "You'll have to hurry or he might be gone when you get there." She put the phone down and pulled David up from the pavement by his sleeve. "Come on, quick!" she said. "Let's get away from here in case they trace the call to this phone box."

Scuttling down a narrow side street lined with parked cars, they didn't see Drax as he turned the corner at the top end and followed them with cautious steps. They found their way to the South Bank of the river and sat on a bench looking at the sunrise. The sky was a soft pink and silver. Somehow it soothed them, and the tension that had gripped them for days started to seep away. They relaxed a little. Drax stood watching from the far side of a parked car about two hundred yards away.

"Let's make a pact," said Dorothy. "We all stick together through thick and thin."

"Agreed!" exclaimed David.

Lucy pulled Paul to her and nuzzled her face in his woolly hat. "We'll agree too. Won't we, Paul?"

"Agreed!" he shouted, and they all laughed.

"Even if we're caught by the Holy Leaders, and even if one of us finds our mother, and even if all of us find our mothers, we'll be blood brothers and sisters for the rest of our lives," said David.

"I'll never find my mother," said Dorothy bitterly, and no-one spoke.

Lucy broke the silence. "You don't really know," she said. "What you heard may not have been true. It may have been said just to frighten you into not being so cheeky."

Dorothy straightened herself up. "Maybe. Anyway, David's my half-brother so I'm very lucky. You are too because you've got Paul. If we're all four of us blood brothers and sisters, we'll have each other, so we'll be even luckier. We'll be a family. Not everyone gets the chance to create their own special family."

A surge of excitement swept through Lucy.

"We really are the luckiest people in the world!" she exclaimed. "We've not only managed to escape, but we've got each other!" She took in great gulps of the sharp morning air. "None of us has ever had a family before."

She dug in her bag for the awl.

"We'd better not actually draw blood with this," she said, "in case we get an infection. But if each of us gives each of the others a poke with it, and says, 'I swear to be your blood brother (or sister) all the rest of my life,' that'll bind us together for ever."

David took the awl. He held Lucy's small hand in his. It was very grubby, but it was warm and soft, and it pleased him to hold it.

"This is a strong, brave hand," he said quietly. "It saved our lives."

Lucy left her hand in his. She was too taken aback to say anything.

Dorothy smiled. "You'll embarrass her," she said. "But it's true."

She turned to Paul and picked up his plump little paw. "This is a strong, brave hand too," she said, giving it a loud kiss, "and it belongs to a strong, brave boy."

Paul beamed with pleasure and pride.

David jabbed the awl gently into the back of Lucy's hand and swore to be her blood brother. He did the same with Dorothy and Paul. The others all took their turn, and the little ceremony was performed with great solemnity. Even Paul managed to jab gently and, with some prompting, recited the appropriate words. When it was over they looked at each other and smiled. Lucy's eyes filled with tears.

"I'm hungry," announced Paul.

"Don't worry," said Dorothy. She spoke softly out of respect for the sacredness of their vows. "We'll find something to eat somewhere, somehow. I know a street with lots of restaurants. If we go round the back there'll be plenty of food in the bins. That's what I did the last time I was around here."

They stood up, and Drax started moving more swiftly down the side street. The children sauntered towards a bridge that crossed the river. A mist rose up above the water to meet the sun's pink morning rays.

"That's the West End over there, the other side of the bridge," said Dorothy. "It's full of restaurants. We'll manage. Now that we're a family we can make a good life for ourselves if we stick together, and we'll probably come across some of my old friends. It'll be an adventure."

Their hearts sang.

The early morning traffic was beginning to rumble

as they strolled along, and they could just see the heads of the pedestrians as they crossed over the bridge on their way to work.

"I'd love to work in an office," commented Dorothy. "It must make you feel so safe. There's a cake trolley, and you can wear nice clothes, and you get paid at the end of each month."

They didn't notice the police car as it drove up alongside them. Father Drax ducked down behind a stationary van.

"Hullo," said a police officer, planting himself firmly in front of the children.

They stopped and looked round. There was another officer behind them.

"Hullo," they replied, politely.

"Are any of you called Lucy and Paul?"

There was no response.

The policeman bent down and spoke to Paul.

"What's your name, young man?"

Paul started to hum.

"Goodbye, we have to go now," said Lucy, hastily grabbing his hand and moving off.

David and Dorothy moved with her.

"Stop a minute," said the policeman, putting his hand on Lucy's shoulder. He spoke kindly.

"We're looking for Lucy and Paul. They're with a friend called David and a young lady called Dorothy who's wearing a bright red suit and scarlet shoes with silver buckles."

Nobody answered. Dorothy looked down at her dishevelled clothes. The shoes still smiled cheerfully up at her. One of the policemen stepped over to the car. He reached inside and produced the baker boy cap.

"Lucy left this behind in the hospital," he said.

There was a pause, and then Paul turned to Lucy.

"Am I Paul, or am I Elizabeth?" he said "Or am I invisible?"

Lucy drew him close to her and put her arm round him.

"It's alright, darling. You're Paul, and that's what you'll always be now. You can forget about being Elizabeth, or invisible. That was just a game. When you're grown-up I'll explain it all to you."

She looked up at the two policemen.

"How do you do?" she said. "I'm Lucy, and this is my brother Paul. These are my blood brother and blood sister, David and Dorothy. We're a family."

"Pleased to meet you," he said. "We've come to fetch you. Would you all like to get in the car?"

The children looked around and then back at the two police officers. There was no way they could escape unless they separated and scattered in different directions – and that they would never do. Lucy held Paul's hand firmly. Dorothy took his other hand, and David took Lucy's.

"Where are we going?" asked Lucy.

"Your mother, Maria, is asking for you."